SWAP CLUB

WRITTEN BY:

LAUREN WISE

D0063163

SWAP CLUB

Lauren Wise

Published by WBS Entertainment

www.worldsbeststory.com

ISBN: 978-0-9958271-0-3

Printed in the United States of America

FOREWORD

…or (in case you start wondering) *Disclaimer*

This book is fiction. I'm not Val, and I never swung (if that is even the word for the past participle of swinging in the sexual sense). I guess it doesn't matter. My point is, this book is *not* about me. It's *not* about my past or present relationships.

This book is fiction. The characters in this story are fictitious. Nothing in these pages is based on true events.

The lack of resemblance to my own sex life notwithstanding, I have nothing against this lifestyle or against consensual multi-partner sex. Even with other consenting married couples.

This book is an escape, something to help take your mind off of everything that's bothering you.

So sit back, light some candles, take your clothes off, and enjoy.

~ Lauren Wise

As she spoke I realized

that her validation

was through his eyes.

She's not dependent on anyone

and yet,

Her beauty only comes from his lips.

Her confidence from his arms.

Her intelligence from his thoughts.

Her control from his hands.

So subtle, almost overlooked,

she hates to be alone,

she hates to sit at home.

When she looks in the mirror, she doesn't see very much

until he stands behind her,

whispers in her ear.

When he's gone,

the music dies

and the reflection feels empty.

Why should she depend on him?

His words only come on a whim.

Who is she?

I want to set her free.

—Anonymous

PROLOGUE

Last night was all a blur. I can't even remember what time we moved to the bedroom and I barely even drank anything. I remember snippets. Fragmented moments when his tongue and lips were between my legs, bringing me to the brink, over and over. Every time my body clenched up, and I held my breath, he'd intentionally stop. He knew my body—its sweet spots and most sensitive parts—like he'd studied it for a test. It felt like we'd known each other forever. I couldn't believe I'd only just met him when he rang my doorbell at 8:02 p.m.

Like an 8mm film, the footage flips through my recall and I can envision the moment when I sat up on my elbows to prop up my torso so our eyes could connect. If I squeeze my eyes shut I can feel the sweat on my back again and the sheets sticking to me.

His eyes were a gorgeous icy blue; his hair was dirty blonde and still full. His skin—softer than any I'd ever felt on a man—was practically hairless, so smooth and warm. Good genes.

Panic came over me as I glanced over at the clock and realized we had only another hour left, and I wasn't sure what to do. I needed to get the beautiful stranger to push me over the edge before he had to get the fuck out of Dodge. I was still new at this.

As his tongue grazed my swollen clitoris, I pleaded with him to let me orgasm, and I didn't realize how desperate I was until I heard it in my voice. Thank God he smiled as he wiped his mouth and crawled on top of me. When his lips met mine, he tasted of me, and I wasn't completely turned off. In fact, I got more aroused the more he kissed me intensely, unabashedly.

I could feel him throbbing against the front of my thigh. All I had to do was bear down on him, and he would glide right into me. He moved his mouth down to kiss my chin; then his lips brushed over my jawbone and traveled the length of my clavicle to my shoulder. He turned his head so that his lips were touching my ear.

He asked me what I needed in a flirty whisper. I told him that I needed him inside me, trying to line up my eager part with his rock-hard part. But he kept it just out of reach.

He took his mouth away from my ear, down my neck, to my chest where he pressed his tongue to my nipple while gently tugging at my breast with one hand. I couldn't take it anymore. I glanced at the ticking clock; the urgency was palpable.

I had an out-of-body experience as I moaned feverishly and literally begged him to have sex with me. My appeal was met with a gluttonous smirk as he flicked my nipple with his tongue. Finally, he looked up, held my eyes, and slowly slipped deep inside of me.

I reached down and added my hand—a move I would never have made three months earlier when I had yet to see my sex life for what it had been: boring. It took no more than four strokes, in tandem with his thrusts, before my whole body was convulsing in ecstasy. I was a live wire. My head felt like it weighed a hundred pounds as it fell back, and my mouth opened wide as all the air in my lungs evaporated while he kept thrusting.

Everything was a blur of motion, sensation, and skin. Time ceased to exist; my post-orgasmic body continued to vibrate with pleasure, like a sustained note, as he ground into me with more and more intensity, until he pulled out, flipped on his back and came on his stomach.

Shortly after the gorgeous stranger went home, while Ryan helped me change our soiled sheets, I couldn't help but pat myself on the back.

Every once in a while I had a good idea.

And this was one of them.

"Ladies and gentlemen, you can't please everyone. Take my girlfriend—I think she's the most remarkable woman in the world…That's me…But to my wife…"
—Jackie Mason

CHAPTER 1

Not Another Tchotchke

An old seventies trend was making its way back into the suburban lives and homes of Montrealers. Husbands and wives were having consensual sex with other married couples and trying to keep the secret under wraps, unsuccessfully. I'd heard rumors about Swap Club on several occasions, and I've learned something about living in Montreal: rumors in this claustrophobically close-knit village of a city were true about 100 percent of the time. Plus, the people who called them rumors were in fact very likely the same people who were involved.

Swapping. Swinging. An organized sex agreement. An opportunity to live out deep-seated fantasies and enjoy the anonymity that allows you to truly let go. The mere idea of this was riveting to me.

I must warn you: I'm about to divulge some very intimate secrets—secrets that are not meant to be shared outside of the Club. I'm not using my real name; my Jewish mother would die if she knew her daughter had enjoyed the lewdest year of her life after she hit forty.

Of course, the past year has also been filled with all the everyday regular moments, too—time spent as a devoted and attentive mom, exchanging new recipes with friends (although I really don't enjoy cooking), shopping at Zara with my sister, Janet, puttering around the house contentedly. Maybe it's one of my strengths that those simple things aren't mundane to me. But I assume you don't really care about that. What you want to know about is the sex, the swapping.

The night I knew I needed more than any ordinary birthday gift for my fortieth, I was doing what I did most nights—lying in bed, snacking on Wheat Thins, watching mindless reality television.

"Here, this is for you." Ryan took the box of Wheat Thins from my hands and replaced it with a gift bag from Holt Renfrew.

"What's this?" I knew exactly what it was as I ripped it open.

"Your fortieth birthday present." Ryan muted the TV, then sat on the bed facing me. He was fidgety and running his hands repeatedly through his hair.

I tugged open the bag, and removed a smaller box wrapped inside. I had been hinting at a diamond tennis bracelet only for the last five birthdays. I didn't even have to open the box. I smiled at Ryan. He got me something I had asked for, something that I had coveted for years.

"Open it, Val." Ryan was excited to see my reaction.

I flipped open the top of the box, and there it lay—the sparkling tennis bracelet. I wrapped my arms around Ryan's neck and thanked him. It was beautiful.

"You like it?" Ryan was proud of himself as he fastened it onto my wrist.

I stared at the sparkling diamonds adorning my wrist and I felt like a fucking liar pretending that it was what I wanted. What I actually wanted was something that I couldn't show off. I had my heart set on something that could destroy my marriage and my family and alienate me from any friend I had ever known, and I was willing to risk it all. I just needed Ryan to do it with me. When is the right time to tell your husband that you want to join a secret sex club? I decided to wait until after he had his orgasm.

We reclined on the bed and kissed for our usual five-minute interlude, which was followed by the awkward removal of pants and socks. I typically kept my pajama top on, hating what the gravitational effects of maternity had done to my once-perky breasts. We got under the sheets, our only barrier against another late-night greeting from one of our children. I tied my hair into a messy bun so it wouldn't get in the way. I needed to wash it. Shit, I'd forgotten to buy shampoo. As Ryan stretched out on his back, I made a mental note to remember to buy it the next day after morning carpool. I started to give Ryan a blowjob, a redundant and tedious feat, but necessary if I wanted him wet enough to glide inside me. The TV was still on. I covertly aligned myself so I could catch just enough of the Kardashian sisters to be entertained while I serviced Ryan.

A commercial for Hamburger Helper chirped away in the background. Do people still eat that? As Ryan grabbed the knot of my bun to better guide my mouth up and down his shaft, I mused about whether I had any ground beef in the freezer. After seven or eight solid minutes of giving Ryan head, I was grateful when he turned me over and slid inside me. I glanced over at the clock. 8:54 p.m. If we finished in six minutes, I could totally catch *The Bachelor*. Ryan thrust in and out of me with vigor, his face planted down into the pillow next to my head. I started to wonder, as I glanced back at the bed sheet slipping off of our bodies, whether I'd remembered to put the towels in the dryer. I was pretty sure I had.

His intensity increased, a sure sign we were almost done. 8:57. Looking good. I tilted my pelvis to step it up. And, in a matter of seconds, we were finished. 8:58, perfect.

After cleaning up, I got back into bed and grabbed the box of Wheat Thins. I adjusted my head on the pillow and caught my TV-strobed reflection in our mirrored closet door. I was startled. There I was: a middle-aged woman with a dirty ponytail in flannel pajamas, with a tennis bracelet hanging from the hand that was shoveling crackers into her mouth, in bed, zombie-addicted to impossibly bad television. The reason our sex life had deteriorated was staring me right in the face.

I looked over at Ryan, who was checking his email. Was now *the* time? I didn't know what his reaction was going to be. I was hoping that he would be happy about it, but then I started to wonder. What man wants to share his wife? Shouldn't he be guarding me, protecting me from other men? Isn't that some kind of natural instinct in the animal kingdom? An alpha male wolf is known for chasing away and killing any other male who tries to mess with his female. And here I was, hoping that Ryan actually wanted to feed me to the wolves.

Sighing, I shook it off, picked up the remote to find *The Bachelor*, and shifted to get more comfortable. Something was pricking my butt. Reaching around, I pulled out the culprit from under me: the big 4-0 birthday card was literally giving me a pain in the ass.

A couple of days later, after the kids left for school, I was pacing around our bedroom while Ryan was in the shower. I had to bring up Swap Club. It was eating away at me and I couldn't take another minute pretending that I was really just preoccupied with mundane mom-chores.

"Hey, can I talk to you?" I pounced the minute the bathroom door opened. I don't remember exactly what I said, or the details of our exchange, but I do remember following Ryan around our bedroom as he got ready for work and then into his car as he turned on the engine.

"Val, I have to get to work. I don't even know what to think." Ryan stared out the windshield as I sat in my pajamas and slippers in the front seat of his car.

"I don't see what the big deal is, Ryan." He turned the engine off and looked at me with his sweet hazel eyes that I fell in love with years ago.

"This is what you want? For me to have sex with other women?"

When I heard the words coming out of his mouth, yes, it seemed crazy. But my mind, my heart, and soul were craving something more—more affection, more attention, more adventure, more sex. But I wasn't ready to end my marriage over it. I remembered the day of our wedding when I vowed to be with Ryan for the rest of my life. I loved him dearly and couldn't imagine life without him. But now, the way I couldn't imagine life without him was more like imagining my life without my favorite pajama bottoms. What I needed to stay in my marriage was to be able to share our sex lives with other consenting couples. Fair game.

"Look, Ryan, I need this," I told him flatly as we sat in the cold driveway.

"You do realize that we took wedding vows, Valerie?" Ryan was clearly disturbed.

"Yes, we took vows, but this doesn't necessarily conflict with the vows because we—"

"In the presence of God, our family and friends, I offer you my solemn vow to be your faithful partner." Ryan quoted the vows we said to each other as

13

if I had forgotten. It wasn't that I was sentimental about our wedding or had an incredible memory for speeches. But our six-year-old daughter, Hallie, was in the habit of begging us to watch our wedding video over and over while wearing her princess costume. "'Faithful,' Val, not 'to have and to screw others from this day forward.'"

"Yes, Ryan, I know. But are we really being faithful to each other if we aren't honest with each other about where we're at in our marriage? And honestly, you can't really tell me that you're satisfied with our current sex life. Once a month, if that."

"Well, no, but—"

"And you can't really tell me that the idea of being with a different woman after having only been with me for the last thirteen years isn't at least a little intriguing?"

"I mean, okay, maybe, but Val…"

"What? I'm not blind. I've seen you look, and that's fine. You're human." I was getting into the groove of my pitch. "I don't think those vows meant we should be faithful to each other at the expense of being unfaithful to *us*, lying to ourselves about what we've become. I need more. I know you do, too. This isn't exactly a traditional solution, but it's something. We'd be doing something for the betterment of our marriage. And isn't that actually being faithful?"

Ryan hesitated. "Maybe." He couldn't deny some of my logic. "But how do you explain this to people?"

"You don't, Ryan. That's the whole thing! We have the chance to explore and help our marriage, and we get to do it in a way that's safe and open between us, but still private."

14

I stared at him silently. I chose my next words carefully.

"And no, I'm not saying I want you to sleep with other women, although that's what will happen. What I am saying is that I want us to confront the issues in our marriage. Our sex life, or lack thereof, is as a good a place to start as any. We both acknowledge that it needs help. This is a way to do that. It doesn't have to be the only way, but it is a way. An opportunity to remind us that we are human and that we have needs." I slowed down and looked directly at him. "Look, we spend most of our time taking care of other people's shit: our kids, our properties, this house. Let's do something for us. If I told you I had knots in my shoulders and wanted to go for a massage, you'd think nothing of it. Ryan, we have knots in our sex life. Swap Club will help us work them out."

Ryan just stared out the windshield that was starting to fog up from our body heat.

We sat in silence for a few minutes longer, and then Ryan shook his head.

"I can't do it, Val, I'm sorry. Call me old-fashioned." And that was that.

"The secret of staying young is to live honestly, eat slowly, and lie about your age." —Lucille Ball

CHAPTER 2

Forty-Nothing

I remember celebrating my mom's fortieth birthday like it was yesterday. It was 1984, I was ten years old, and my dad had rented out the private party room at Ruby Foo's Hotel.

He spent weeks on his Commodore 64 designing invitations in The Print Shop. My mother pleaded with him to just go buy a package of Hallmark fill-in-the-blank invites, but he insisted. Once they were finally printed, neither she nor I, even at the age of ten, could bear to tell him they were littered with spelling mistakes.

Back then, printing one copy took at least ten minutes. I can still hear the sound of the ink being pressed back and forth onto the perforated paper. *Eeeeeeeeh Oooooooooh. Eeeeeeeeeh eh eh eh Eeeeeeeeeeeh.* It must have taken days to print up all twenty-five misspelled invites.

Come Celebrate Carol's fourtieth birtday

Please RVSP no later then March 18th.

Ruby Foo's Hotel

Saturday March 24, 1984

7pm Sharp

Not gifts please, just bring your favorite wine.

My father came from the WASP-iest of Westmount households. He went to all-boys' private schools his whole life and then met my gorgeous wallflower of a mother, who had grown up in a traditional Jewish home in Côte Saint-Luc. All the private schooling in the world and my father still spells tomorrow with two *m*'s and one *r*.

My mom introduced him to matzo balls and knishes; he introduced her to cocktail onions and crudités. My late maternal grandfather initially hated him. My father was always too formal and uptight for my grandfather's taste. That is, until my grandfather learned that my dad knew how to make a killer Manhattan. My father attended all of their Shabbat dinners in a suit, holding flowers for my grandmother and a jar of maraschino cherries for my grandfather's drink. I think he asked my dad to come for Friday night dinners just so he could make the drinks.

The night of my mom's party, an arch of turquoise and silver balloons adorned the mahogany walls of the burgundy-carpeted party room at Ruby Foo's. The round tables were covered with white tablecloths, and the plates were adorned with white napkins that had been folded into ornate little boats. Anyone over the age of fifty-five will tell you that Ruby Foo's attracted an affluent clientele; it was considered to be the go-to venue for weddings, sweet sixteens and, in this case, my mother's fortieth birthday.

It was the eighties. Women were sporting chopped, layered hair and makeup so thickly applied that husbands could barely recognize their wives when they got into bed. Shoulder pads were not just a fashion statement—they were a way of life. My mother used to add shoulder pads to every outfit, even her sweat suits.

The men wore pastel suits over T-shirts à la Don Johnson. Unfortunately, they looked more like Don Johnson's ugly half-brother than Miami Vice himself. My dad went the other fashion route: the multi-colored Cosby sweater. My mom always told him he looked "sexy." (These days, I'm not sure "sexy" would be the descriptor used for a Cosby reference.)

My mom took my little sister, Janet, and I to get our hair done, which meant French braids and the highest waterfall of bangs one could create from teasing the front-most section of our hair. I remember getting up from the hairdresser's chair after being lacquered with Aqua Net and holding my neck stiff for hours so that my hair would stay perfectly in place. In retrospect, I could've stood in a hurricane while a tornado sucked me into its vortex, and I still would've had a perfectly teased hairdo two weeks later.

Even at five years old, Janet was already the star of the show. She was what most people call the epitome of confidence. I'm serious. I'd describe five-year-old Janet the same way I'd describe the now-thirty-five-year-old Janet: she had her own style and dressed in whatever she wanted. My mom knew better than to fight with Janet over clothes. This is what my parents referred to as "choosing their spot." Arguing with Janet over what she wanted to wear was not a fight my parents had the energy for. Even with her ridiculous outfits, Janet still looked like a kid on the cover of *Teen Beat*. Always cool. Way cooler than me.

The wait staff wore tuxedos and stood quietly on the sidelines as my family and my parents' friends stuffed their faces with roast beef and burnt-end eggrolls. My aunt read her cheesy poem, which began with the old classic: "Lordy, Lordy looks who's forty!" I remember listening to my aunt quip about gray hair and Avon ladies selling wrinkle creams and thinking to myself how old forty was. But on the bright side, I mused, when you hit forty, you got a big party.

Fast forward to 2013. My fortieth looked nothing like my mom's. Because of the Christmas holidays, we never celebrated my birthday in December. Typically, it would get acknowledged by February, and I'm pretty sure one year Ryan completely forgot. It wasn't his fault. Ryan just wasn't a big birthday guy. To make matters worse, he was born in July, so his birthdays, in the middle of his summer vacation, were always kind of nebulous. Most of the time, my birthday party was ultimately just an excuse to see our friends.

To celebrate my fortieth, Ryan made a reservation at El Taqueria. This was all because I'd mentioned one time on a vacation a few years earlier in Cancun that the resort's guacamole was delicious. One time. Ryan has a memory for details. Of course, the guacamole comment was in contrast with all the rest of the food at the resort, which made Ryan either super attentive or completely oblivious, I'm still not sure which. There was also the distinct possibility that he chose this place because it was very easy to get a last minute reservation in December for a sizeable group, and then decided to justify the choice based on the guacamole. I'll never know.

I'd mentioned several times in the year leading up to my fortieth that I didn't want a big party. I didn't want our friends to have to bother with babysitters and gifts and all the hoopla that went along with the invitation. I told him over and over that all I wanted was for the two of us to eat dinner at my favorite Italian restaurant, Bottega. I even left the number on a Post-it note stuck to his wallet. Okay, maybe that's not all I wanted… I was hoping that Swap Club was still open for discussion.

Also, Ryan probably should have checked with me about the scheduling; I was getting my period any second. On the one hand, we were celebrating my birthday in December, which never happened; on the other, I was wavering on a thin line between raging arousal and raging fury.

We arrived at the restaurant and waited at the bar for everyone. The décor was a stereotypical take on the "authentic-looking" Mexican restaurant. Strands of green and red fairy lights were slung from the wood beams, oversized sombreros hung on the walls next to painted wooden maracas and colorful woven Mayan blankets. El Taqueria for my fortieth birthday. No misspelled invitations, no catered dinner with tuxedo-clad waiters and no cheesy birthday poem. Just cheesy.

The wooden door blew open and in walked my oldest friend, Melissa, and her husband, Jeff. They stomped the snow off their boots as they entered the restaurant. I could see Melissa as she glanced around at the décor, and I knew she thought that she would rather die than celebrate her fortieth here.

"Hi! Happy belated birthday lady!" Melissa hugged me and then whispered in my ear, "Maybe next year we can go to the Mexican Riviera instead of eating Mexican?"

Jeff greeted me as Montrealers do, pressing his cheek against each of mine and making the kissing sound with his lips. The scruff on his cheek made me wince.

"Happy Birthday, Val!" Jeff said, completely oblivious to having given me the equivalent of a chemical peel with his beard, and then shook Ryan's hand. I caressed my cheek, hoping that the prickling sensation wasn't translating into crimson-colored scratch marks.

The handsome host greeted us at the bar and asked us to follow him to our booth. His gorgeous long, silky black hair reflected the greens and reds of the hanging fairy lights as we followed him. I'm not usually attracted to men with long hair, but damn, I would've had to be dead not to find him attractive. He had full lips, a perfect body, and massive triceps rippling his tight black T-shirt. I enjoyed following his toned frame to our table.

"Val? You okay with this booth?" Ryan snapped me out of my preoccupation with our host.

"Yup, looks fine." I smiled wide at the host. I couldn't help but wonder... if I couldn't be a member of Swap Club, then would I constantly be on the prowl? I needed a drink.

We slid into the brown leather horseshoe booth where we were able to sit side by side and people-watch. Awesome. The host strode back to his podium, causing females at each table to track his movement.

The tables were filled with, dare I use the term, "lumber-sexuals" in tight plaid shirts with thick beards and perfectly parted *Mad Men* hairdos sitting across from hot-looking tousled-hair girls wearing tight pants, leopard, black or some variant of such.

A non sequitur: It had recently been pointed out to me that since the nineteen fifties there has been an inverse relationship between women's pubic hairstyles and men's facial hair. Just something to consider.

We were still missing Tanya and Harry and Helen and Steve. Our waiter, who introduced himself as Roberto, came over to take our drink order. I needed some tequila in my system to help with my nerves. I suffer from a classic case of social anxiety that Ryan thinks stems from an awful slumber party Melissa and I attended when we were in elementary school. I'm not sure, I might just be wired that way. Maybe both. The funny thing is, I have no recollection whose house we were at; I seemed to have erased certain parts of this trauma to cope. We had just finished watching the movie *Grease 2* with Michelle Pfeiffer. The part I remember vividly was when it was time for bed, we lined up our sleeping bags in a row. I went to the bathroom to brush my teeth, and when I came out, all of the sleeping bags were shifted to one side of the room, all of them except for mine. Mine was left by itself all alone on the opposite side of the basement.

"Stop it! You girls are being so mean." Melissa tried shaming the flock of girls chuckling at me.

Ten girls watched and snickered as Melissa and I lifted my sleeping bag off the carpet and moved it closer to theirs. Then, like a drum-line, all of them, lifted their sleeping bags and moved them away from mine.

To this day, I remember crying myself to sleep. Melissa kept whispering for me to stop crying, that I was making it worse and she was right. The next morning I woke up with red swollen eyes that I couldn't hide from my mother when she came to pick me up.

"What happened?" she asked as I put on my shoes in the vestibule. I couldn't find it in me to tell her what happened. I was afraid she would think I was a loser.

"Will someone please tell me what happened?" I sped out of the house and left my mother inside looking for some explanation.

It's amazing how one small event could have such an impact, but every time I enter a room full of people my mind is already calculating all the ways I might be vulnerable. I learned that night about "mean girls" and how debilitating that slumber party would be for me later in life. I had my tools in place should a panic attack arise: Werther's Originals to suck on for dry mouth, and peppermint lip smacker for dry lips. Apparently peppermint doubles as a sensory distraction. But in this setting, having Ryan on one side of me, Melissa on the other, and tequila in my hand made me feel safe enough to take some of the edge off.

Roberto's humor was pleasant and upbeat despite the chaotic hustle and bustle, mariachi music and all surrounding him. Also, his reference to me being a "beautiful lady" definitely scored him some major flattery points. I was still waiting for Ryan to notice my new low-cut Zara top, miniskirt, and knee-high hooker boots that I bought this afternoon—a direct response to the bad-bun, flannel-pajama-wearing woman eating Wheat Thins in bed I had seen in the mirror the other night.

As usual, the men started their testosterone-driven sports-filled banter, and I was left with Melissa to gawk at the young and the restless beauties across the way.

"Sorry, sorry, sorry, we are late!" Helen and Steve swooped into our table like a tornado, her curly blonde hair bouncing around as she did away with her coat like a caped matador about to taunt a raging bull. She almost knocked the man sitting at the next table in the head. Steve grabbed her coat and tucked it over a free chair.

Steve had long ago gone fully gray, and yet I was still surprised how much grayer he was from the last time I saw him. He's no George Clooney, but the gray did make him look quite dapper.

"Cool place!" Steve lied. I can't always see through people, but Steve was too easy.

"What are we having? I'm ravenous!" Helen sat and thumbed through the menu.

"Tacos," I replied flatly.

"Where are Tanya and Harry?" Ryan asked me. As if I should know—he was the one that did the inviting.

"I don't know. Why don't you call her?"

"She's your friend, just call her." Ryan looked at me like he was making perfect sense.

"My friend?"

And this, by the way, was exactly how it was. Even after thirteen years of marriage, we have *his* friends and *my* friends. There were no *our* friends.

"So, you want me to call my friend and ask her why she is late for my birthday party, instead of you calling her and asking."

Ryan took his phone and begrudgingly called, but not before saying, "I don't know what the big deal is for you to call her."

Just like I expressed in the car not long ago: "I don't know what the big deal is for us to have sex with other people."

But, of course, just as he was listening for Tanya to pick up, she turned the corner with Harry.

"Hi! Awesome place!"

Liar.

"I'm so sorry we are late," Harry apologized.

Now, Harry was an anomaly, or rather a glitch in the aging system. His hair seemed to get fuller with age—or what I have come to think of as a proceeding hairline. It actually looked like his eyebrows were going to soon connect to his hairline.

"Our sitter showed up at 7:30!" Hairy—ahem, I mean *Harry*—said as he crossed his wrists and shrugged indicating he was captive to the babysitter.

Tanya interjected as the two of them squished in with the rest of us, painting me into the corner with no escape.

"I told Flaca ten times to come at 7:00, but she insists that I said 7:30. Is there any reliable help out there?" Tanya blew kisses at us. "Happy Birthday, Val."

Tanya was the kind of friend who dropped bags of apples off at our house like clockwork in September after apple picking, the kind who remembered our anniversary and never got mad about canceling a lunch date an hour before. I had a soft spot for her even with her questionably obtuse disposition.

Roberto swung around with a tray filled with umbrella-clad drinks of various colors. He even had the brains to have enough for all of us.

"Can I get *mi hermanos* some salsa and tortilla chips? Some guacamole?"

Ryan took the reins. "Definitely some guacamole for the birthday girl!"

I could feel my chest tighten.

"Why don't we add some beef tacos and chicken *fajeetas?*"

I wanted to crawl under the table. Ryan's inability to speak Mexican food was excruciating.

"Oh, you have to see this." Helen pulled out her phone to show us something. I was hoping it was some celebrity nipple slip or maybe even a leaked Oprah and Stedman sex tape. (Another consequence of wanting to become a member of a sex club was, apparently, the assumption that everyone else was also fixated on sex.)

"It's just the most amazing thing, I have to find it."

Tanya, Melissa and I sat and waited while Helen searched on her phone for, hopefully, another picture of Anne Hathaway, Britney Spears or Lindsay Lohan "accidentally" exposing her lady bits while getting out of a car.

"Maggie sang the most adorable song the other day when she was in the bath."

Come again? I took the umbrella out of my Windex-blue drink and downed it. My adult party was quickly turning into just another night out with my *normal* friends.

"Amazing, can't wait to see it," I managed through clenched teeth. I looked back at Ryan who was sipping his emerald drink, his lips turning the same green because he had taken the straw out. That was my sexy husband over there, turning into the Hulk. Minus the full head of hair, muscles and ability to punch through cement walls. With his penis.

Ryan was politely listening to Steve's riveting story about a fence.

"So, I told my neighbor, if you don't like the fence then don't fucking look at it. I mean, how the hell do they expect me to put in a pool without a freaking fence?"

Where was Roberto? I needed some more Windex. Stat.

"Wait, where is it?" Helen was still looking for that video of her kid singing. Shoot me, please. I tried to convince her she'd already shown it to me, or, better yet, to the world.

"The one you posted on Instagram? I saw it."

Nope, that did nothing. Helen was still searching.

"It's the law, you know, and because the pool is so fucking big, the fence has to be big."

My choices were listening to Steve rant about his fascinating fence or watch the video of Helen's kid in a bath. Where was Roberto?

"Oh, here it is!" With a plastic smile, Helen held the phone to show us. We all looked attentively. Rather, we all looked like we were looking attentively.

"You know? It's a safety pre-… safety pre-...?"

"Caution." Helen had ears everywhere, even while showing the terrible-quality video of her little girl singing off-key.

"Yeah, a fucking safety precaution." Steve caught Helen's intervention.

Was this how I was spending my fortieth? What was going on? Even Ryan must have thought it was horrible.

"I mean, how does he expect you to swim in your pool without a fence? What a prick." Ryan spoke between sips, oblivious to the bright green mess happening all over his mouth. He looked like he just ate out a Muppet.

Nope, Ryan didn't think my birthday dinner was horrible. I needed Roberto. My dad threw my mother a beautiful party, he sent out invitations, albeit homemade, but he sent out actual invitations to a party, with balloons and tablecloths and here I was at a taco shack with my oblivious friends talking about pool fences. Where was my fortieth birthday poem?

"Oh hey, kids!"

And just when I thought my birthday couldn't get any worse, Sabrina Weinstein, the most vicious female living in Montreal, was standing at my table.

"Hi, Sabrina," I muttered as Roberto touched down with my Windex.

She was dressed for the Golden Globes. Perfectly curled hair, perfectly flawless skin, and then my eyes zeroed in on the three perfectly matching tennis bracelets on her wrist.

"We have our friend's fortieth tonight." Sabrina motioned towards a table of attractive couples doing tequila shots. At least I wasn't the only sucker celebrating forty at this small step up from Applebee's cliché of a restaurant. Maybe Ryan was more hip than I gave him credit for.

"What's your excuse for being dragged to this horrible taco stand, Val?"

Maybe not. I could have killed her. I wanted to rip the tennis bracelet from my wrist. I wanted to be nothing like Sabrina Weinstein.

"It's Val's fortieth birthday!" Tanya piped in.

"Fortieth? Val? I thought you already turned forty."

Oh no she didn't.

"Nope, I turned forty a couple of days ago." The drinks weren't strong enough.

"Well, Val, you don't look a day over thirty-nine."

My brain was already justifying my earlier anxiety and making notes to be more on guard next time while simultaneously making a case to just stay home. Part of me wanted to call Sabrina a bitch to her face, tell her she should really go fuck herself with her Chanel, but the mariachi band decided at that very moment to march by us with their trumpets and it was too loud. They were headed right for Sabrina's table.

Also, that part of me usually really only wakes up after the moment has passed. My snappy comeback for the obnoxious guy in line at the ATM always comes when I'm three blocks away. I had no doubt I would be dreaming up retorts for Sabrina Weinstein in bed that night.

"Ugh. Can it get any worse? See you fogies later." And with a flip of her hair she continued to sashay to her table.

One of the mariachi singers dropped a sombrero on Sabrina's friend's head and the band started singing "Happy Birthday" in Spanish to her. I downed my Windex and stuck my hand up for Roberto to grab me another.

"I can't stand her," Melissa confessed.

"Whatever, she's harmless." I tried to mask my indignation. If I acted like Sabrina bothered me, I felt like it was showing weakness.

"Yeah, harmless, until she's sleeping with Ryan," Tanya spat out.

Ryan, who now looked more like the Jolly Green Giant, looked stunned at the notion.

"Sleeping with Ryan? You think I'm threatened by Sabrina?" I had to ask Tanya because Tanya was my "call 'em as she sees 'em" kind of friend, and if she thought I was threatened then I had to put an end to that line of thought.

"No, seriously." Tanya added, "I heard she swings."

"Now we're talking." Harry excitedly perked up.

"Swing? Yeah, right. And if that were the case, if Sabrina were fucking Ryan, that would mean I would be fucking her husband."

The whole table glanced over at Sabrina's gorgeous husband. Ryan awkwardly shifted, his green mouth in a grimace. He looked utterly ridiculous.

"It's true! Some kind of secret swingers society! I heard it from Claire who heard it from Janice," Tanya said.

"Well, if you heard it from Claire who heard it from Janice—" Jeff teased.

"Who heard what from who?" Harry asked. Ryan continued shifting in his seat like a kid in synagogue. I just stared at Ryan. So much for the super-secret sex club.

"Does it really matter?" Tanya asks. "The point is everyone is talking about it." Ryan looked like he was going to puke up the Chicago River on St. Patrick's Day.

"Everyone is talking about it because it is absolutely a crock of shit. There is no swingers club in Montreal," Ryan said flatly, as if he hoped that would put an end to it.

"Well, if there is a secret club that has married people having sex with each other, then I think it's fucking gross." Melissa seemed completely mad at the whole idea.

But her husband seemed to think differently. "Oh yeah, it's fucking gross to have sex with other women. Consensually. Without getting into trouble. Like a permanent hall pass."

Just as Ryan looked as if he was going to burst, Roberto placed the guacamole, tacos, and *fajeetas* on the table and everyone dug in. The timing was impeccable.

The evening continued with inane chitchat. But I was feeling restless. And edgy. (Thanks, period.) And horny. (Thanks, gorgeous host.) I had to turn things up. I wanted to get my mind off of the conversation. Not to mention, I was dressed to the nines (okay, maybe my version of nines, not necessarily up to Sabrina Weinstein's standards) and wanted a little attention. This couldn't be all I had to look forward to tonight. Guacamole, Windex and some video of Maggie singing in the bath? What had my life become? I had to do something to get this night turned around. My fortieth birthday celebration should be a night I wanted to remember. I was going to show Ryan that I was serious about spicing things up.

Under the table, I mischievously put my hand on Ryan's crotch. He got startled and his guacamole almost came out his nose. He shot me a crazy look as he grabbed a napkin.

Melissa picked up where we left off earlier. "Not that there is a secret swingers club, but if there was a secret club then how do you get in? I mean, my sex life is fantastic—I am not asking for me."

Jeff patted himself on the shoulder.

Under the table, I slid my hand back up Ryan's lap, between his legs, and started rubbing his crotch. But he grabbed my hand and swiftly rejected my advance.

"What are you doing?" Ryan whispered under his breath into my ear.

"Just playing." I winked at him, but he looked away and discreetly crossed his legs away from me and moved slightly closer to Tanya.

Maybe Ryan wasn't attracted to me anymore. For some reason I decided the best way to be sure at that moment was to take Ryan's hand and put it between my legs.

"I couldn't do it. Have sex with a different guy every month? No way." Tanya spoke with her mouth full of guacamole.

"You mean I could be having sex with a different woman every month?" Harry joked. Tanya shot him a look.

Ryan and I were keeping our composure, but below sea level, Ryan was resolutely trying to pull his hand away from my firm grasp.

"Excuse me? Are you not satisfied?" Tanya quipped back.

I pretended to be interested in hearing Harry's response about his sexual satisfaction while Ryan kept pulling his hand away from between my legs and simultaneously swiping my intrusive hand from his crotch. What guy wouldn't want this?

"Will you stop it?" Ryan snapped at me.

Just then, an extra large sombrero was suddenly on my head and a flan with candles stuck in it was placed in front of me. The mariachi band belted out *"Feliz Cumpleanos! Ole! Feliz Cumpleanos! Ole!"*

I'm not sure if it was the four Windex drinks I downed or the chaos at my table, but all of a sudden, my vision began to get foggy and my hearing became impaired. I looked over at Ryan and his scowl reminded me that my dissatisfaction in our sex life was clouding my judgment. My anxiety was repeating "told you to stay home" while my brain was calculating possible exits.

The mariachi band was drowned out by the sound of the people laughing at the other table. All I could do was wish I were anywhere but here.

Then the silence. They waited for me to blow out my candles. I could feel my heart thumping against my chest as I looked at Ryan's face, distraught but forcing a smile. I felt like he resented me; he just didn't want to admit it. Forget him. I resented me. Who was this person I had become? I didn't recognize myself anymore. How could it be possible to be perfect on paper yet still feel such a tremendous void?

I had to get out of there. I quickly blew out my candles, leaving a few burning. I tugged my skirt down and then took off still wearing the sombrero.

As I ran out of the restaurant, the gorgeous host yelled after me;

"Happy Birthday! Come again!"

In my low cut top, mini skirt, and knee-high boots—and still wearing the sombrero—I looked like a fucking crazy Mexican hooker running up

Ste. Catherine Street in the middle of winter. But I didn't care, because as long as I was running away, I felt like I was running back to me.

The next morning I woke up with the most intense headache. Ryan left the door to our bedroom closed to let me sleep off the night before. I got out of bed and listened. I could hear the voices of the kids faintly and, as I opened the door, Ryan getting them dressed in their snowsuits to play outside. He was warning them to leave the yellow *and* blue snow alone.

The aftermath of my fortieth birthday party was spent in bed sipping coffee and eating saltines. I got several texts from Melissa and Tanya asking what happened to me. I texted back with a martini glass and sad face emoji, then turned my phone on silent. I was even too worn out to dream up witty comebacks I could have said to Sabrina Weinstein.

After my sudden birthday party exit, Ryan combed the streets for me in his car. He finally found me a few blocks from the restaurant, not running anymore but barely walking. If only I had sneakers on, I would've been home before him. My new hooker boots were "sitting down and eating" hooker boots, not "running a half-marathon" hooker boots.

Ryan pulled up alongside me and yelled, "Val, get in. You barely have any clothes on!"

So he finally noticed my new outfit. I ignored him as the tears welled in my eyes.

"I need more, Ryan. I need more than this. I know it's out there. I know it seems irrational and risky but it is what I need."

Ryan put the car in park and climbed out. He walked over to me and placed his coat around my shoulders. My feet were killing me, I was cold, and I knew Ryan was attributing my impulsive behavior to the Windex I had been downing all night (thank you, Roberto).

"I'm forty, I have everything I could ever want, and you're an amazing husband and father. If you just give me this, I will be forever grateful."

Ryan stared at the pavement. He couldn't make eye contact with me. I mean, here I was, literally begging him to let us have sex with other people. What kind of wife asks that of her husband?

"I know I'm asking a lot, and I know how crazy this sounds. I'm just asking you to trust me and give me what I need."

"Let's go home, Val. Let me think about it."

I got into the car and we continued home. Every block closer to the house, my mouth became dryer and my neck got sweatier until we finally pulled into our driveway, where I swung open my door and puked blue all over the snow on our front lawn.

"For she's a jolly good fellow, which nobody can deny…"

"I can remember when the air was clean and the sex was dirty." —*George Burns*

CHAPTER 3

A Celestial Meeting

Ryan agreed to meet with Celeste, the "Madame" of Swap Club, the week after my party. The day Ryan and I went to that fateful meeting happened to coincide with the very first time I'd ever skipped a waxing appointment with Svetlana Chesnokov, the coveted Russian esthetician known for her Brazilian bikini-waxing prowess. Here I was, trading in the long-lost hope that a well-manicured muff would be enough to inspire us under the sheets to become part of a consensual sex ring.

How did I find Celeste? Well, being the resourceful person that I am (I really should have been a private investigator), I was able to set up a meeting with her after three days, six phone calls, and four emails. I can't tell you any more than that. This is a secret club after all, and Rule #6 was put in place to respect the privacy of its members.

Celeste—if that's even her real name—had flawless ivory skin and wild red hair. She reminded me of Susan Sarandon in *The Witches of Eastwick*. She must've been a cool chick in the nineties, the kind who loved a methed-out, coked-up Steven Tyler and knew about raves before they were a thing.

She welcomed us into her charming Victorian home in Westmount: creaking oak wood floors, ornate crown moldings, and the smell of lavender in the air. I'd heard lavender was used to calm nerves, so I took some deep breaths, hoping it would help calm mine.

Celeste looked directly and deeply into our eyes, first Ryan's, then mine. When we locked gazes, I felt like she could see all the lies I'd been telling my whole life. I had the urge to confess all my dirty secrets to her and let her bear the burden of all my sins. I pluck my body hair. I sit on my ass most days while my kids are in school and my husband is at work. I eat chocolate for lunch and then complain at suppertime that I didn't eat lunch. I PVR porn and watch it at 11 am, and then erase it. I hate some of my friends. I love doing absolutely nothing. I have brown spots on my skin that I don't want to get checked just in case they are cancerous. I tried Indian food once and loved it, even though I was sick for hours after. Pepto is a staple on my grocery list. I pretend to listen to people when they talk to me. My mother scares me. Most of the time I say yes because I'm too scared to say no.

"So, you think you want to be a part of this club?" Celeste's question must have been rhetorical because she continued speaking before either of us could open our mouths. "This is a very strict club. There are no second chances, and one broken rule will get you expelled."

"Expelled?" Ryan asked. "Sounds like high school."

"Something like high school, if you're referring to the raging hormones and hot sex." Celeste had made this spiel before. I could tell just by her quick wit and ability to shut Ryan up.

Unexpectedly I became tense. It was weird; I was the one who wanted this! I'm the one who convinced Ryan that this would be good for our marriage, and here I was utterly perplexed. I couldn't tell if it was the stiff antique chair, but I was extremely uncomfortable. Was this actually happening? The last time I'd been in a meeting like this we were at the notary for our pre-nup. Now we were listening to Susan Sarandon explaining the rules for consensual adultery. My moral compass was being muddled by my need to rekindle my sex life.

"The rules of Swap Club are very straightforward," she went on. There were six of them in total:

1. No exchanging phone numbers with new partners.
2. No socializing as couples with other Swap Club couples outside the Club.
3. Only attractive couples can be members.
4. The contract is good for one year.
5. All participants are required to undergo physicals before being accepted. Sexual relations are permitted only with Club members and spouses for the duration of the contract.
6. No disclosure of the Club or its members to anyone, period.

The third one was a stinger, especially if we weren't accepted. It was common to hear rumors circulating about the Club, especially among the less attractive and overweight demographics, or anyone who drove a Hyundai, Honda or a Kia. (My apologies to anyone who drives one of these cars, but the honesty I'm offering is probably why you're going to keep reading.) Besides, I didn't make the rules. I just broke most of them.

The fifth one was a bit disconcerting—I hadn't thought about STDs in years—but definitely a necessary health precaution, especially since condom use couldn't actually be monitored. I guess it was also important to figure out which women were on birth control and who got their period when. Sheesh. It appeared sex was never easy breezy, even when it was an organized sport. But I appreciated the Club's rigor. As long as no one cheated outside the Club, everyone was safe. Kinda.

The swap happened the second Saturday of every month, so there was some semblance of organization. Celeste would send a text message to the husband's cell phone the day of with the designated address for the 8 p.m. rendezvous. No names were given, no back-story, just the address.

The men must leave their assigned addresses by 11 p.m. sharp or else their Mercedes, BMW, Range Rover, or Escalade (fill in your luxury vehicle of choice here) would turn into a pumpkin. Kidding. This was to avoid having men cross paths and prevent the awkward post-coital walk of shame witnessed by the freaking couple's other half.

So, to be clear, we were given three hours to fuck someone else's husband while our husband was off fucking someone else's wife. I'll let you chew on that for a moment.

Celeste placed a stack of papers on her coffee table that looked as legally binding as any contract I'd ever laid eyes on. My body was frozen. I imagined it was possible to mistake my deer-in-the-headlights paralysis for calm, but I was actually using every ounce of self-control to not throw up on the coffee table. I'm not sure Celeste would let you have play dates in the fancy sex club if you heaved your lunch all over the contract. Was I really going to do this? Could I really do this? I wasn't sure I'd even know where to begin with another body that wasn't Ryan's.

"Take this home, read it over, and if you think you can keep a secret and abide by the rules, you may sign it and drop it off with a certified cheque for two thousand dollars."

"That's it?" I asked, surprised. The notary had gone through our pre-nup line by line and asked us a million probing questions.

"That's it?" The fee surprised Ryan. "What's the two thousand dollars for?" Celeste looked at Ryan and then leaned over her desk and spoke directly to him.

"The cost of keeping this Club exclusive so that you don't have a Steve Buscemi or a busker fucking your wife, Mr. Martin."

And with that, Ryan sat back and never uttered another word about the membership fee again. Not to mention his golf membership, which he'd used a total of one time last summer, cost way more than this. And I was sure he planned on using this membership a hell of a lot more than one time.

I couldn't believe that was the extent of our interview. My pre-interview anxiety-addled brain, as it does so often when I don't know what's coming, had conjured much more intimate methods for screening couples—like Celeste, cigarette dangling from her long fingers, asking us to strip off our clothes as she slowly circled around us in her silk bathrobe, scrutinizing our bodies and educating us about the virtues of erotica and sex toys. I pictured Ryan nervously standing naked in her secret sex room; she would demand that I get him hard. Of course, that's not how it went down, thank God, because I would never have made it through.

I caught a glimpse of myself in the mirror on Celeste's wall while Ryan asked a few more questions about the safety of the Club and the importance of privacy. The image immediately morphed in my brain and there I was, in all my domestic glory, sporting a dirty ponytail, flannel pajamas, and cracker crumbs collecting under my collar. I could feel the fear of my dissolving marriage, of societal judgment and scrutiny all beginning to grip me.

"Yes, that's right. The other members voted. Majority ruled," Celeste responded. I'd missed Ryan's question.

"Majority ruled? So, you mean the others want us in?" I asked confused.

"Just keep your mouths shut." Celeste smiled and then pushed the paperwork closer to us.

Lightheaded from the influx of all the Swap Club information, I stood up and put my hand out.

"Thank you for meeting with us. We will talk it over and get back to you." Celeste smirked at me as she shook my hand.

"Looks like there'll be no need, Valerie." Celeste pushed the contract over in front of me.

I was confused, and then looked down at the contract where the ink from Ryan's signature was already starting to dry. Turns out Ryan had bigger fears.

Too afraid to say no to my deep-seated desires, Ryan was saying yes to it all.

"I know a man who gave up smoking, drinking, sex and rich food. He was healthy right up to the day he killed himself." —Johnny Carson

CHAPTER 4

Screening and Shouting

We were in.

Almost.

The bank teller stared at me from behind her dark rimmed glasses as she stamped the cheque. I just smiled coyly. Little did she know that the cheque she just certified for two thousand dollars was being used to improve my sex life. Even if I had indulged her, she didn't strike me as the type that would have cared.

As I left the bank and drove myself to Celeste's to drop it off, I was having an imaginary argument with my mother.

"Most people spend more than that on gas in a year. Beats the hell out of gym memberships, mammograms, dental visits, and all the boring stuff we pay to put ourselves through!" I was arguing with myself in the rearview mirror. The stress was getting to me.

Only one thing left to do. Ryan and I had to be screened for STDs, and I needed to take a pregnancy test. Funnn.

We were given the address to a private home in Outremont, one of the neighborhoods in Montreal most highly populated with Orthodox Jews. Was the doctor going to check me through a sheet with a hole?

Ryan took off early from work, something he rarely did. But we were keen to start the Club in January, which meant we had just two weeks to get the medical side of things organized. Once Ryan decided to do something, he hated to wait. The night he decided we needed a larger car, he posted my sedan on Lease Busters before I had finished brushing my teeth.

Ryan was a CFO at one of Montreal's larger real estate companies. He didn't have to answer to anyone and could quite literally work from his car if he wanted. In spite of that, he worked between seventy and eighty hours a week, and never once in the thirteen years we'd been married had he taken a sick day.

As we pulled into the driveway in front of a statuesque home on Bloomfield Avenue, I was Rolodexing through the countless school functions, friends' birthday dinners, and family barbeques Ryan couldn't make because of his crazy workload. We could barely schedule free time together, let alone while the kids were at school. Yet here we were, making time to see each other during the day so we could see other people at night.

As I slammed the car door shut, another wave of doubt washed over me. I'd been fighting these waves since signing the documents at Celeste's a few days earlier. Fear is a fickle motivator. We'd already given her our two thousand dollars; it was non-refundable. And we were about to submit voluntarily to STD testing like a couple of awkward college students—and in someone's private home, no less. Someone who knew exactly why we were there. Oy. The whole thing was hideously embarrassing.

As we waited on the front stoop for the door to be answered, I broke into a high-pitched giggling fit.

"What?" Ryan looked at me. "What's so funny?" His face darkened; I could see him shutting down. "What the hell, Val?"

I actually didn't find any of it funny at all, but I couldn't help it—I'm that person who laughs uncontrollably when I'm nervous or uncomfortable. My nerves were vibrating through my organs at an 8.2 on the Richter scale.

I tried to stop myself from laughing, but the more I tried, the more I laughed. Here I was—the girl who wore flip-flops in hotel showers, carried Kleenex in every coat pocket, whose knuckles were drier than a nun's vagina from washing them so often with soap (and Purell)—standing outside some fancy off-the-books doctor's house to get screened for an STD. Gals like me didn't get STDs. And we certainly didn't join sex clubs.

The door opened, and thankfully the guy looked nothing like a rabbi—more like David Duchovny with a stethoscope. His eyes were a smoky green. He was actually kind of hot. I stopped laughing immediately. I was still quite nervous, but now I was also focused.

Dr. Krief introduced himself and walked us up his stairs into a home office where a handsome woman in her late fifties was already waiting.

"This is Dr. Houde. Mr. Martin, please follow her into that room. Mrs. Matthews, you can come with me."

To say I was thrilled would be a serious exaggeration. It didn't quite add up. Why was I going with him, and Ryan going with her? I shot Ryan a look. I didn't want to be the one to ask if Swap Club was starting now. Truth be told, if it was starting, I was definitely winning with Dr. Krief. But I wasn't mentally or physically prepared to begin the sexfest today. I still needed time to prep. Maybe I could ask to use the bathroom and give myself a quickie French bath and freshen up the underground a bit.

"Dr. Krief, if you don't mind me asking, why is my wife not being seen by Dr. Houde?" Maybe Ryan had a little jealous in him after all.

"I don't mind you asking," answered Dr. Krief flatly. "I'm a gynecologist, and Dr. Houde is a GP. So, unless you have a vagina, Dr. Houde will be more than happy to do your exam."

Dr. Krief took the folder with my name on it and asked me to follow him. And so I did, but not before I turned back to see Ryan dragging his feet as he followed Dr. Houde across the hall.

We entered a room that looked exactly like every other doctor's office I'd ever been in. The exam table was classic, accessorized with metal stirrups for Dr. Krief's viewing pleasure. I had no idea I was coming here for an internal. Fuck me.

"Have a seat on the table, and I will be back in a minute." Dr. Krief left the room, and I immediately started to get undressed. Good thing I wore jeans and a T-shirt, nothing too difficult to unhook or undo. I was wearing some really cute pink underwear with mini ribbon bows down the backside. I slid them off and tossed them on top of the pile of clothes on the chair. I have a thing for underwear; I've never been able to wear just any old pair. They had to be pretty, if not downright sexy. I've honestly never been sure whom I'm wearing them for. It certainly wasn't Ryan. Whenever we had sex, he was about as interested in my underwear as a kid is in the ribbon on his birthday present. It was just one more obstacle to overcome on the feverish warpath to the booty, so to speak. I guess it's more like a weird extension of some old motherly anxiety: always wear nice underwear in case you get into a car accident.

I made myself comfortable on the table and sat there naked, waiting for him. I hadn't been naked in front of another man in forever (with the obvious exception of Dr. Rosenberg at my yearly physical—where I still cringe at age forty.) I was shivering with nerves—and maybe anticipation?—as I lay like a piece of smoked meat on the cold, crinkly wax paper covering the examination table. I wished the doctor would skip the physical exam and just take my word that everything was fine.

My mind cycled back to the spring of '85 when my non-existent boobs turned into swollen nipple bumps. Too small to wear a bra, and too obvious not to wear anything. I remember cringing as my family doctor, Dr. Rosenberg, who looked like everyone's dad, did his routine exam and lowered my gown and pressed his cold, thick fingers on my nipples. I was mortified. As soon as we were in the elevator heading back down to the car, I begged my mother to switch me to a female doctor. And so she did. My mother found Dr. Helen, a woman doctor that called my vagina a *weewer* and my breasts *bumpaloompas*.

I quickly switched back to Dr. Rosenberg and have been with him ever since. At thirteen, having a woman touch my boobs was basically just as terrifying as having a man touch them. At forty, having anyone touch my boobs was comedic. After breastfeeding two kids, my breasts looked liked the droopy dog from *Tom and Jerry*.

I heard the tap of Dr. Krief's Oxfords on the wood floor making their way to the door. My palms and thighs were soaking a hole in the hygienic exam table paper. Hideously. Embarrassing.

I was still wondering whether Dr. Krief was going to break me in for Swap Club. My anxiety about Swap Club had me convinced that everything was going to be some kind of wild sexual episode. Listen, when you sign up for something crazy, you can't be sure when the crazy is going to begin.

Okay, I had to calm my nerves before the exam table paper disintegrated beneath me. I started thinking about his eyes. Man, those smoky eyes. Just as I was readjusting my pose on the table, Dr. Krief walked in and quickly shut the door.

"So we have to do the questionnaire first," he told me, motioning to the paper he'd gone to retrieve while I'd been stripping down (prematurely, apparently).

"I'm sorry, you didn't need to undress yet," Dr. Krief said, as he handed me the gown that had been hanging an inch from my face the whole time. I wasn't positive, but I think I caught him giving me a quick but full once-over as he handed me the gown.

I awkwardly unstuck myself from the paper and tried gracefully to wrap myself up, blushing with embarrassment. Dr. Krief wheeled over his chair and began to ask me questions about my medical history and sexual experience. It was super detailed. He wanted to know whether I had any allergies. Ah, there was still hope for Ryan's backdoor exit! If part of the screening process was an allergy test, Ryan would for sure fail and get us kicked out, and then we would just go back to our normal, sexually impaired marriage. Ryan would be sure to remind me that he tried to make my wish come true, but unforeseeable circumstances stood in our way. Win-win for him.

"Have you ever been screened for HPV? Gonorrhea?" I fixated on his moving lips and started to tune out. They were full lips. I kept on nodding my head and began to wonder if he was a good kisser. My mind kept wandering to his different body parts and at some point—maybe it was the current line of questioning?—as my brain traveled further away, I found myself trying to guess his stance on licking ass. Not that I'd ever had this done to me, not by Ryan or any previous boyfriends, but I'd recently watched an episode of *Sex with Sunny Megatron*, and she devoted a whole segment to anal pleasure. She talked about there being a second G-spot in there. I've never had much success with the first G-spot. Who would know better how to find it—or them—than a doctor?

The next part of the screening went more routinely, and all my sexual curiosities evaporated the minute the syringe penetrated my vein and drew two vials of blood from my arm. I also discovered there was no seductive way to get a Pap smear, or to pee into a cup for a pregnancy test. Nothing about handing over a steaming cup of piss, even to hot Dr. David Duchovny, was the least bit sexy.

As I was getting dressed, and Dr. Krief was stuffing my report into an envelope (for, I could only assume, Celeste) I heard a yelp. Apparently, Ryan was getting his blood work done. He'd never been a fan of needles, even so the scream was pretty loud.

I waited for Ryan in the makeshift waiting room. He emerged about ten minutes after me and kept fidgeting with his pants. He didn't look well, and Dr. Houde was holding a glass of orange juice.

"Are you okay?" I asked, concerned, but he wouldn't look at me. He just walked past and said over his shoulder, "You better drive." He continued right down the stairs.

I turned to Dr. Houde. "What happened?"

"Mr. Martin fainted. Twice." Dr. Houde gestured to the orange juice in her hand. She explained that Ryan had to have his urethra swabbed with a Q-tip to check for gonorrhea, chlamydia, and herpes. That's why he fainted the first time. Dr. Houde cautioned that we could both be randomly selected throughout the year for another round of tests. This was how Celeste kept the members in the Club, and deadly sex-related diseases out. And that's why Ryan fainted the second time.

I put Ryan's Audi A5 into first gear. I forgot how feisty the car could be, and did my best to act cool as I struggled to remember the subtle maneuvers of driving stick. But my anxiety had also reached a fever pitch. So, like any mature and evolved partner, I drove home that day apologizing the whole way and telling Ryan how much this meant to our marriage as he lay on the backseat in silence, too embarrassed to criticize me for grinding the gears all the way back to NDG.

A few days later, Ryan was helping our ten-year-old son, Michael, with his science fair project, an extra-credit assignment from his teacher, Miss Clarice, who (in my opinion) had it in for Michael. Last year, Michael had Miss Gemma, a sweet, mild-mannered, soft-spoken lady. This year he has Miss Clarice, whose name, to be honest, I couldn't say without thinking about *Silence of the Lambs*. Miss Clarice (suck on teeth) decided that instead of giving Michael a detention for an unfinished book report, she would enroll him in the grade four Science Fair. And by enroll Michael, I mean enroll Ryan, Michael, and myself.

The topic of choice: using pulse rate to measure emotion. Michael (Ryan and I) will spend the next few months documenting if pulse rate is a good indicator of fear or excitement.

Just as Ryan and Michael were learning how to take their pulse, Ryan got the text from Celeste welcoming us to Swap Club for the next twelve months. I nodded at the information and wandered mindlessly into the powder room on our main floor. I'm sure Ryan's heart rate changed accordingly.

Things were starting to get very real. I stared at myself in the mirror, trying to do the math. How had my life gotten here? Meet a nice boy, get married, have kids. Check. Join an organized couples' swap and sleep with other people's spouses. WTF? This was not one of the milestones I'd fantasized about as a little girl. The forty-year-old woman in the mirror staring back at me realized, almost for the first time, that her marriage must be pretty messed up if she thought that other women sleeping with her husband was going to fix things.

My eyes unfocused, and I could feel the weight of everything pushing down on me. This was crazy. Swap Club was crazy. I had no idea how I was going to do it. My brain started charting escape roots. I could fake a kidney stone and get Ryan to drive me to the hospital. What if I just didn't answer the door?

Sex might be a very good distraction. Deep breaths. I decided to focus on the sex. All the sex I was going to have. After all, I used to really like sex. When my mind had been open and carefree, I daresay I was a sexual person. Things were different now. I wasn't in my twenties. But sex had been good once. It could be good again. Maybe it would energize me, make me less cranky, and turn me into a happier, more lighthearted person. I took one last look in the mirror and left the bathroom with a bit of resolve. If nothing else, it seemed like it would take my mind off Ryan having sex, which was going to happen unless I pretended to have a collapsed lung.

I kicked into logistics mode. First, I'd call my mom to make sure the kids could sleep at her house on January 11. Second, I'd call Svetlana Chesnokov to book an appointment for a Brazilian.

My daughter broke my train of thought.

"Mommy, you didn't flush."

"Oh, right. Sorry, honey."

"If you are always trying to be normal, you will never know how amazing you can be." — *Maya Angelou*

CHAPTER 5

Swap #1: January 11, 2014

Not Your Average Joe Blow

"You are not cheating, you are not cheating, you are not cheating," I kept repeating, like a mantra, desperately trying to hypnotize my brain into submission. Call it cheating or not, it didn't change the fact that I was about to have sex with not-my-husband for the first time in over fifteen years. I'd honestly never actually considered having sex with another man. Sure, I'd imagined doing it with my fair share of celebrities. Zac Efron, Bradley Cooper, Gordon Ramsay, Simon Cowell (the last two must be the submissive in me)—they all got my juices flowing.

There were even a couple of guys from my past I'd cycle through in some of my fantasies. But those were just that: fantasies. Like having sex in Buckingham Palace, my daughter winning the Nobel Prize, or ditching my life to run a kayak rental shop on a beach in Bora Bora.

In just a few minutes, there was going to be a strange man in my house, and I had already tacitly agreed to have some sexual interaction with him. What if he wasn't attractive to me? What if he wasn't attracted *to* me? Did we have to have sex? Would we have sex? My head was running laps. I needed to pull it together.

Before Ryan kissed me goodbye, "Business Ryan" wanted to have a talk.

"Val," he said, "I've given this a lot of thought, and I want us to make a pact that we don't discuss what we do during our swaps."

"Business Ryan" put his hand out for me to shake, and then "Husband Ryan" gave me an encouraging hug and kiss before finally leaving.

The road getting here was a bumpy one, but now we were on this journey together, and I was nervous as hell. I sat on the couch, staring at the walls filled with our wedding pictures and vacation snapshots. The unnaturalness of what I was doing was surfacing in a serious way just minutes before my first swap was about to arrive. I've never jumped out of a plane, but I imagine something similar happens at the moment before that plane door opens at ten thousand feet. People aren't meant to fly. And, if they happen to be flying, they aren't expected to jump out of the plane. The problem is, that's what's happening so the only thing left to do is double-check your gear. I decided to do the same thing and redirect my attention to my outfit of choice.

Tight blue jeans, sheer white T-shirt and a hot pink bra with a matching G-string I'd bought years ago when I still cared what Ryan saw me in. That was before I'd realized how little he concerned himself with my undergarments. He was fine with whatever I wanted to wear. The understanding was that if I wasn't wearing clothes, I was up for having sex. He couldn't care less what he had to remove from my body to get in. So underwear became just *my* thing. Now I had the chance to show off for someone who might care.

I wondered if my too-casual style might not be as cool as I thought it was. Maybe I should have worn something edgier, something unexpected. So much for keeping my brain in check. This is the thing when you're a worrier—you worry. So I got up and checked myself in the mirror. "You look great!" I was the only one on hand to give my forty-year-old self a pep talk.

Before I had time to analyze that last thought, my ruminating was shattered by the familiar sound of the doorbell. Except it seemed like the doorbell sounded different this time. Almost like it was summoning me in a flirtatious, teasing way. I had a sudden rush of anticipation. My stomach fluttered as I took a deep breath before opening my proverbial threshold. My heart pounded against my chest as the door opened, and my eyes fell on Joe. I could hear each rhythmic beat in my ears so loudly, I was certain Joe could too.

His eyes smiled as he recognized me. Joe and I had known each other since we were eleven years old. Of course. Quintessential Jewish Montreal. My moral dilemma and anxiety were eclipsed by the familiar—and attractive—face in front of me. Never mind that we'd known each other forever, Joe had also been my first kiss in grade eight! I couldn't believe it. My first swap was my first kiss. I hoped this time would be more relaxed and have less teeth banging.

The extra crazy part was that I'd always had a soft spot for Joe. Not like an active fantasy—he was just one of those people that you always have a connection with because of your history. His once-brown hair, now a sexy shade grayer, was shaved on the sides, and the tuft on top of his head hung casually but strategically to the left. He looked like a model. He always had, but now he looked like a distinguished Calvin Klein model. Jackpot.

"Thank God," he whispered loud enough for my ears to hear over the heartbeats, which, if it were possible, were hammering even harder now.

"Thank God?" He was standing so close; I could feel his breath on my face. His eyes were smoldering. He was insanely sexy. It was at that moment that I discovered that lust is stronger than a lot of other feelings. I'm not proud of that, but there it is. My next thought was whether I should just rip off my clothes right there and let him have at me. At least that's what happened in *9 ½ Weeks*.

"You look exactly the same," he breathed. Not to sound conceited, but I was accustomed to people telling me that. Joe's attempt at pushing my flattery buttons didn't necessarily go the distance he probably hoped it would. Or I hoped it would. It dawned on me that I was yearning to be seen as more than just "the same." Something more like, "God, you're sexy," "You're so sexy," or "You're so fucking sexy." I would've been happy with any of those.

Joe and I stood in my entrance, our noses practically touching, eyes locked on each other, and for a minute all my brain could think about was the next time I'd bump into his wife, Denise, at our local market. Joe's hand found its way onto my shoulder. He examined my arm and made his way down to my hand. I almost panicked because my hand was a bit sweaty, but then again, so was his.

In one fluid gesture—a move I could only imagine he'd been practicing over and over—he pulled me in and kissed my lips with his eyes wide open. I'm sure he thought there was no need for small talk; we were in this for one thing and one thing only, and there wasn't any time to waste. My head was still trying to interject with questions and worries, but since my lips were enjoying themselves, my brain had to take a back seat.

His mouth was moist and warm. His tongue tasted sweet. The minute his hand pulled my head closer to his, I lost all feeling in my legs. I couldn't remember the last time I'd French kissed. Never mind that, I couldn't remember the last time a kiss caused my lady parts to tingle. I was going to be in trouble tonight. I had to pace myself. After all, it was only 8:13 p.m.; I had access to Joe's body for another two hours and forty-seven minutes.

Joe and I stopped kissing just long enough for me to offer him a drink.

"Can I get you a vodka? Wine? Anything?"

Joe thought for a second and then pulled me in for another kiss. He wasn't here to drink, he wasn't here to talk; he was here to get something he couldn't get at home and, according to my contract, it was my job to give it to him.

I don't remember how it happened, but before I knew it, we were on my barely-ever-used living room couch. As I straddled him in the same room where Ryan and I read our books and talked about trivial bullshit, and where my cousin slept when she visited from the States, I'd never felt more sexually alive.

Joe was in control. His hands explored my neck, back, and ass while I tried to mimic all those trashy movies I'd watched late at night while Ryan was snoring because of allergies or some deviated septum he believed he had. Still fully dressed, Joe and I were getting hot. The sweat from my nerves was now sweat from my hormones and the heady mix of our raging pheromones.

I felt my hair sticking to the back of my neck and my T-shirt clinging to me. Every so often, we would stop kissing and rest our foreheads on each other. It was time to move to my bedroom. Panic-stricken, I felt my heart start to thump again. I didn't know if my legs were capable of bringing me up the staircase. The sweat dial switched back from hormones to nerves. My brain turned itself back on full blast, and the only loud sound I could hear was an exaggerated Woody Allen version of my late grandmother's voice:

"This is vat you vant? Kissing vith a stranger?"

"It's not a stranger, Bubby. It's Joe. Remember Joe?"

"Ach. Pheh. I never liked him. He had no ambition, and he was just trying to get in your pants."

"He was fourteen! And besides, that's precisely what he's here for!"

"This is marriage? To have sex vith some strange man in your bed? This is the marriage you vant?"

"I don't know. But this is the marriage I have."

Shaking, I somehow managed to extricate myself from his lap and, turning my back on him for the first time since he walked through the door, took him by the hand and led him up the stairs. I was conscious that he was examining my ass, my legs, my thighs. I was sure he was comparing me to his more voluptuous wife. I took a deep cleansing breath; I made a mental note to buy some lavender plug-ins.

Joe sat down on the bed, the same bed I've shared for thirteen years with Ryan, the same bed where I file my nails, check Facebook and watch the Kardashians. Now it was about to become the bed I would—I hoped—have mind-blowing sex in. With Joe. If I had to have mediocre sex, it might as well have been with my own husband. For free.

"Do you mind?" Joe pointed to a frame on my nightstand, an old picture of Ryan and me on our honeymoon in Rio.

"Not at all," I replied and flipped it over.

"Come here." Joe smiled, staring straight into my eyes. He was really into the eye contact thing. And then he said it:

"I think you're so sexy."

There they were. The words I'd been dying to hear. I hadn't realized how much I needed to hear them. Maybe it was worth the wait? It didn't hurt that they were coming out of the mouth of someone who looked like Joe.

I, Valerie Matthews, was sexy? My brain shut down, and my body took over. He pulled me in and slid his way back onto the bed. I crawled on top of him.

After that, it was all a bit of a blur. I'm not sure whose shirt came off first, whose pants were ripped off first, or at what point I was trembling in ecstasy, but somewhere between 8:46 and 8:57 p.m. we were completely naked in my bed and losing all our inhibitions.

I even took my bra off, something I haven't done during sex in years. I mean, who wants to see my natural, saggy boobs? Apparently Joe did; he couldn't keep his hands off them.

Joe knew where to put his hands, how to hold my face while we kissed, how to take me in his mouth slowly and take his time while giving me oral pleasure—something I hadn't experienced with Ryan in years. With each nibble, touch, and lick, I was quivering from head to toe. I rolled on top of him, my hair a mess as he held it off my face, and I rubbed myself against him.

All the pre-swap moral dilemmas and deliberations had been eviscerated by this point. I could never have predicted how the sheer power of physical lust would affect me once I'd opened the door to it. I was ready, and I wanted him inside of me.

He slid in, slowly, and both of us exhaled in total euphoria. I rocked gently on top of him and moved my hips just enough to make both of us moan in pleasure. I'd forgotten about this position. I never wanted Ryan to get a good look at my body while we were having sex, so we stuck with missionary under the covers.

The room was spinning. I couldn't take it anymore. I wanted passion. I wanted rough. I wanted sexy, sweaty, hot fucking. So did Joe.

He flipped me over, and there I was, face down with Joe on top, taking me from behind. He cupped my breasts in his hands and kissed the back of my neck as he thrust inside me. I was going to come, and just as I was reaching my orgasm, Joe took one hand off my breast and began to rub me below.

The more I got off, the more he did too. We were about to climax at the same time when I briefly started calculating how many more hours we had together, how many more times I could plausibly reach this kind of orgasm before he'd have to leave.

Joe's kisses turned into gentle bites along my neck, back and side. He was about to come, and he did exactly what I expected him to. He got on top, missionary style, and looked me right in the eyes as he came on my chest. I could feel the warm come running down my sides; I was too exhilarated to care. I loved it.

9:27 p.m., one hour and thirty-three minutes until I had to let him go. We lay on our backs, catching our breath for a few minutes, giggling as we looked at my stomach. Joe got up to get me a towel from the bathroom. Usually, I wouldn't dare wipe come with my good Neiman Marcus bathroom towels, but on this night, I didn't even think about it.

"I'm so thirsty. Want some water?" I asked. Joe nodded, and we headed down into the kitchen wrapped in my sheets. Once again, not something I would ever do. I always thought people wrapped in bed sheets after hot sex were just in movies.

I sat on the island in the kitchen, and Joe sat on the stool between my legs. We stared at each other as we chugged down our glasses of water.

"That was quite a workout," Joe joked.

"I'm still shaking," I confessed. "That was really good."

"We make a good team. It's a shame we only have 'til eleven." Joe was saying the exact words I'd been feeling since the moment he walked through the door.

"What if I don't let you go?" I teased.

"You're amazing, so fucking amazing."

Joe's well-manicured fingers were touching my thigh. He opened the sheet, and there I was, sitting on my kitchen counter, completely naked. I made a slight move to cover my breasts, but Joe stopped my hand.

"You have a beautiful body, Val."

"Are you kidding? I hate what I look like." I really meant it. I used to have pretty nice breasts, and now I was ashamed of them. I hadn't worked up the nerve to ask Ryan for money for a boob job.

"Are *you* kidding?" Joe retorted. "My wife's boobs are sagging and lopsided from breastfeeding. Yours are nice and firm."

"Are you kidding me?" I couldn't tell if he was serious.

"All you women are the same. No matter how much we compliment you, you never believe us. Val, you're beautiful. Your boobs are great, and man, that ass." Joe got up and started back upstairs. "Are you coming? We still have some more time." I checked the clock. We had one hour and nine minutes.

"Let's have some fun," he called down to me.

I jumped off the counter and scrambled up the stairs, still wrapped in my sex toga. I found Joe in my bathroom where he'd started to run the bath. He'd already lit some candles and was immersing himself in the warm water. I followed suit, and before I knew it, we were having sex again, in the bath.

He was throbbing. I was reeling in ecstasy, and for what it's worth, I couldn't imagine how my vagina was going to hold up. Also, I'd never had sex in a bath before for two reasons: 1) I was told by my friends in high school that having sex in water could cause suction and the penis could get stuck, and 2) I had vivid memories of watching *Showgirls* with my Nana—we'd thought it was a musical—and as we awkwardly watched the sex scene in the pool with Elizabeth Berkley, my Nana let out an inadvertent comment about how impressed she was with Elizabeth's coordination.

9:56 p.m., one hour and four minutes left.

So, the urban legend about penis suction in water—not true. It wasn't true the first time Joe and I had sex in my bathtub, nor was it true the second time. We were lying on the bathroom floor, wrapped in towels, when Joe leaned over and wiped my face.

"You're all black," he said tenderly. I jumped up to check my reflection in the steamed up mirror. I'd forgotten to wash off my mascara and looked like a hung-over raccoon.

"Ugh, I'm so embarrassed," I said, scrambling for a Kleenex to wipe away my stained cheeks.

"You look fine. Please don't get self-conscious on me now. I still have some things I want to try with you." I spun around.

"What kind of 'things'?" Joe was smiling. He managed to look sexy even wearing one of my magenta bath towels.

I noticed that he had a tribal tattoo on his arm. Ryan would never get a tattoo. The closest thing Ryan had to a tattoo was a chicken pox scar on his arm from 1983.

"We have less than an hour," I warned, squinting at the clock. I wanted nothing more than to keep Joe in my bed until morning, but I was starting to wonder if my lady bits were up for any more pounding. I actually surreptitiously felt my clit to see if it was swollen or maybe even falling off.

I used to be quite athletic, naturally slim and toned. At forty there were no real glaring errors, besides my boobs (according to me, apparently). I went to Pilates pretty regularly, more as a social activity than a physical one, but now I was starting to think I shouldn't have wasted all those opportunities to increase my stamina for Joe's three-hour sex session. I didn't think I was up for another round. All I wanted to do was crawl into bed and let him caress and cuddle me and tell me over and over how sexy I was.

"Come here," he demanded. I liked it, and just like that, I was turned on again, despite my sore vagina.

"What do you want?" I breathed into his ear, as he pulled me close and unraveled my towel.

"I want you to go into your room and put on the dress you wore to the event last month at the school."

It hit me then and there just how goddamn surreal my life was in that instant. On a normal evening at 10:30 p.m., I was already in bed watching a PVR'ed episode of *True Blood* and playing Candy Crush on my iPad. But here I was, sore from two plus hours of wild sex I hadn't even thought I wanted up until the moment the doorbell rang. And now I was about to play dress-up with my grade-eight boyfriend. Whose life was this?

"You remember what I wore?" I was impressed that he'd even noticed.

"It was blue and tight, and your ass looked amazing in it."

I went into my closet and grabbed the dress, and as I was pulling it over my head, I heard noises coming from downstairs. It sounded like Joe was chopping garlic on a cutting board. *Chop, chop, chop, chop.* What the hell? Was he cooking all of a sudden?

I followed the sounds into the living room, surprised to find him sitting naked on my couch and hunched over on my coffee table. As I approached Joe from behind, I caught a glimpse over his shoulder: lines of cocaine were decorating my imported Indian coffee table, and the cute metal bookmark that my mom had bought me at a quaint gift shop on Sherbrooke Street was being used as a razor blade.

"What is this?" I asked, sounding as dumb as ever.

"A little blow. You mind?"

I felt betrayed by him, and not just because he was snorting coke in my living room, but more because of whom I thought he was. He had a gorgeous family, three beautiful kids, a house in Westmount, and a Porsche Cayenne. And here he was, snorting away my fantasies on my barely-ever-used living room couch. I was turned off.

How could I be so naïve? Everything Joe said to me tonight was a façade; the drugs were talking, saying only what would make Joe have the night he needed.

10:37 p.m.

Twenty-three minutes until I could get rid of him. Send him back to Denise, who probably emotionally eats her sadness away while her husband does lines of cocaine all over their perfect life.

Thirty-three minutes until Ryan would come home to me decontaminating our cocaine-tainted coffee table, wearing a cocktail dress with a face covered in smudged mascara, with wet tangled hair and a sore vagina. Awesome.

"A couple nights ago, I was licking jelly off my boyfriend's penis. And I thought,

'Oh my God — I'm turning into my mother!'" —*Sarah Silverman*

CHAPTER 6

Carol, My Mother, and Undiagnosed Bat-Shit Crazy Person

I typically have lunch with my mother, Carol, at least once a week. She doesn't usually tell me anything over lunch that she hasn't already called to tell me three times. My mom has undiagnosed OCD, especially when it comes to being on time.

It doesn't matter what time she tells me to meet her; I can bank on the fact that no matter what, she'll text me thirty minutes earlier than our set time to tell me she just got a table, not to rush. Or that she just parked at the mall, not to rush. Or my all-time favorite: I'm here (meaning outside my house in the car), not to rush. Which of course means, "I'm here, move your ass."

My mother has lived in Montreal thirty years longer than I have, and she still believes it takes an hour to get from her home in Côte Saint-Luc to everywhere on the island. Sometimes I want to make her sit in my driveway or the restaurant or wherever she's waiting for me for the entire thirty minutes, but I don't. I move my ass.

There was one time, and one time only, that I remember my mom ever fucking up. I was about five or six. I was sitting at our kitchen table eating a piece of celery with peanut butter while my mom was chatting away on the phone with her friend Shirley. If I close my eyes, I can see my mother twisting and untwisting the coil telephone wire that attached the receiver to the base. I took a bite out of the celery, and a stringy piece went down my throat and got stuck. I couldn't bring it back up, and I couldn't swallow it down. Most importantly, I couldn't breathe.

I started banging my hands on the table trying to get my mother's attention. She wouldn't look at me, so I started smacking the table harder but she thought I was just being loud and waved her hand behind her gesturing me to keep it down.

"Sorry, Shirley, they always want your attention the minute you get on the phone."

I could feel the tears rolling down my cheeks as I gasped and choked. But still, my mother was so engrossed in her conversation that she kept on talking.

Finally, in one last desperate attempt to get her attention, I banged the table so hard that my mother turned around in a rage.

"What is with you? Can't you just eat and be quiet!" And then realization set in and she saw me turning blue. "Oh my god, Shirley, Valerie is choking!" She flew over, reached down my throat and pulled out a piece of celery the length of a pinky finger from my throat.

Maybe she didn't fuck up. Maybe she saved my life. Depends on how you look at it. To this day I have conflicting feelings about my mother. I love her. I resent her. I love her. I need her. I hate her. I admire her. Why can't I be more like her? Thank God I'm nothing like her.

Another thing about my mom: she's decided she's gluten-intolerant. Not allergic, because that would mean she actually got tested and is factually unable to eat gluten. She blames her constant gas pains and bloating on gluten, not her kale salads mixed with broccoli and the other gaseous roughage she eats on a daily basis. She insists that there must have been gluten hidden in something else when she holds her stomach and shakes her head.

Our lunch date that day in January was strategic. I arrived half an hour early—i.e., right on time—and brought her a loaf of the gluten-free bread she loves from the bakery around the block from my house. I placed it on the table in front of her as I sat down.

"What's this for?" Like a pro, she sniffed out that there was a hidden agenda. I needed to get the kids out of the house for our Swap Club meets, so I wanted to make a monthly arrangement. She also knew the minute I said "every second Saturday" and "once a month" that something was up. I had to play this one very carefully.

"Why every second Saturday? Where are you going? Why can't I babysit at your house? Why do they need to sleep over?" Her questions came at me with the speed of an automatic rifle.

"Because that's when we need you." "Because we are going to go out." "Because we need one night off." "Because. Because. Because."

My mother studied me; she knew I was holding out on her.

"Well, I'm not doing it unless you tell me what's really going on." She sat back, smug, her hands still cupping her coffee mug. She was pleased with her maneuver.

The woman did save my life, so I told her the truth:

"Fine. If you have to know, Ryan and I are having some marital issues, and we would like to address them by devoting one Saturday night a month to focus on them." It sounded sincere enough. I wasn't completely lying, so I was fine with it.

Besides, she did ignore me when I was choking to death.

She started in. "Your generation doesn't understand what marriage is. When your father and I, may he rest in peace, took our vows, we understood it meant forever. When your generation takes their vows, you think it means 'for now.'"

She always said "may he rest in peace" when she brought up my father. She says it as though her words form a protective barrier that magically illuminated over his grave. My father died the year I was engaged to Ryan. A sudden heart attack in his sleep. My mom has never looked at another man since.

My mom let go of her mug and crossed her arms. She was thinking about what she needed to say to drive her point home.

"Valerie, I hope that whatever is going on in your marriage, you can work it out and stick together. Marriage is a little about love, but mostly it's about forgiveness. Ryan is a good man. I would never have let you marry him if I didn't think so."

Yes, Mom, he is a good man. For my fortieth birthday, he bought me a $2000 membership to a sex club, and that's why we need you to babysit.

After my mom shared her Dear Abby wisdom, checked her teeth in her compact, and then reapplied her cherry-red lip liner and lipstick, she signaled the waiter to bring the bill. She'd said what she needed to, and I got what I was looking for: a commitment from her to watch our kids while Ryan and I had sex with other people.

"Before you diagnose yourself with depression or low self-esteem, first make sure you are not, in fact, just surrounded by assholes."

—Tweet From: Notorious d.e.b. @debihope,

Time: 12:23 PM, Date: January 24, 2010

CHAPTER 7

Swap #2: February 8, 2014

Just Shut Up

Two weeks later, and thirty minutes early, I watched from the window as Michael and Hallie climbed into my mother's car. I could see that she had lined the backseat with towels. Undiagnosed OCD means my mom has preserved her 1999 Mercedes as though it never left the dealer's lot.

Weirdly enough, I was more nervous this month. I had greater expectations and couldn't imagine a more awkward ending to a long night of sex. Last month, Joe was so high when he had to leave, that I had to help him get dressed and call him a taxi. I saw his wife drive him over the next morning to get his Porsche as I hid in the shadow of my living room drapes.

To better prepare for swap number two, Ryan and I decided that over the course of the next few weeks, we had to have sex a few more times than we usually did. I even turned my clock around to face the wall so I wouldn't get hung up on how long it took. I mean, athletes train hard for the Olympics, and as far as I was concerned, three hours of sex should be an Olympic sport. Ryan and I still needed work on the passion and romance in our sex life, but our stamina also needed improvement or else I would be nursing a sore vagina month after month.

Reeking of Drakkar, Ryan came into the bathroom as I was primping to kiss me goodbye. The nostalgic stench hit me like a wall, and suddenly I remembered every teenage boy I'd ever slow-danced to Aerosmith with in my friends' basements circa 1990. I was certain Ryan had hung on to the same funky bottle from high school.

"Honey, you stink!" Ryan's insecurities immediately surfaced.

"Seriously? Maybe I should shower."

"Shower? You have to be there in ten minutes. Just take a washcloth and wipe yourself down." The irony that I was helping my husband prepare for his evening tryst was not lost on me. Nor was the humor when Ryan started scrubbing at his neck with one of the magenta bath towels Joe and I had wrapped ourselves in a month earlier, possibly even the very one I'd used to wipe the come off my stomach. (I washed them. Don't be gross.)

I went into our bedroom to get dressed, my DVF wrap dress waiting patiently for me on my bed, alongside a new black lace bra-and-panty set. I slid my towel off and pulled on my bra. I stared at my vagina, which was almost entirely bare.

"Seriously?" Ryan stood just outside our bathroom. I was hoping he was upset I'd bought more underwear, but I realized he was staring at my naked body.

"When did you do that?" Ryan looked at me as though I had betrayed him. "We just had sex the other day, and your... your... did not look like *that*!"

He cared. Ryan was jealous! I know it sounds mean, but I was so happy. I wondered if the once self-proclaimed "old-fashioned" Ryan still cared that I would be sleeping with other men. It seemed he did. And I was thrilled. That little bit of satisfaction made me willing to embarrass myself to save his feelings.

"Ry, it was a complete mistake. While I was showering, I used my razor to neaten up and took a little too much off one side." I twisted towards him to give him a better look. "Then I had to even it out on the other side, which resulted in a very uneven landing strip."

I looked at him hoping he could see the humor in this, but he was still distraught. I had to throw in a joke.

"Needless to say, next time I plan on borrowing your nose trimmer to do the job unless I feel like looking like Hitler from the belly button down." And then he smiled. Phew.

"You're going to be late!" I said, changing the subject and pointing at the clock.

"Take it easy this time." Ryan smiled awkwardly. His voice was tinged with something that could have been concern or might have been a remnant of jealousy. He went downstairs, leaving me alone with my newly, practically hairless labia to decide which it was.

At 8:05 p.m., I was getting antsy. Whoever was supposed to be here was late, and I was growing resentful with every minute that passed. What if I got stood up while Ryan was off with another woman? Not fair. Maybe we should have made a rule that if one of us had a no-show, the other wasn't allowed to have sex that night. Then I realized there was no real way of implementing this, so I opted for pacing back and forth and checking the window for oncoming headlights. The street was dark. No car in sight.

By 8:09 p.m. I was starting to get insulted. What was the protocol for a no-show? Did I report him to Celeste? Did I ignore the doorbell when it rang? I sat with my iPhone and checked Instagram to take my mind off of the potential rejection. I'd posted a picture earlier of the kids and me at the planetarium for my instafriends. Fourteen likes, three comments. #notbad.

I heard a car pull up. I looked through the window but couldn't make out the person sitting in the dark Mercedes. Snow was falling lightly, impairing my view of the man who had the nerve to show up twenty minutes late. I ducked just as the car door swung open. I didn't want him to see me waiting, so I crawled through my living room into the hallway just as the doorbell rang.

Once again my heart was pounding like a jackhammer. "You are not cheating, you are not cheating, you are not cheating." I put my mantra on autopilot to try and drown out the sound of my nerves.

My palms clammed up as I opened the door to Sam, who was standing on my porch holding the most beautiful bouquet of flowers.

"I'm so sorry I'm late. I stopped off to buy you these."

Instantly forgiven. But holy shit, my best friend Melissa's older brother was my swap date tonight.

"It's okay. And thank you, that's very sweet." I was waiting for him to react, but I got nothing.

"Can I come in?" Still examining the flowers, I'd forgotten to invite him inside. I was trying to remember the last time Ryan bought me flowers and couldn't. It was probably the bouquet he bought me for my first Mother's Day.

"I bought you some calla lilies and roses. They seem to be the popular winter flowers."

I smelled them again. They were gorgeous.

"You're not allergic, are you?"

Was Sam too caught up in the flowers to realize who I was?

"I'm Sam. What's your name?"

Well, there was my answer.

Granted it had probably been twenty-something years since we'd had any real contact. Melissa and I used to hang out in his basement apartment in grade ten, smoking joints, while he was having sex in the room next door. Packs of cigs were seven dollars at the time. We'd split the cost; I'd take the left side, and she'd take the right. During moments of teenage boredom, we would light the aluminum paper and watch the white paper burst into flames and then disappear. When he'd come up for air, he'd terrorize Melissa by smelling his finger and then chasing her around the room until she let him have a cigarette from our shared pack of du Mauriers. Not the most refined, but that was before he got his degree from Princeton.

"I'm Valerie, Valerie Matthews…?" I watched for a sign of recognition, but Sam was too busy checking out my house. I could tell he was sizing us up.

"Nice house. I love this area." The small talk was making this even more awkward. I just wanted him to shut up and act sexy.

I decided to pretend I didn't know him; it seemed more fun— and easier—that way.

Sam was tall and light-eyed, and his dark black hair seemed a little too black. As he stepped into the light, I wondered if he was one of those guys who colored his hair at Le Pascha, the salon in Montreal that catered to men only.

Sam followed me in, and it wasn't long before he was giving me an explanation about my street name's origin.

"Can I offer you a drink?"

I was trying to remind him of why we were here. If I'd wanted a small-talk session, I'd have made a lunch date with my mother-in-law. He was killing me with his follow-up lesson to my street name's origin with a tutorial on wainscoting. I was going to have to drive this baby home. It was already close to 8:30, which meant Ryan was probably already deep into foreplay. There was no way he would be having more sex than me tonight. After all, this was *my* birthday present.

"Sam, why don't we have a seat?" I led him into my now-used-every-second-Saturday-of-the-month living room.

"Vodka? Wine?" I offered as he unbuttoned his top button.

"A vodka soda would be great, thanks."

I nodded and walked over to my bar.

"So Valerie, have you lived here long?" Are you kidding me? I decided this guy must be a nervous talker; it was going to be a long night.

"Here, let me know if you like it." I handed him his drink and licked my lips seductively. The same way Olivia Newton-John licked hers right before saying, "Tell me about it, stud," in *Grease*. I had to draw him out of the rabbit hole and refocus his attention on the main attraction.

"It's perfect," he replied as he stared at my lips. Then his eyes lowered towards my dress and landed on the tied bow falling on my hip. "Nice dress," he said flirtatiously.

"You like this?" I flirted back, twirling the loose part of the belt. It was the perfect dress for a mini-strip tease, but I didn't know if I could actually do it.

I'd never stripped for anyone except the couturier who had made my wedding dress.

Sam leaned in and tugged the bow loose. This was happening. I took his drink from his hands, helped myself to a swig and placed his glass on my desecrated coffee table.

"Do you want me to strip for you?"

Who was this woman talking? It was as if I were having an out-of-body experience, and someone else was taking over. This newfound confidence was refreshing. Maybe it was my freshly shaved vagina.

"Strip? Sure, should I get my wallet?"

What a dumbass. The perfect arm-candy guy, a catch so long as he didn't open his mouth.

"No wallet needed here, Sam, just your hard... cock."

What the hell was coming out of my mouth? His eyeballs nearly fell out of his head.

"Whoa there, Val, you have a dirty mouth."

Yup, apparently I did. I was as shocked as Sam was. I either had to back-pedal my way out of this or forge ahead.

"Do you like the dirty talk? Or would you like me to act more like your wife?" And there it was: the mean streak.

"No, no. I like it," he said, panting. "Just as much as you're going to like my hard *cock* in your mouth."

I didn't know if I was shocked, offended, or turned on, but all of a sudden Sam was hitching himself to my ride and putting it into gear. He stood up and walked past me, into the hall, then up the stairs. I held my dress together with my hands and followed him. *Holy crap, holy crap, holy crap.*

I found him in my room unbuttoning the rest of his shirt. I was impressed with his body; it was chiseled and not too hairy. I walked over to him and put my hands on his chest, as he removed my dress and placed his hands on my ass. He pulled me close to him, pressing his boner against my pelvis.

"Feel what you did to me."

I have to admit, I was proud of myself. I hadn't even laid a finger on him, and this guy's penis was reaching his bellybutton. I started to unbuckle his belt. The weight of his hands on my shoulders was sending me a clear message: he wanted me on my knees.

"You want me to suck your dick, don't you?" I heard the words come out of my mouth but wasn't 100 percent certain it was me talking.

"Yeah. Suck it."

So, at Sam's request, I undid his zipper and pulled down his fashionably torn True Religion jeans. His penis was probably the largest I'd ever seen, but not in length—I'm talking girth. It in fact, looked like Danny DeVito. It kind of gave me the creeps, but there I was, putting it in my mouth.

I faked a few *mmm*'s and *ohhh*'s as I licked his fat stump. As he closed his eyes and dropped his head back, I made my hands wet so that I could replicate the feeling of my mouth with my bare hands. It must have been years since his last blowjob. He kept saying:

"Yeah, suck it like that, mmm that's good, keep going, baby."

Was this a joke? Apparently, I gave good fake blowjobs. Who knew? Man, I could've saved my poor college self a ton of energy and a whole lot of lockjaw.

"I'm gonna come, I'm gonna come…" Was he serious? Did I just rub this guy out in four minutes flat?

I could tell Sam was about to burst—his nubbin was pulsating in my hand. I cupped my hand over the top and waited as he ejaculated all over my palms. Sam quivered with the release. I couldn't believe how much come came out. Those pipes must have been backed up for at least a month.

"That was incredible," Sam moaned. "You should give lessons." His compliments seemed premature, as though we were done for the night.

"I'm glad you enjoyed it." I couldn't think of what more to say or how to proceed. I figured there had to be some kind of rule for reciprocation. If there wasn't, maybe I should suggest that Celeste write one. Do I ask him to return the favor, or should I simply rip off my G-string and stick my pelvis in his face?

"So, Sam, is there anything *you're* incredible at?" His eyes lit up with the challenge.

"I'm amazing at everything I do," he boasted. Typical overachiever.

Sam laid me down on the bed; he kissed my legs my knees, and then used his tongue along my inner thigh. With his hand, he grabbed the material from the bottom of my panties and used his knuckles to rub me. He did this ever so slowly—so slowly, in fact, that I felt myself gyrating against him, hoping he would pick up his rhythm. It felt good, though, I had to admit. He was making me wet and I was wanting more.

As he made a move to take off my panties, he paused for just a moment to run his hand appreciatively along the black lace. I couldn't say whether it was explicit admiration, but I felt pleased that someone had noticed my underwear. It almost made the uncomfortable lace worth it. I couldn't wait to get the bra off. Any woman who's ever worn a lace bra can vouch for how itchy it makes our nipples.

He slid off my panties, opened my legs, kissed my pelvic bone and then worked his way down towards my clitoris. He took me into his mouth and then started to suck on me like a tootsie pop. I kept getting distracted by the slurping sounds; it was killing the mood for me. After about three painful minutes of listening to Sam *cliterally* eat me out, I pulled him on top of me and "surrendered" to wanting him inside me "so bad," I could "hardly take it anymore."

Lucky for me, Sam's manhood was quick to recover. He slid inside of me easily; I was already up to my knees in his saliva. It felt pretty good as long as I closed my eyes and imagined it was Zac Efron until I climaxed and then pushed him off of me.

As we lay on our backs, the sound of Sam's heavy breathing was making me nervous.

"Are you okay?" I asked carefully, worried he'd be insulted.

"I'm great. I could really use a smoke." By the sounds of his lungs gasping for air, I couldn't imagine that a cigarette was the answer.

"You still smoke?" The words fell out of my mouth before I even had a chance to think about a retraction.

"Still?" he asked.

Sam sat up and took another look at me.

"You know me?"

His eyes had worry in them, peppered with embarrassment.

"Seriously?" I asked him, staring right into his eyes.

"Seriously."

I got up, but my thighs were sticking to each other. I felt so gross; all I wanted to do was get into a hot shower. I was afraid Sam would want to join me, though, and I had zero desire to see his stunted shaft in its soft state.

I walked over to my shelf and pulled out a photo album. As I flipped through the pages, I grabbed a towel from my bathroom.

"Here."

I handed the album over to Sam, opened to the page where there was a picture of Melissa and me in his basement apartment. Our hair was teased, and we each had a du Maurier hanging from our lips.

I wiped myself with the towel and watched Sam's face as the realization set in. His eyes widened, and so did mine.

"Unibrow Val?"

I couldn't believe he was referring to my fourteen-year-old nickname twenty-six years later. In my huff, I'd also failed to notice that I was using the Drakkar-drenched towel to wipe up my vag. Not only was it starting to burn, but now it smelled like a nineties pool hall.

I wanted him and his chubby dick to leave, so I pretended I was dejected by the fact that he didn't remember me and asked him politely to "just go." It was almost 11 p.m. anyway.

I tweezed my eyebrows as I waited for Ryan to return. Swap number 2 left me with not only a damaged vagina once again, but worse, a damaged self-esteem.

Sticks and stones? Bullshit. Words hurt.

"I think we can all agree that sleeping around is a great way to meet people." —Chelsea Handler

CHAPTER 8

Swap #3: March 8, 2014

The Perfect Fucking Boy Next Door

I've always been a big dreamer, and I don't mean metaphorically. From as far back as I can remember I've had hyper-vivid dreams. The one I had a few nights after the swap with Sam was no different.

I was sitting on the edge of an indoor Olympic-size pool that had no water in it. I wasn't alone; people were hanging around poolside, talking and just taking it easy. I kept looking down into the dry concrete, wondering where the water was. It seemed like I was the only one who thought it was weird that we were all in bathing suits, but there was no water to wade in.

An obese teenaged boy in an oversized swimsuit caught my attention as he huffed and puffed his way up the ladder to the diving board. I started to panic. Was this kid really going to jump off the diving board into the empty pool? I looked around to see if anyone else was concerned. No one appeared worried. They looked anything but. They seemed entertained by the prospect of a fat boy jumping off the diving board to what could only be his certain death.

I tried to stand up, but my legs didn't want to support me. I watched as the weight of the boy caused the diving board to bend downwards.

He had everyone's attention; he smiled and waved as everyone looked at him, cheering and applauding. I wasn't enjoying the show at all. I was concerned and utterly distressed as the kid stepped off the diving board and plunged to the bottom of the pool, smashing into the concrete and causing it to crack along the sides of the deep end.

He stood up, clearly hurt, but the sound of the crowd cheering him on seemed to buoy him. So he got up, limped out of the pool and climbed back up the ladder to do it again. And he did.

I once took a course at Marianopolis College called "Dreams, A Way of Knowing," taught by Sister Mary Stuart. I took the course because it was CEGEP (in the province of Quebec, CEGEP is like mandatory Junior College), I needed an elective, and I thought it would be an easy A. It turned out that I learned one thing that would change my perspective on dreams forever.

Sister Stuart believed that everyone in your dream is you. That resonated with me and I spent the rest of the day after having that dream trying to decipher why my brain made me an overweight teenage boy.

In my past, I have been guilty of Mom Syndrome, suppressing my needs while I focused on pleasing others, saying yes to carpools and neon yellow nail polish instead of corporate hours and a nanny. It's what I wanted. I chose to be a mom. But a few months into Swap Club I was realizing that I left a piece of myself in the maternity ward when I brought my son Michael home.

I made it okay to put myself at the lower end of the totem pole. Now I was allowing myself the top spot one Saturday night a month, and you know what? I was starting to believe that there was nothing wrong with that.

So far, Ryan and I had been pretty good at keeping the discussion about swap dates to a minimum. I don't think either of us wanted to hear the play-by-play. When he got home, we'd change the sheets, then I'd shower first and wait in bed for him while snacking on Wheat Thins while he showered. We'd watch *Saturday Night Live*, he'd give me his customary shit for eating in bed, complaining that the sheets were covered in crumbs, and then came the habitual snatching away of the box.

It was our third Saturday. At 5:15 p.m. the phone rang, and Ryan answered.

"Your mom says she'll pick them up in a half hour." Time to shower, shave, primp and get my vagina ready for swap man number three. I watched as Ryan hung up. He took a big breath and stretched his back.

I was studying him, trying to pick up subtle clues about how he was feeling about Swap Club from his body language. Ryan has lots of tells. Slow blinking means he's annoyed. Rubbing his hair means he has something he wants to say. Scratching the back of his neck means he's ready to change the subject. Unfortunately, he was giving nothing away this time.

At 7:56 p.m. my house was so quiet I could hear the hum coming from the air ducts. I was on Facebook looking at pictures I'd posted a few years back. We'd taken our kids to Lake George, a three-hour drive from Montreal. I couldn't believe how quickly the time had passed since that trip.

I remembered my mom once saying to me, "The days are long, but the years are short." For the first time, I understood what she meant. I had a lump in my throat. One day my children would hopefully be married with kids, and I'd be in my sixties thinking back on the year Ryan and I decided on a "sex-positive" lifestyle, and screwed other people.

I closed my computer, went straight to our bar and opened the bottle of tequila. I had a moment of hesitation, remembering the finale to my Mexican Windex night. So I opted for a shot of Jack. I downed it and I shivered as it hit my stomach.

I paced around my main floor. Michael's science fair project was sitting on the dining room table. He and Ryan had been spending a lot of time working on it, and I hadn't really understood until that moment what it was all about.

There was a graph, one side of it listing activities: riding a bike, playing soccer, and jogging. On the other side of the graph were different activities: going on a roller coaster, watching a horror movie, and going to the dentist. Along the bottom of the graph was the pulse rate for each activity. Riding a bike, pulse rate of 98 beats per minute. Soccer, 102 beats per minute. Jogging, 107. No pulse rates were recorded for the roller coaster, horror movie, and the dentist.

I picked up a piece of paper with Michael's handwriting on it.

Fear is an emotion that is more than a reaction in your head. It's an automatic adrenaline rush that your whole body responds to, especially your heart. We've all experienced that pounding feeling in our chests after someone or something has scared us. But what happens when we are just mildly frightened, or even just a little excited about something? Does our heart rate change? I have decided to focus my science fair project on fear and our heart rate and see whether or not scaring someone to death is even possible.

The headlights of a car lit up my living room window, and almost reluctantly I put down Michael's project to get ready to answer my door. "Here we go," I whispered out loud. "You are not cheating, you are not cheating, you are not cheating."

I harmonized my mantra with the rhythm of my nervous, pounding heart. Pulse rate if I had to guess? Well over 100.

The man who stepped into my doorway was a complete stranger. I had absolutely no idea who he was, and he had no inclination about me either. This was hopefully going to be better.

As I shut the door I knew, just by looking at his spotless truck, that whoever he was, he lived in Côte Saint-Luc, Hampstead, NDG, or Westmount. Montreal March weather is notorious for slush and muck. One trip on the Décarie expressway and your vehicle is completely mud-bogged. This truck had not touched a highway to get to my house.

He was 5'10", had light hair and eyes, and smiled as he hugged me hello.

"Nate."

"I'm Val," I said, hugging him back.

The adorable stranger looked like the person cast for the part of the "boy next door." His soft cheeks rubbed against mine; I felt like I'd just met my new best friend. I liked him immediately, and my nerves intensified once I'd gotten that instinctual hunch that this was a guy I could very easily have a Hollywood crush on.

"Please, come in," I said, beckoning him over my shoulder. "Can I offer you a drink? I already helped myself to a shot of Jack. Not that I'm a drunk or anything. I was just trying to take the edge off." *Oy vey, Val, just shut it.*

"Sure, I'll match your shot and then have a drink with you."

Nice guy. He knew I was nervous and was trying to make me comfortable. Ugh, the tables had turned. I was acting like a blubbering idiot and was going to ruin this for him.

"This is actually my first swap," Nate confessed. "You'll have to go easy on me."

I was astonished.

"I'll go easy, I promise," I said, trying hard to play it cool as I led him directly upstairs to my bedroom.

"The drinks are in here?" Nate's voice pitched high, like a kid's after he'd been coaxed into a van with hard candy.

"Oh, no, they're downstairs, I'll get them." I left him standing with his coat on in my room. "Shit-shit-shit-shit-shit-shit-shit-shit," I kept repeating under my breath, as I ran down the stairs, grabbed the bottles and glasses awkwardly and ran back upstairs.

"I'm so sorry. I can't lie, I'm pretty nervous," I said, deciding it was just best to be honest. I placed the bottles and glasses on my nightstand and sat on the bed. I figured the only way to come back from coming off like a wreck was to own it and surrender.

"I'm nervous, too," he said and sat down next to me on the bed. I put my hand on his lap and smiled at him.

"You're very cute," I said sweetly, trying to climb back out of the hole I'd dug. Nate's eyes shone.

"Cute? Isn't there a rule about using the word cute to describe a grown man?"

We both laughed, and I poured him a shot. As he threw it back, I could tell he'd once did shots like these every Friday at Angel's on St. Laurent Boulevard, the happening strip when I was old enough to go out. Everyone went to Angel's, Di Salvio's, or Cafeteria. I started to wonder how many times Nate and I had potentially been in the same place at the same time over the years. If you grow up English and

Jewish in Montreal, you more or less know—or know of—everyone in your cohort, plus or minus five years.

Just as I was about to make a comment about him tasting my vanilla lip balm, my cell rang. I didn't know whether I should answer it. I could see the word "Mom" shining brightly on the screen and knew it must be something important, perhaps that one of the kids had shoved a raisin up their nose.

I grabbed the phone while Nate sat awkwardly on the edge of my bed.

"Hi Mom, everything okay?" I said, slightly annoyed, expecting to hear my mother's voice.

"Hi, Mommy! You know that hair clip you bought me?"

"Hallie, sweetheart, hi. Mommy is busy right now, can we talk about this tomorrow?" I smiled nervously at Nate.

"Why, Mommy? What are you doing? Can I say hi to Daddy?"

"Umm, Daddy is in the bathroom..."

"Okay, well, good night, Mommy. I love you."

"Good night, Hallie. I love you too!"

"Oh and Mommy?"

"Yes?"

"I'm sorry about the stain on your new coat."

"What stain?"

"Good night, Mommy."

I turned the ringer off on my phone and slid back next to Nate. He was smiling; the call didn't bother him one bit. I, on the other hand, was stuck in mommy-brain. It was taking every ounce of willpower not to run down the stairs to the front closet and check my new suede coat. The suede coat I had been eyeballing for over a year. The suede coat I finally convinced Ryan I needed. The suede coat that apparently now had a stain on it. How does one get a stain out of a suede coat anyway? I would have to ask my mom tomorrow. She would know how to get it out, or who to pay to get it out at the very least.

"So, Val, how does this go?"

Oh. Yes. Nate was here, waiting for me to have sex with him, and all I could think about was:

1. Hallie.

2. My suede coat.

3. Should I put my belongings that cost over $500 under lock and key?

4. Could I slip out for just a second to take a peek at the stain?

5. How badly stained was the coat?

6. Would it be weird to try and use one of my fifty stain removal products now?

"Val?" Thankfully, Nate interrupted my thoughts just as I was starting to spin out of control.

I looked at him playfully. "Well, you get to have sex with me tonight, and then go back to your wife."

"I know the logistics of the swap, Val. I meant how does this go?"

Nate was gesturing at the space between him and me. I could only assume he wanted to get things under way, so I got closer to him. So close, in fact, that our mouths were locked before I could give the stained suede coat another thought.

I know this sounds weird, but Nate's tongue was the perfect size. I've kissed enough frogs to know this for a fact. There are men who have long pointy tongues. Some men have dry and bumpy ones. Others have bulbous and thick tongues. You know the thick-tongued guys—they're the ones who have trouble pronouncing words like "pastrami sandwich."

Nate's kissing technique was perfection. Slow, sensual and calming. I could imagine lying in bed with Nate and just kissing for hours until our lips got chapped. He put his hand on my thigh; he was making the first move, and I felt like I was suddenly sixteen again. I panicked for a minute as it dawned on me that I'd skipped the G-string altogether this time. I decided it would be a sexy move to go commando under my mini-skirt. Should I tell him?

As his hand slowly made its way higher and higher up my thigh, our kissing grew more intense. Nate's hand was seconds away from discovering my bare essentials, and I was pulsating with anticipation.

I opened my eyes to see his reaction as his fingers met my lady muffin. He opened his eyes as well and laughed.

"Wow, I wasn't expecting that," he said as he continued to kiss me. We reclined on the bed where he proceeded to finger me like we were in grade ten making out at the Westmount lookout. The kissing and his hand moving up and down—both felt amazingly good. I couldn't take how badly I wanted this Dawson Leery look-alike inside me.

Nate lowered his body all the way down, spread my legs apart to make room for his face, and then replaced his finger with his impeccable tongue. I reached down and encouraged him to keep his hand there as well—it had been doing such an excellent job already—to push me over the edge. Between his fingers and his tongue, it took no more than a few strokes before my whole body was shaking in ecstasy.

I rolled on top of him; I could feel his stiff penis through his pants. Like any other Jewish girl, I enjoyed a good high-school dry hump, but I wanted to feel his skin against mine.

I pulled off his T-shirt and couldn't believe how formidable and soft his chest was. Not a freckle or a blemish—his skin was perfect. Nate lay back as I undid his cargo pants; he smoothed my hair away from my face as I pulled them down.

He was wearing boxer shorts, something I hadn't seen in years. Ryan wore boxer briefs because as his balls got older (or heavier), they kept hitting his inner thighs, and he needed the extra support.

Nate had the kind of perfect penis I didn't mind sucking on. It was well groomed, lean and easy to wrap my mouth around. Perfect skin, perfect tongue, and perfect penis. There had to be something wrong with this guy.

I took him in my mouth over and over. It was flattering to see the level of pleasure he was getting. He was also such a gentleman: he held my hair back as I blew him. I wondered if this was a thing a mother taught her son.

"Honey, you have to open the car door, bring her roses on Valentine's Day and hold her hair back while she sucks your dick."

Nate moved me over, then got on top of me.

"I want to fuck you so badly," he breathed.

I appreciated his use of the word *fuck*. I was starting to think this Kevin Arnold guy was too good to be true.

"You want to fuck me?"

I could feel the tip of his penis teasing my labia.

"I do."

He slid right in, and I lost all feeling in my toes. With every thrust, I could feel the room spin. This was what sex was supposed to feel like, complete and utter euphoria. His hips swiveled in sync with mine; I could barely form a thought as he plunged deeper inside of me. My stomach tightened as I held my breath tightly. I'd forgotten what it felt like to be on the brink of such an intense orgasm.

"I can't take it," I cried.

"Let go, just let go," he coaxed me. He wanted me to climax and was waiting for my release. He held my hands above my head against the pillow.

"Let go, Val."

And I did.

And then Nate did.

My toes curled as my whole body shook in exhilaration. Nate collapsed on top of me. His lips found the side of my neck.

"That was … incredible," he said. "Thank you." He'd barely caught his breath. Then he turned his head to look at me directly. "I'm not sure how anyone else is going to compare after this."

My stomach tightened again. Was he kidding me?

"That was amazing. I wish we could meet like this every time." The words tumbled out before I could help myself. It was the truth, but I probably shouldn't have said it.

Nate leaned over and took my iPhone off the bedside table. He dialed a number. A second later I heard a muffled ringtone coming from the cargopants heap on the floor.

"Now I have your number," he smiled, shrugging coyly and ending the call. "What can I say? Rules were made to be broken."

Nate maneuvered his body between my legs. We had just enough time to play a little longer, so I closed my eyes and focused on his tongue and lips between my legs. He teased me bringing me to the brink, over and over. Every time my body clenched up, and I held my breath, he'd intentionally stop. He knew my body—its sweet spots and most sensitive parts—like he'd studied it for a test. It felt like we'd known each other forever.

I sat up on my elbows to prop up my torso so our eyes could connect. I was so sweaty the sheets were sticking to my back. As his tongue grazed my swollen clitoris, I pleaded with Nate to let me orgasm.

"Please, Nate." I didn't realize how desperate I was until I heard it in my voice.

He smiled as he wiped his mouth and crawled on top of me. I could feel him throbbing against the front of my thigh. He moved his mouth down to kiss my chin; then his lips brushed over my jawbone and traveled the length of my clavicle to my shoulder. He turned his head so that his lips were touching my ear.

"What do you need, Val?"

"I need you inside me."

Finally, after what seemed to be a torturous amount of time he looked up, held my eyes, and slowly slipped deep inside of me.

I reached down and added my hand. It took no more than four strokes, in tandem with his thrusts, before my whole body was convulsing in ecstasy. I was a live wire. My head felt like it weighed a hundred pounds as it fell back, and my mouth opened wide as all the air in my lungs evaporated while he kept thrusting.

Time ceased to exist; my post-orgasmic body continued to vibrate with pleasure, like a sustained note, as he ground into me with more and more intensity, until he pulled out, flipped on his back and came on his stomach.

Nate stood up, cleaned up his mess with a tissue and got dressed. I was still limp; I couldn't move a muscle.

"I'll be in touch," he said, as he leaned down and kissed my lips tenderly. I didn't want him to go. He rubbed his soft hand against my cheek and left my bedroom.

I heard the door shut as I lay in bed, just reveling in satisfaction, until, a minute later, my brain turned back on. I ran downstairs and whipped open the front closet. There it was, my brand-new coat. I was almost too afraid to look. I pulled it out and examined it top to bottom, both sides. I don't know how I didn't see it at first, but then, there it was: Hallie's black handprint smack dab in the middle of the back of my suede coat that still had the price tag hanging from it. The post-orgasm euphoria was gone.

About half an hour later, after Ryan and I changed the sheets, I lay in bed munching crackers watching doe-eyed Rachel McAdams fawn over the dapper Ryan Gosling in *The Notebook*. Damn you, Nicholas Sparks. No man will ever live up to Noah Calhoun in the scene where he's hanging from the top of a Ferris wheel, bartering his life for a date with Allie Nelson. Damn you. *Crunch, crunch, crunch.*

My Ryan, not Gosling, was in the shower washing his Rihanna-nailed lady-fuck off of him. I'd noticed some crazy fingernail scratches all over his back. He must have had quite the date. Was I jealous? *Crunch, crunch, crunch.*

When he came out of the bathroom, I took a jab at him:

"You really got scratched up there." *Crunch, crunch, crunch.*

"Yeah, she had these crazy talons."

"Aw, poor you." My mock sympathy was not subtle. He flashed me a look.

"Are you jealous, Val?" Ryan was smirking.

"Jealous? Is that a joke?" (Yup. I was jealous.)

"I hate when you eat in bed," he shot back as he climbed under the covers next to me. I took another bite and exaggerated the crunching in Ryan's face before he grabbed the box and tossed it on the floor. I was done anyway.

"I love that you're jealous," Ryan said as he zoned out.

"Whatever." I couldn't lie, so I changed the subject. "We have that birthday party tomorrow," I reminded him. Ryan wasn't responding, probably relishing the idea that I was envious of whomever used him as a scratching post for the last three hours. I knew he wasn't listening to me.

"We have that instructional conference tomorrow in the Kama Sutra." No reaction.

"I'm pregnant with someone else's baby." Finally, he looked at me. Annoyed, but at least he looked.

At 3 am, my phone beeped. My first text message from Nate.

Want to feel you again, it said.

I put my phone down quickly and stared at Ryan fast asleep. Riddled with anxiety, I didn't know what to feel. On one hand, Nate had turned Swap Club on its head for me, and that felt great! On the other hand, breaking the rules and bantering via text with one of the members felt like cheating, and that felt terrible. I decided to focus on the positive, and act accordingly.

You never know…:) I typed back to him. *Happy effing fortieth,* I thought as I sunk back into my pillow, smiling.

After tossing and turning for over an hour, I took out my phone and deleted the message. My conscience was able to handle consensual swinging, and nothing more.

"Imperfection is beauty, madness is genius and it's better to be absolutely ridiculous than absolutely boring." — Marilyn Monroe

CHAPTER 9

A Dildo in the Shower

Kate was Ryan's college roommate's girlfriend. Ben (the roommate) and Kate had been dating for years, and everyone just sort of assumed they would just carry on in typical Quebec fashion and remain "common law" spouses. And then one day, after having lived together for nearly a decade, Ben proposed, totally out of the blue. Kate's mother-in-law's invitation to the bridal shower, mailed not even a week after we'd heard the news, reeked of, "Thank God it finally happened, let's celebrate before they change their minds."

My initial instinct was to decline graciously. Kate's friends weren't really my crowd, and truth be told, I did better at social events when I had a wing woman or was with Ryan. If I went, though, that would mean some time off from the weekend grind. Ryan could deal with the kids for a few hours on a Sunday while I got buzzed on mind-numbing small talk and Prosecco.

The thing was I actually liked Kate, so I sucked it up and RSVP'd "attending" to her soon-to-be mother-in-law, Mrs. Gold.

As it goes with bridal showers, the invitation instructed me to buy a particular type of gift: something for the honeymoon. At least the shopping would be fun. I could do double duty and hit a fun sex shop. I'd already felt like I'd gone through my assortment of sexy things to wear on my swap nights, so it was a good excuse to add to my supply.

So I justified sneaking away from my mundane mom-chores—two fresh piles of laundry that needed folding, a fridge that desperately needed purging of last week's leftovers, and a kitchen floor that needed some serious Swiffering—to brave the perpetual traffic on Autoroute 40 in search of the perfect honeymoon gift.

Montreal's east end is home to the notorious Salon Triple XXX, which is basically the equivalent of a massive Costco stocked with 18+ equipment. I really should have been grocery shopping. Aside from the ancient leftovers, our fridge was practically empty—but I found myself excited, if not a bit intimidated, by the prospect of box-store bulk sex shopping instead.

For a minute, I reneged on my plan to buy Kate sexy lingerie. I mean, what forty-year-old woman doesn't already own some? Maybe I should get her a set of furry handcuffs and some flavored massage oils. While I was deliberating the virtues of different synthetic flavors, I suddenly found myself smack in the middle of the strap-on aisle.

I couldn't help but gawk. I reached out to touch one of the bulging packages and caught myself blushing. Whatever, Val, how could this faze you? You're freaking swinging, for Christ's sake! Maybe a new vibrator would be fun for my next swap. I'd pick out something for me and then find a gift for Kate on the second floor in the clothing section.

The dildos came in all shapes and sizes—from replicas of Sam's dwarf thumb to ones that rivaled Big Gulps—and a full rainbow of colors, from Albino pale to 70 percent dark chocolate and everything in between. Some of them even had holes in the packaging so you could feel for yourself the "natural" sensation of silicone. An interesting marketing idea, although I wasn't sure how much sensory information I could actually obtain from poking the tip of my finger through a little hole.

As I examined one called "Cyberskin," a young woman with several face piercings, Wilma Flintstone–red hair, and Amy Winehouse eyeliner began to talk to me about the dildo I was holding.

"Cyberskin, just so you know, is the most life-like, texture-wise. If that's what you're going for," she explained, casually. "It's a porous material, which means it can't be sterilized. So you should probably stay away from anal with that one. Also, it gets sticky after you wash, but if you dust it with cornstarch, you shouldn't have a problem. Also, if you like it rougher, be careful because it's a bit delicate. More prone to rips and tears than silicone dildos."

I just stood there, staring at Wilma Winehouse, as I held the Cyberskin dildo shaded "Indian Summer" in my hand.

"Which would you suggest as a first-time purchase?" I couldn't think of anything else to ask.

"I prefer the silicone ones if you want my opinion. Less maintenance if you want to use it several times over the course of a day". She paused to give me a once-over and then kept on with her pearls of wisdom. "Some women prefer these smooth ones with no veins. They come in purple or pink. Personally, I prefer having something with a little more grip, slightly more life-like." She handed me a super veiny one.

And with that, Wilma turned and started to move away down the aisle.

"If you have any questions or need some lube suggestions, just come and find me," she called back.

I decided that Wilma's recommendation was on point. Who doesn't like something with nice veins and a good set of balls? I dropped the heavy, ten-inch "Vanilla Cream" silicone dildo in my basket (face down) and then took the escalator up to the second floor.

The clothing aisles were organized according to fetish. You had the romantic red and black satin section, the S&M black leather and studded accessories section, and the dress-up fantasy section—slutty French maids, slutty superheroes, and slutty candy stripers were all well represented.

I found my way over to the racks of matching bras and panties. This was in my wheelhouse. They looked relatively normal to me until I started trying them on in the dressing room. It was only then that I realized they were all crotchless.

I tried on a pair of large-loop black fishnet thigh-highs, a garter, and black leather lace-up corset. I could see why women wore these centuries ago: my otherwise saggy boobs were miraculously up to my chin.

I chose a tasteful black lace negligee with matching crotchless underwear for Kate, and just for giggles I tossed in a feathered garter, lube, and a leather flogger.

I carried the pile that had accumulated on the stool in my dressing room down the escalator and headed to the checkout counter. I pulled out the cash Ryan had given to me for groceries. No paper trail, no evidence.

"Do you guys wrap gifts?" I asked Wilma.

"We sure do."

I separated the piles, and watched as Wilma carefully folded each item and made two beautiful gift bags for me to carry out and hide in my closet.

The day of the shower, I spent an hour getting ready. I was feeling anxious. I wouldn't know anyone except for Kate, and I'd probably spend next to no time with her, since she would have to split her attention socializing with all the guests. What had I been thinking RSVP-ing to this?

I kept changing my outfit. My black pants to beige pants to a skirt, back to the black pants. I was trying to find the perfect outfit to blend in seamlessly with the furniture. I opted for a pale blue blouse, black skinny pants, and black booty heels. I added a sheer burgundy lip balm to color to my pout. No simile here. I was actually pouting.

Ryan took Hallie and Michael for brunch, and then they were going to spend the early afternoon with Melissa and Jeff and their two kids. I had the house to myself. On a *Sunday*. I fantasized for a minute about just staying home, running a bath, and flipping through the three weeks' worth of *Us* and *People* magazines that had been collecting dust on the kitchen counter.

But I didn't. I unstuck myself from the edge of my bed, grabbed the gift bag, forced myself down the stairs and pulled my floor-length parka out of the closet. The sun was shining, but it was still minus twelve. Ah, late March in Montreal.

The shower was called for eleven, so I left my house at 10:45. An older woman whom I could only assume was Mrs. Gold opened the stately glass front door to an elegantly decorated home. I looked past her shoulder to see if I recognized anyone. The house was empty except for the caterers.

"Kate should be here shortly," Mrs. Gold said, as she took the inconspicuously wrapped lingerie from my arms and closed the door.

Not only was I the first one to arrive, I was also there before the guest of honor.

"Make yourself comfortable," Mrs. Gold said, pointing to the empty living room. "I've just got to check on the last of the hors d'oeuvres."

"Someone had to be first!" I joked to Mrs. Gold's back. She was already halfway to the kitchen. She looked stuffier than a private school librarian, blonde hair neatly twisted into a bun, Hermes scarf draped around her neck, and a silk blouse tucked into her light wool slacks. (She wore slacks. Everyone else wore pants.)

I took a seat in the living room and immediately began to sweat. What was wrong with me? A bartender in his mid-to-late fifties stood behind the rented bar. He stared at me. I was sure he was judging me for being that person—the anal one who shows up early to everything. Just like my mom. I felt the sweat pooling in the dip in my neck and trickle down my cleavage. I tried to casually mop my neck with my hand and rearrange my blouse so that it hung away from my skin as much as possible. Blue blouse. Brilliant choice.

I had a friend at McGill named Kenny Switzer. Really sweet guy, but he had a severe sweating problem. In June of third year, we were outside the Shatner (yes, *Star Trek* Shatner) Student Union building discussing job prospects when he ran me through the Switzer interview dress code: always wear dark pants (spills don't show); always wear a watch (makes it seem like you are punctual); never wear blue or grey shirts (they turn sweat stains into dark blotches). He went so far as to tell me that before he bought any dress shirt, he would discreetly put the sleeve in his mouth and suck on the fabric—while still in the store—to see if the material would darken when damp. It only took one more look from the bartender to make me decide to hide in the bathroom.

I snuck down to the basement like a creep, locked myself in their carpeted bathroom and removed my shirt before really drenching it. I looked at myself in the mirror.

"What is wrong with you?" I thought as I stared in the mirror. "Get it together, Val. Get. It. Together." I slid down the peacock wallpaper onto the floor and sat there, trying to take deep breaths to calm myself down. I was about to have a panic attack. I had to fight it. I'd been here before, in a total state of panic in a bathroom. I couldn't even count how many times I'd left Ryan sitting somewhere alone to calm myself down in a bathroom. At weddings, on airplanes, in restaurants, at gas-station restrooms. This was familiar to me. At least this time the floor was carpeted, and it smelled nice.

I took out my phone and did what any normal woman would do to distract herself from a full-blown panic attack: I went on YouTube and searched "puppies." I sat on that floor for a good ten to fifteen minutes, and after my seventh puppy video, I finally heard enough high heels tapping on the wood floor above my head to know it was safe to reemerge. No longer the first to arrive, I was now fashionably late.

I patted my armpits dry with a decorative towel and refolded it over the metal hoop it was hung on to look at but not touch. I put my damp-ish blouse back on, smoothed my hair, and went upstairs. I slowly opened the door to the basement and waited until the coast was clear to nonchalantly saunter in as though I'd just arrived. Through the crack of the door, I could see Mrs. Gold was still busy in the kitchen. I quickly slinked back into the foyer and pretended like I'd just walked in.

"Val!" Kate spotted me stepping out of the foyer. "Come on in!" Phew. "I'm so happy you're here, come meet everyone!" Kate took me by the hand. She marched me down a line of women and introduced me to them, one by one. My mind played a trick on me, and there they were: the nine-year-old versions of these women lined up on their sleeping bags.

"Val meet Crystal, Jocelyn, Erica, Randi…" I put on a big smile and said my hellos. Each of them said a perfectly friendly hello and then turned back to the conversations they were having with each other.

The front door opened again, and Kate went to greet the new guests. She was so warm and gracious. She made it look so easy. I looked around to see if there was a good place to situate myself, but everyone was standing and talking. I couldn't just go sit on the couch by myself. My heart started to pound again. I could feel the bartender's eyes burning a wet hole in my blue blouse.

I pretended to look for something in my purse. I was just about to pull out my phone and feign typing an important text message when Sabrina Weinstein, bitch queen extraordinaire, sashayed into the living room. Fuck me. I should have known she might be here. She seemed to always cross a room like she was walking the red carpet.

"Hey, Val! I didn't know you were friends with this crowd," she fake double-kissed me hello, as she waved to some of the other women. I needed this to end.

"I love your top, Val. Is it designer or just something from H&M?" Sabrina asked, just loud enough for everyone around us to turn their heads and wait for my answer. I actually wanted to hit her. I started picturing the scene from *Mean Girls* where Lindsay Lohan's character dives through the air in the cafeteria and wrestles the bitch to the ground.

"Sabrina, you are such a snob," Kate teased, coming to the rescue. I remembered why I was torturing myself: Kate was the kind of friend who had your back.

"Hey Val, come grab a plate with me," she said, ushering me away from the throng. Kind and considerate Kate had intuitively clocked my social anxiety. She must have seen the sweat marks beginning to stain my H&M shirt.

After one more trip to the bathroom to do a few lines of puppy videos, it was finally time to open gifts. Kate sat on a large tufted chair, and all the women sat around with their coffees and looked on.

She first opened boxes that were from people who had been assigned "living room": nice candelabras, candy dishes, photo frames. Then she opened boxes designated "kitchen": beautiful flatware, cake trays, serving platters. So far, mostly benign, practical fare that I couldn't imagine she didn't already own at forty. I was actually looking forward to the honeymoon gifts. I really needed the comedic relief, and this stuffy crowd could certainly use it, too.

Mrs. Gold stood up to announce the next set of gifts: "honeymoon." The honeymoon people lined up their gifts in front of Kate.

She picked up the one closest to her; it wasn't mine. A cotton nightgown with a picture of a kitten wearing sunglasses.

Then she opened the next one. I was hoping this one would be a bit spicier, but it was matching bride and groom T-shirts.

Oy vey.

Kate reached for the next gift.

Dear God,

Please, I beg you. Let that be a vibrator and anal beads, and I promise to take Michael and Hallie to have their teeth cleaned.

Amen.

Scented candles. I was going to die.

Kate reached for the last one. It was mine. I thought I was going to have a heart attack. The armpits on my pale blue top were now a dark navy.

"Kate, maybe open that one when you're alone," I whispered to her, trying intercept. I pulled the bag away from her. I mean how was I supposed to know that "honeymoon" actually meant things for the honeymoon!

"Don't be silly!" Kate laughed and tried to get the bag back.

"No, seriously. Please don't open this here." I was trying to reason with my kind, considerate friend.

All of a sudden, Sabrina snatched the bag.

"What's the big deal, Val? Just let her open it." Sabrina was proud of her intervention and smiled deviously.

I sank back into the couch. Even if I'd wanted to dig a hole through the carpet and disappear into it, my energy was sapped. Like these women have never seen crotchless panties?

Kate opened the box, and her jaw dropped. Her cheeks turned beet red; her eyes darted at me. So, I guess Kate has never seen crotchless panties. Sabrina, never missing an opportunity, grabbed the box and held it up like a trophy for the whole Prada shoe– wearing crowd of respectable doctors, lawyers and philanthropic women to see. My ten-inch vanilla cream cock was flapping above Sabrina's head. People gasped. Some just stared, mesmerized by the giant phallus, while others whispered to the person next to them. Could saying, "It was for me, not for Kate!" make things better? The humiliation was complete.

After a few half-hearted attempts at jokes and many sincere apologies, I insisted that Kate let me get her something else. I said my goodbyes to Kate and her friends. I couldn't wait to get home and recover. Mrs. Gold stood at the door holding a swag bag.

"Thank you again, Mrs. Gold. It was a lovely party." I didn't want to look at her, so I took the swag bag and opened the door.

"Excuse me, Val?" Mrs. Gold said in a hushed tone. Reluctantly, I turned to look at the flawless lady. Three hours later and she still looked immaculate.

"That girl, Sabrina was it?" she asked me.

"What about her?"

"You represent what she wishes she could be. I know jealousy when I see it. The next time you see her, just smile and remember that."

"Jealous of me?" I asked, astounded. " No way. Sabrina is just a bitch."

"A bitch? Yes. But only a bitch to the one that intimidates her."

As I walked out of Mrs. Gold's doorway with my giant dildo under my arm, the cold March air felt refreshing against my flushed cheeks. I turned back to Mrs. Gold and smiled at her. She winked back. She was the breath of fresh air I needed.

Coolest woman on earth: Mrs. Gold.

"...decide...whether or not the goal is worth the risks involved.

If it is, stop worrying...." —Amelia Earhart

CHAPTER 10

Swap #4: April 12, 2014

It's All In The Modern Family Ties that Matters

It was already 3 p.m. and Ryan still had no message from Celeste with an address. I was starting to get paranoid that she found out I had exchanged numbers with Nate. Although I never replied to any of them, he sent me a few flirty texts here and there, and when my curiosity got the better of me, I looked him up on Facebook and played Jewish geography. Boy, did I regret that.

Lo and behold, I went to elementary and high school with his wife, Kelly. But it was worse than simply knowing her; she was the daughter of one of my mother's close friends, and for years my mother insisted I be nice to her. My mom was at their wedding, for God's sake! How many times I heard about Kelly's "Chanel red" bridesmaids' dresses?

Kelly was a nose picker in kindergarten, and ironically enough, thinking of her reminded me of the summer of '89 when a handful of girls went to Dr. Gaston Schwarz for nose jobs instead of summer camp when we turned sixteen.

On our first day of grade eleven, Kelly came to school with a new nose, something I never thought needed fixing in the first place. Kelly walked into class and acted as if nothing was different about her.

You can't change a piece of your face and then not acknowledge it to everyone who has to look at you.

"Hi Kelly, how was your summer? Do anything special?" I asked in homeroom as I stared at the pinched nostrils and perfectly chiseled bridge.

I think she replied, "Oh, nothing special. Just chilled."

I sometimes ask myself why some of the prettiest girls in Montreal ever went under the knife in the first place. It was almost like a trend that only caught on with the wealthier demographic in our age group. I'm glad I was part of the demographic that spent my summer in camp for eight weeks with counselors who smoked at the activities and taught me words like "felch," "rim-job," and "trib." (Don't be embarrassed if you have to stop to Google "felch" and "trib.")

Kelly and Nate had one kid and lived in Hampstead, and as I crept through his Facebook photos, I learned that they met at Western, moved back to Montreal in 2006, took a family vacation on a Caribbean cruise, and enjoyed Beauty's for brunch. I browsed many, many pictures of him camping wearing those cargo pants I peeled off of him last month. Ah, Facebook—the equivalent of a department store display window of people's lives. My mom would be thrilled to learn that Kelly and I had indirectly kept in touch by both being members of Montreal's elitist sex club.

"Mom?" Michael stood in the doorway holding the TV remote.

"What's up, Mike?"

"Dad is busy with work, and I started this movie that's a bit—" Michael seemed jittery.

"A bit what?" I wasn't sure what he wanted. Michael is typically the kind of kid who knows what he wants and just speaks his mind. This kid standing in my doorway was uncomfortable and awkward.

"Mike?"

"This movie is fricking scary, Ma. Can you come watch it with me? It's for my science project."

"Of course. What's it called?" I hated horror movies growing up. My sister Janet loved them, of course. While she watched them, I would cower in my room for the two hours because even the music freaked me out.

"*Nightmare on Elm Street.*" Michael was on edge. He was already a half-hour into the movie and hadn't realized what he was getting himself into. So, I put on a brave face, told Ryan to keep Hallie upstairs, popped some popcorn, and I went with him into the basement to watch Freddy kill people while they sleep. (Not before turning on every light and opening every window shade. About twenty minutes later, I sent poor Michael upstairs and watched the rest by myself. Miss Clarice's (suck teeth) science fair project was turning into a Martin family affair.

Horror movie heart rate results and findings for Valerie Matthews (forty-year-old mother): Pulse rate of the subject increased from 77.6 beats per minute when she was watching calm scenes to 110.1 beats per minute (41.9 percent increase) when she was watching scary scenes in the same film.

At 5:45, Ryan's phone finally beeped with a text message.

Please come as a couple to the St. James Hotel in Old Montreal at 8 p.m., present yourselves to the concierge and mention my name.

Ryan read it aloud, and I immediately panicked.

Heart rate results and findings for Valerie Matthews, (forty-year-old mother): Pulse rate of the subject increased from 77.6 beats per minute when she was calmly emptying the dishwasher to 2000 beats per minute (2477.32 percent increase) when her husband read her the text message.

"I don't want to mingle with the wives!" I was on my feet and pacing up and down our hallway.

"Hi, how are you? I had your husband last month, who did you have?" Ryan did what he often does; he leaned against the wall calmly and watched as I unraveled. His lax attitude, in general, was one of the things I often appreciated about him.

"Val, this was your idea. You need to calm down." Sometimes his lax attitude just made me more anxious.

"Calm down? We signed up for Swap Club, not Orgy Club, Ryan! I don't want to be in the same room as you while you have sex with other women." I mean, I had my limits, and this wasn't part of the deal.

"This isn't an invitation to an orgy, Val. Let's go check it out and if there is more than one person waiting to have sex with us, then we can leave. Okay?" He looked at me, eyebrows raised, "Okay?"

"Okay."

Ryan gave me a hug and kissed my forehead. "You're going to be fine, Val. Remember this is part of the adventure you wanted." Ryan went upstairs and left me in the only-used-every-second-Saturday-of-the-month living room.

We bumped and vibrated up the cobblestone road to the upscale stone hotel set in a restored building from the 1800's and let the valet take our car. As we climbed the steps to the entrance, I was surprised that we were the only ones on time. I imagined that there would be a lineup of Mercedes-Benzes, BMWs, and Range Rovers. Ryan and I made our way through the sophisticated lobby and approached the concierge.

"We're here to meet Celeste." Ryan spoke matter-of-factly to the lady behind the counter.

"Your first names, please?" She had her fingers on the computer keyboard ready to type. She looked as if she had done this before, several times.

"Valerie and Ryan."

The concierge typed in our names and then looked at us as she slid two key cards to us.

"Room 607 for the lady and 807 for the gentleman, your meetings have arrived." We looked stupefied at the cards lying on the counter.

We got into the gorgeous mirrored elevator, and each pressed our designated number. As the doors to the elevator shut, we had no choice but to stare at our reflections as the bell chimed every time we passed a floor. I couldn't tell if we looked happy, sad, excited, anxious, or altogether desperate. What I did know was, when the door opened on the sixth floor, I was relieved.

I stepped out of the elevator and turned back as it closed. Ryan lifted his hand and waved goodbye just as the gold door sealed shut, and I was again looking into my reflection. I walked up the swanky hallway, dimly lit and actually the perfect "look" for this occasion. I remembered I had a piece of gum in my mouth, so I quickly tossed it into a flowerpot.

Feeling a bit uneasy, I got to door number 607, and my legs started to shake. I was barely used to swapping in the comfort of my house. At least there, I had the ability to watch them pull up in their car and size them up before they rang my bell.

Here I was entering the lion's den blind, and my trepidation was getting the best of me.

Take it easy, Val. Relax. I took a few deep breaths and put my card in the slot. I opened the door slowly and announced my presence.

"Hello?" I didn't hear anyone respond, so I closed the door behind me and walked into the beautiful suite.

"Hello?" I repeated as I explored this stunning hotel room, a room I have only seen in movies. It felt like a mature room, a room that has never seen a crayon or sippy cup. A room decorated with a creamy duvet, matching white couches, and drapes with gold furnishings to accent. Clean and pristine in disparity with the debauchery it would soon host. The inconsistency was comical.

"Hey." I turned to find a familiar man standing in the doorway of the bedroom.

"Neil?" I nearly died on the spot.

"Valerie, I can't believe this." Neil and I are sort of related, but through marriage, not blood. Ryan's step-sister married his brother. This meant there was a colossal chance that Ryan and I were about to have sex with semi-relatives. Unless of course Ryan had no memory of meeting Neil's wife, Julie, at his step-sister's wedding, which was entirely possible.

"What the hell!" We both started laughing hysterically. "Are we alone?" I had to make sure.

"Yes, we are alone. Why, were you expecting a third?" Neil looked worried.

"No, I just didn't know what to expect really," I said, relieved.

Neil was the meaning of tall, dark and handsome. He was H.O.T. Hot. I always flirted slightly at the pre-wedding events, and Neil and I had a shot together during the cocktail hour the day of the wedding. As I managed to choke down the hors d'oeuvres, we made jokes about the stale Moroccan cigars and inedible shrimp cocktail.

During the ceremony when the bridesmaids walked down the aisle I had to bite my lip. I made eye contact with Neil at a certain point, and we both nearly burst out laughing at the zipper on one of the dresses, looking like it was fighting for its life. Not that the girl was overweight in the least. It was just a cheap zipper that seemed to have lost its battle with her supersized silicone breasts.

"Swap Club? You?" Neil made his way over to me and sat down on the couch; he was wearing an amazing pair of jeans and a cardigan. I loved it.

"What? Are you that surprised?" I questioned as Neil leaned on his knees and stared at my lips.

"You not as much. But Ryan? That's pretty shocking."

He just said Ryan's name. It was a sudden jolt back to reality.

"I'm about to have sex with someone that knows my husband personally. Although we aren't actually related, and it's not like we do the holidays together. Right?"

"Val, let's order dinner and watch a movie." Neil grabbed the phone and ordered us some plates of French fries, spaghetti and meat sauce, some crusty bread and chocolate pudding for dessert.

An hour later, the empty plates covered the coffee table, our shoes sat in a pile on the floor, and Neil and I were watching the remake of *Psycho* with Vince Vaughn and Anne Heche. I kept gazing over at Neil. In actuality, I had always been secretly attracted to him. What better opportunity then tonight to at least kiss him? But how could I? Where was my nerve?

"Listen, Neil, I think you're very—comfortable?" I managed to say.

"You find me comfortable?" Neil was smiling.

Ugh. I wanted to say *sexy* or *hot*, but the word *comfortable* flew out of my mouth faster than the blue Windex drink post–Mexican fiesta.

I laughed. "Um, not so much comfortable as I would say handsome." The word *handsome* barely made it out of my lips.

"Really?" Neil looked at me and smiled and perked up. "How attractive? A nine? A ten?"

I laughed again. "I didn't say attractive, I said handsome. And more like an eight point oh, but the personality brings it to an eight point five."

We both laughed, and then a thick silence fell on the room. Neither of us knew what to do, so I got up to pour myself a drink out of a mini bottle of gin. I never had gin; the little bottle was charming, but the feeling of the gin on my esophagus, not so much.

About ten minutes later, Neil and I were sitting next to each other on the loveseat. He was sipping his drink while we teased each other.

"You were a huge flirt at the last wedding." Neil said, provoking me.

"Me? What are you talking about? You were the one that got me drunk at the bar."

"It was an open bar, Val. You were drunk before the ceremony batting your lashes at me and—"

"Batting my lashes? What are you talking about?" I knew he was right. I totally looked forward to the humdrum family events just so I could see him.

Another silence fell on the room, and then our eyes met. His eyes were smoldering, and before I could think about anything I could say to break the silence his mouth, tongue, and body were passionately engaged with mine.

Neil stopped kissing me and stared in my eyes.

"Wow, I thought it would be weird, but it's definitely not." Neil stood up. "Wait here for a second." And then he left me alone on the loveseat to ponder whether or not this was considered good family values.

Before my conscience got the better of me, Neil reemerged from the bedroom and made his way over to me.

"Come with me." Neil took my drink from my hand and placed it on the table, then led me to the bedroom where Sade was playing in the background.

"Sade?" I asked flirtatiously.

"I made a playlist, is it too cheesy?' Neil asked, unable to read me.

"No, not at all." I was totally into it and wanted to reassure him.

I turned to Neil, wrapped my arms around his shoulders and kissed him while we swayed to the music. As our kisses became increasingly wild, I found my fingers had a mind of their own, unbuttoning Neil's cardigan, then pulling his T-shirt over his head, and before I knew it, Neil and I were dancing topless as Sade poignantly sang about the sweetest taboo.

Neil lifted my hair and kissed the nape of my neck. I felt the chills from my spine spider their way up my back, and as far as I can remember, I believe this was when I lost all control.

Neil and I had made our way over to an open wall. I felt my back against the cold wallpaper. Neil stopped kissing my lips, and trailed his mouth down my chin, my neck, my chest and took my bare breast into his mouth and sucked on my nipple. I closed my eyes and saw stars lighting up inside my eyelids. As his tongue licked the hardest part of my nipple, his hands were unzipping my pants. He kissed my navel in perfect sync while his hands lowered my pants to the floor and had me standing in only my satin pink G-string.

Neil turned me around to face the wall, raised my hands above my head and held them with his hand. His other hand traced a line down my back, right through the crease of my buttocks and then spread my legs with his palm cupping my pulsating under- carriage. I was positive my panties were already soaked as he rubbed me, still kissing the back of my neck.

My knees were buckling; I could barely concentrate on standing as his hand rubbed me so intensely I couldn't help but moan with every stroke.

"I think you like this," he whispered in my ear. I nodded my head, unable to form any kind of sentence.

My legs were shaking. My arms were becoming limp, still fastened above my head with his firm grip.

"I think you'll like this better." Neil lowered himself to the floor and took a seat under me as he leaned against the wall.

He stared up at me as my arms fell to my sides, and I watched him peel off my G-string. I knew what was to come, only I didn't think my legs would hold me up. Neil pulled me closer to his mouth, stuck out his tongue and teased my clit with it.

"You want more?" I nodded as I stared back at him.

He pulled me closer and took my clit into his mouth. My head fell back as I stood there, trying to concentrate on the moment and not falling right onto my ass. His tongue and hands continued to stimulate me, licking, rubbing, sucking. I was going into a complete state of ecstasy.

"Neil, I want you inside me," I managed to blurt out.

"Come here." He unzipped his jeans and pulled out his magnificent-looking cock. He used his other hand to pull me down to the floor and straddle him. His penis entered into me, we both let out a huge sigh, and then I began to swivel my hips. He had a firm grip on me, from his lips to his hands, to our most private bits. Neil and I were in complete rapture; I barely noticed us make our way to the bed.

Neil climbed on top of me, spread my legs with his hands and fingered my swollen clit as he slid back into me. In perfect harmony with his penis and hands, Neil brought me to a state of euphoria.

We lay in bed joking around post-coitally (I made up that word).

"How the hell are we going to keep this a secret?" We were destined to see each other again, and I didn't know how I would handle being in the same room as his wife, Julie.

"Shit." Neil grabbed his phone while still keeping his other arm around me. "I'm going to text Julie to stay behind fifteen minutes, so you don't bump into her, and I don't bump into Ryan."

"Smart thinking."

A little while later, I met Ryan in the lobby, and I wanted to burst. How was I going to keep this secret from him? I just had sex with a family member. I would have to keep quiet and keep my distance from him tonight. Nervous that we would bump into members of the club, we got the hell out of there and went straight home.

When Ryan and I got back from the hotel, he was starved so he went straight to the kitchen and made himself something to eat while I showered and got into bed with an old family album. I initially pulled out the album to see if there were any pictures of Neil and me, but as I thumbed through the photos of our family, I reminisced about all the wonderful moments I'd had with these nutballs. Vacations, holidays, school concerts, and every cockamamie family shot of nothing brought me back to a warm and fuzzy place I almost forgot about in my journey to fill a void that in actuality might not really be empty.

A few nights later, I had a horrible dream. There I was, standing on a busy street corner with Hallie. As I looked at the oncoming traffic speeding past us, I watched as Hallie was inching her way off the sidewalk, looking at me right in the eyes. I yelled, "Hallie, move back!" but she just kept staring at me with a glazed-over look in her eyes and continued to disregard my plea to keep her out of harm's way. My legs felt like cement pillars, unable to move closer and grab Hallie by the collar and move her back onto the sidewalk. I yelled and I yelled, "Hallie! Get on the sidewalk! Move back!" But Hallie wouldn't listen. She just looked at me and blatantly ignored me as she stepped right out into the road.

I woke up screaming, "Move back!" and startled Ryan awake.

Sister Mary Stuart would probably tell me that the dream of Hallie walking into traffic was the two parts of me in conflict. The simple, straightforward child part of me was longing for freedom, trying to move forward, not seeing the risk ahead, and the jaded grown-up part of me was holding back, afraid of the risk. The risk is crystal clear.

This Swap Club thing was about sex. But freedom? I'm not so sure it's as simple as that. I see the potential risk! For crying out loud, I just had sex with Ryan's step-sister's brother-in-law! I was going to bust every time Ryan looked at me. I had to tell him. It was the middle of the night, but we were both up and clearly my experience with Neil was weighing on me.

"I have to tell you something. I can't take it anymore."

"What? What is it, Val?" Ryan sat up and flicked on the lamp.

"Okay, I know we made a pact about discussing the swaps, but I have to break it. My swap at the hotel was with Neil." I froze and waited for his reaction.

"With Neil?" Ryan popped out of bed and began pacing back and forth.

"I know! I had to tell you!" I just sat there trying to read whether Ryan was angry or not.

"Wasn't it weird?" Apparently Ryan wasn't angry so much as he was curious about my moral compass.

"Yes, it was weird, but I rationalized that it wasn't blood exactly, and it was technically your family through marriage, and that only makes it my family through marriage, through marriage."

"What the hell are we going to do if my family finds out?" Ryan was genuinely concerned, realizing for the first time how tiny Montreal is, especially when you're screwing your way through a small demographic within a five-minute radius of the Décarie Expressway.

"We all signed contracts, and I highly doubt Neil would want your family to find out either. I'm sure our secret is safe." I had to reason with him. I couldn't keep this secret from him, but I didn't want him to resolutely quit Swap Club only four months in.

"Are you mad?"

"This is wild, Val. I'm not mad at you. I'm just a little in shock, that's all. I mean, Neil? You had sex with Neil!"

Ryan surrendered to the idea that I was going to have sex with other men, and now he had to succumb to the idea that the other men could potentially be relatives. I didn't blame him for being conflicted.

"Are you having second thoughts about Swap Club?" I asked worriedly.

"Yes! I'm only human, Val. I don't think it's unreasonable for me to be a bit freaked out about Neil."

"I understand, I guess that means you didn't sleep with Julie." Ryan shook his head and then I had a thought. If I was just partnered with a relative, it could be plausible that I knew someone Ryan had slept with, hence his restraint. I wanted to test my theory. "Ryan, it was just sex. It wasn't anything more than that, no more than it was just sex with the last three guys before him."

"Great, Val. Were there any other groomsmen from my step-sister's wedding I should know about?"

I frowned. What a low blow. I threw it right back at him. "No, Ryan, what about you? You've also slept with four women now. Anyone I know?"

We were squared off, ready to pounce. When Ryan hit me back, I was knocked out. "You really want to know about the girl you did Mom and Tots with?"

"Who? Elisa? Jacklyn? Carolyn? Who?" I named everyone in my class, but Ryan's poker face was too good.

"Who, Ryan?" I tried to picture him with each of those women, and the more I thought of it, the more I realized I didn't want to know. The nail marks on his back were still healing, and now I was trying to remember which one of my mom-friends had painted claws.

"You want me to tell you? It was…"

"Don't tell me! Don't tell me!" I plugged my ears and shut my eyes like a toddler."Lalalalalalala don't tell me!"

When I opened my eyes, Ryan was laughing at me. I unplugged my ears and realized how ridiculous this was. Ryan sat next to me on the bed as if we were sitting next to each other in a movie.

"This is what we signed up for," Ryan said calmly. "We signed up to spice up our sex life, and who better to spice it up than my own brother-in-law's brother?"

I rested my head on Ryan's shoulder, and we just sat there for a few minutes.

"Let's just hope that's the last family member I have to sleep with or else Michael's bar mitzvah is going to be fucking awkward."

We laughed, then quietly thought about the prospect and shuddered.

"Let's vow that from now on, family member swapping is off-limits," I said, and then we shook on it. Then I placed my head back on Ryan's shoulder and contemplated the notion that we just vowed to stop sleeping with each other's relatives.

"Everything will be okay in the end. If it's not okay, it's not the end." —*John Lennon*

CHAPTER 11

Swap #5: May 10, 2014

Douchebag McMoneybags

A few weeks later, while I was examining my pores and crow's feet in the mirror instead of folding the laundry I left in the dryer from the day before, changing the bed sheets, unloading the dishwasher, vacuuming, or mopping, I got an email from Michael's teacher, Miss Clarice (suck teeth), requesting us to come and meet with her. I promptly scheduled the meeting for Wednesday, mostly because I was procrastinating folding laundry, changing the bed sheets, unloading the dishwasher, vacuuming, and mopping.

The problem with being a stay-at-home mom is, when the children are doing well, I'm feeling great about myself. In that case, I'm doing a great job. But, when the kids are fighting, the kids won't listen, the kids won't eat, the kids won't get into the shower, the kids won't get out of bed because they went to sleep too late, the kids' rooms are a mess, the kids are disruptive in class, the kids stuck a piece of gum in their hair and used kitchen shears I left on the counter to cut five inches of hair out of their head because they USED THE KITCHEN SHEARS I LEFT ON THE COUNTER... I become super hard on myself for not "doing a great job."

I met Ryan a few days later in the school hallway, which smelled exactly the same as it did when I was in elementary school. A hint of urine, some white glue, and a dash of apple core rotting in the garbage can.

Miss Clarice sat at her large wooden desk, and Ryan and I sat on the little metal desks in the front row. Miss Clarice. It was a little idiosyncrasy of Michael's school, all the teachers being addressed as "Miss" or "Mister" and their first name.

She was quite pleasant-looking with shoulder-length gray hair and hazel eyes. She wasn't what I was expecting. The description Michael gave us had her with wild, twisted wires coming out of her head, gray skin, and fangs dripping with drool.

Miss Clarice opened up the conversation. "So, as we discussed over the phone, Michael is a very smart boy. I just would like him to stay focused. Michael is easily distracted and can be lazy at times, and it's so sad to me because he is so bright." I felt like Miss Clarice was talking about me.

I started to fidget. My mom defenses were kicking into high gear, and all I wanted to do was drop-kick Miss Clarice in the face. My imagination was running away with me, as Miss Clarice's lips moved, all I could hear was; "You're a terrible mother. You're a selfish mother who cares more about getting laid than her son's reading and writing skills."

I could feel the sweat building on my neck and the blood pumping through my veins. Puppy videos as a distraction were out of the question, and I needed to think quickly before my nerves kicked into high gear and a full-blown panic attack set in.

What if Michael flunks grade four? Then he won't go to high school, and if he doesn't go to high school he has no chance of getting into Marianopolis, and if he doesn't go to CEGEP he can't get into McGill, and then he will live in our house until he's in his forties, and then he'll never get married because what woman would ever marry a forty-year-old man who still lives with his parents?

"Valerie?" Ryan snapped me back into our meeting.

"Oh, yes, sorry." Miss Clarice waited for me to answer. All I could think of saying was, "Yes." But she didn't look convinced.

"Yes?" Miss Clarice sought clarity. But I was so confused. This was much more fun when I wasn't actually there. Good thing Ryan piped in to help me out, although he looked mortified.

"No, Miss Clarice, the answer is *no*." Ryan shot me a look and then continued, "And I think to alleviate any additional stress on Michael, we should cancel this science project thing."

"But he worked so hard on it, Ryan!"

"Here's what we can do so all of Michael's hard work won't be wasted. I'll let him present his science project next year, in the grade five science fair in November. He will have the extra time to work on it over the summer, and time to focus on getting through grade four."

Before I even had a chance to weigh in, Ryan closed the matter. "Great. Perfect. Let's do that, Miss Clarice. We appreciate it."

What happened when we left the class was a classic cargument.

"Yes? What were you thinking? Yes, you would like Michael to repeat the grade? What is wrong with you, Valerie?"

Ryan was pissed. He used my full name, and now this was a full-on fight. I couldn't tell him that instead of paying attention and talking about the well-being of our son, I was ruminating about middle-aged Michael living in our basement, and that I couldn't think of the male word for a spinster.

"She's a bully, Ryan. Michael is a good, smart, and caring boy. That old hag has a problem with him. None of his other teachers do. Maybe it's her, not Michael.

I can't believe you signed him up to work on that stupid science fair project through the summer!"

"That old hag controls whether or not our son repeats the grade. Who cares about the science project? You heard what she said about his math marks, they're not good enough and it could impact his chances of getting into a good high school! What the hell, Val! Don't you check his homework book?"

"I do," I lied. I couldn't remember the last time I checked Michael's homework book. Ryan was right. I needed to do more than watch horror movies for him.

"You're such a flake sometimes." It was the last thing I remembered him saying. I didn't even defend myself because he was telling the truth. I was a flake. As he continued towards our house, I caught myself counting down the hours until Saturday.

Seventy-eight-and-three-quarter hours later, Ryan left for his swap and left me sipping a glass of white wine in my kitchen while I waited for mine. The minutes seemed to go by so slowly, and at 7:50 p.m. when I still had about ten minutes to kill, I found Pink's "So What" on YouTube and danced around my kitchen to distract myself from contemplating the logistics of Swap Club twenty-nine years down the road, if Michael was still living with us.

The doorbell rang at 7:59 p.m. This guy was eager! I counted to ten so I could catch my breath and then went to the door. My heart was still pounding in my ears, but my nerves had calmed down a bit.

I opened the door and found Mr. Moneybags standing on my porch with his stunning Porsche shining in the background. He had no idea who I was; why would he? But I knew *exactly* who he was.

At twenty-seven, he had already been featured in endless write-ups in the *Gazette* and *Forbes* magazine and was interviewed on Bloomberg TV. This guy was a self-made millionaire. I can't tell you what he does—it would be a dead giveaway—so for the sake of confidentiality, let's say he buys startups, brands them, and then sells them. I had no idea he was even married; I thought he was a bachelor for life.

I invited Moneybags into my home and watched as he looked around.

"Beautiful home. It reminds me of a place I spent some time at in Spain." I couldn't tell if he was showing off or just making conversation. Time would tell if this guy was a douchebag.

"The minute I drove up and saw this Victorian gem, I could smell the Spanish air." About four minutes later I came to the conclusion that he was absolutely a douchebag. "Even the wainscoting is the original, I'm telling you. It's like I've been here before."

He named about six cars that he owned, three homes he built around the world, and his favorite chef who does house calls especially for him. The last thing I wanted to do with this guy was have sex with him. I wanted to fake a stomachache or pretend to get my period; I had to think of something. I regressed into my former teenage self and decided to do to him what I did to my prom date: start a fight and get him to storm out. The residual aggravation from the meeting with Miss Clarice and the cargument with Ryan was enough for me to use as inspiration.

"So, Mr. Moneybags, do you ever stop talking about yourself?" He looked at me with a jolt.

"What?" He literally seemed unsure if he'd heard me correctly. I too was unsure if I heard myself correctly.

"I asked you in a nice way if you ever shut up because you haven't since you walked through my door five minutes ago." Moneybags was astonished. I watched as his cheeks turned red and his eyes glazed over.

"Wow, you say what's on your mind, don't you?" I have to say, I was a bit surprised that he didn't talk back, tell me to fuck off, or call me a bitch.

"But seriously, in five minutes you've managed to tell me where you live, what you ate for breakfast, and how many Hugo Boss suits you own. You haven't even asked me my name, or if I give a shit about the jet you just flew yourself to Rome on."

Moneybags was speechless, which made me even more confident. I liked this game, and I was going to keep on with it.

"Let's make a deal." Moneybags' mouth was hanging open. "The next time you talk about yourself or tell me something that I didn't ask you about, I'm going to smack you across the face." Whoa. Did I just say that?

I waited for a reply, a rebuttal, a *go fuck yourself*, but nothing came out of his mouth. The silence was amazing. His shoulders slumped a little and then he sat down at my kitchen table defeated. Did I just muscle Moneybags into submission?

"I feel like such a dickhead. I apologize. Can we start over?" Yep. I muscled Moneybags into submission. Go me!

I thought for a minute. He was attractive (when he wasn't talking), he had a nice body, good arms, good hands. Maybe there was a way to turn this night around.

"I have an idea." I took him by the arm and led him to my front door. "Now, get out."

He looked at me in total shock.

"You're kicking me out?" He reminded me of the kid in elementary school who got punished and had to sit in the hall.

"Nope, I am giving you a chance to start this night over."

I held the front door open.

"You're kidding, right?"

I didn't look at him and just stared out the door. Moneybags begrudgingly stepped onto my porch.

"Now, count to ten and ring my doorbell again."

Sometimes people need a second chance, and I was willing to give this guy the opportunity to prove he wasn't such an ass-head.

The doorbell rang again, and when I opened the door, Moneybags was on one knee with his hand on his heart.

"My lady, your knight in shining armor awaits." That was better, and I had another idea.

"Stay here." I closed the door and ran back inside to get a sweater.

"Isn't this against the rules?" Moneybags asked a few minutes later as he pulled away from the curb.

"I didn't read anything about sex in cars being off limits." Moneybags looked at me like I was insane.

"Sex? In my $150,000 car? You got to be out of your mind!"

I wanted to smack him across the face like I said I would, but I didn't have the nerve to follow through. Apparently my parenting and "dom" skills were consistent with each other.

"I don't care how much your car costs, and if you don't want to get laid in it, you should be driving a Kia."

I looked around and remembered a quiet dead-end street at the top of Westmount near St. Joseph's Oratory.

"Go up here. I know a good spot."

We pulled onto Surrey Gardens. I felt like I was in high school all over again, only I wasn't in my friend's Honda Civic this time smoking a joint and listening to Alanis Morissette on full blast.

"Pull over there." I instructed Moneybags to the exact spot that I figured would give us the most privacy.

"Are you serious? What if we get caught?"

I didn't have an answer for him, so I pretended like I didn't care.

"What's the worst thing that can happen? We get a ticket? I am sure you can afford it."

He pulled over to the end of the street and turned off the engine.

"So, now what?" Moneybags had no idea how to romance a lady. Not that this was a romantic situation, but my God, he was as suave as Gary Busey.

"Why don't you lean over and kiss me for starters."

We took off our seatbelts and leaned in towards each other when our lips touched, I felt absolutely nothing. There was no excitement; it was like kissing a mannequin. I had to get creative, so I told him to move his seat as far back as it could go. He hesitated as he looked at his dashboard, so I gave him a slap and then he did as I said.

I crawled onto his side of the car and straddled him. This tight area might not be the most conducive to car sex, but I had to make it work.

It took a little bit of time, but the tighter I squeezed my eyes shut and the more I envisioned Zac Efron, the easier it became. I imagined we were somewhere in West Hollywood, we had just finished dinner, and Zac could barely wait to get me home. The scenario was working. From this point on, this swap was with Zac, and no longer Douchebag McMoneybags.

Our kisses became more energized, the touching more intense, and I felt his rock-solid pecker pushing against his Armani jeans. I leaned down and pressed a button to recline Zac's seat backward.

"Ah, that's better," he said, reminding me once again that I wasn't actually with Zac. I had to regroup. I closed my eyes and started kissing him again, thinking about the shower scene in *The Lucky One*; it was working.

Zac unbuttoned the front of my shirt, exposing my sexy pink satin bra with lace trim. We continued to kiss as he caressed my breasts with his hands and managed to slip his tongue under the cup. His tongue on my nipple caused a physical reaction directly in my clitoris. I can't explain any better than that. I literally felt my clit pulsate when he sucked on my nipple. A new sensation that I never really took note of before—a plausible consequence of my preoccupation with my deflated boobs.

The windows of the Porsche were getting steamed up and I was in the mood to feel Zac's billion-dollar body part inside me. I was growing bored of the foreplay and wanted to move on to more serious bases. Five swaps in, and Val Matthews wasn't afraid of wanting more.

I slid into the tiny back seat and unzipped my pants. I teased him with a little peep show of my string underwear just barely covering my lips.

"Do you want to see more?" I asked in the sexiest voice I could muster from my position crumpled in the backseat with my legs up to my chin.

"I want a taste."

Zac turned himself around and placed his face right between my legs, his lower half still in the front seat. He licked me with my underwear still covering my most sensitive parts. I actually thought it was amazing. Just the teasing and the "almost-there" anticipation made me squeal every time he took another taste.

"You like that?" he kept asking me, and I kept nodding.

Slowly, Zac slid my string underwear off my legs and spread me open. I wanted his tongue on my bare skin so badly; I was holding on to the back of his head when he finally made contact. He spread me wide open and licked me up and down; I didn't even notice that I was moaning so loud that he had to put his hand over my mouth to absorb the noise.

"You're going to get us caught!" He was somewhere between worried and flattered, so he kept his hand over my mouth while he gave me the best oral pleasure I have ever had… in a Porsche.

Things got tricky when it was time to return the favor. I had to climb back over to the front seat, naked from the waist down, and maneuver my body around the stick shift. I unzipped his jeans and carefully pulled his johnson through the top of his underwear's waistband. There was no way to pull his pants down; I wasn't even going to try.

I was surprised to see that Zac completely trimmed his hedges. His five-inch penis looked about eight inches with all the manicuring that he had done. Good on him. This was the cleanest cockpit I had ever visited.

After a couple of licks and sucks, Zac placed his hands behind his head and lay back. He was so quiet that I couldn't tell if he was falling asleep or dead.

"Is this OK?" I asked a bit insecurely.

"Oh yeah, I'm just enjoying. Keep going, baby."

I proceeded to do my best work, the type of work that had all the other men barely able to hold their blow. But no sound of enjoyment was coming from him.

I had to up my game. I took his testicle into my mouth, and it felt like a plum inside a Ziploc bag, absolutely clean-shaven. I sucked on his balls, licked between them and moaned as I practically ingested his scrotum.

Nothing.

"Are you alive?" I asked, completely insulted.

"Yeah! Why did you stop?" He seemed just as perplexed as I was.

"You aren't making any noise. It's like blowing a corpse."

I was back with Moneybags again, no matter how hard I tried. The only time I could actually fantasize about Zac was when my eyes were closed shut.

"Baby, it feels phenomenal, trust me. I'm just quiet."

I couldn't argue with this guy. What was the point? So I continued to give him head until my jaw, neck, and hips started to hurt from the contortion of my body around his car.

"Climb back on top of me," Moneybags requested as he took a condom out of his pocket. "I just need something to catch my come in, can't get it on the leather. Come here." The moment was already dying, and the hot pink wrapper of his cherry-flavored condom was killing the mood even more.

I climbed over to his side, and then barely slid him inside of me. I had one leg along the doorframe, and the other on the inner compartment where he kept his gum. My back kept hitting against the steering wheel and my head smacked the roof every time I stretched my back. Regardless of how awkward the positioning was, Moneybags was fully getting off, and he was only halfway inside of me. I couldn't lower myself enough to get him completely covered.

I looked over my shoulder at the clock, and after four minutes and eighty-seven thrusts (yes, I counted), Moneybags came. I fell off of him and back onto my seat.

"Man, that was fucking unbelievable."

I could barely get my clothes back on. My legs kept sticking to the seat as I tried to pull my pants back up. My moist nether-regions were leaving wet marks on his leather seat, and I couldn't help but grin as we drove all the way back home in his $150,000 car.

When we pulled up to my house, Moneybags got out of the car, came around to my side, and then opened my car door for me.

"That was… interesting." He put his hand out to help me up.

"Did I mention that your house reminded me of a place I used to stay at in Spain?"

"Yes," I said, rolling my eyes. "You did mention a vacation home." I couldn't believe he was trying to impress me again.

"No, not a vacation home. My late grandparents had a home in Seville and I used to spend my summers with them when I was a kid. Your house made me think of them. Man, I miss my grandparents. I think about them all the time. The sacrifices they made for my parents so that we could have a better life in Canada…

I promised my grandfather on his deathbed that all his hard work wouldn't be in vain." Moneybags was about to turn and walk back to his car, but before he could, I grabbed his arm, pulled him in and gave him a hug.

Maybe he wasn't a complete douchebag after all.

"Fantasy is a necessary ingredient in living, it's a way of looking at life through the wrong end of a telescope." —Dr. Seuss

CHAPTER 12

Swap #6: June 14, 2014

I Got Schooled

The bruises on my legs and back finally healed from the last swap. I had to assure Ryan over and over that it wasn't intentional.

"I'm okay, I promise, Ry. Porsches are really not made for fucking." I figured if I joked about it, he would believe me and just drop it.

"Thanks, Val. I really wanted to picture you having sex with some guy in an exotic sports car."

"At least I kept my promise and didn't tell you *who*, I only told you *where*."

I met Melissa, Tanya, and Helen for brunch, something we rarely do, but because of work schedules it was our only chance to see each other in weeks. I was anxious all morning. I was going to see Melissa for the first time since I banged her brother a few months ago. I usually see her on a weekly basis, but with the construction going on in her house, it had been months—probably a good thing.

I wondered all morning if maybe Sam told her that we were members of this secret club and that a few months ago we were fucking in my bedroom while Ryan was off doing the nasty with God-knows-who. Maybe that was the real reason I hadn't seen her, and she was just blaming it on the renovations. I would never know. There's just something so bizarre about having direct connections with the members of the Club (even if they have no recollection of knowing you).

In the one hour we spent together Melissa managed to send her food back twice, but not before complaining about Jeff's post-nasal drip keeping her up at night and her mother-in-law visiting from out of town, and although the built-in babysitting service was welcome, the twenty-four-hour surveillance on her marriage and family life was not. Helen complained about her nocturnal lactose intolerance, her asymptomatic psoriasis, and that she gained five pounds on her 100-pound frame.

And then, when I thought our lunch couldn't get any shallower, Tanya started complaining about her cleaning lady, Flaca.

"We all have our problems, I know. First World problems, but problems I have to deal with nonetheless." Tanya pushed her egg whites around her plate. "Flaca was upstairs cleaning our bathroom when I came home from running errands. As I was in my bedroom getting changed, something she did in the bathroom caught my eye. I was hoping I was wrong, but I wasn't."

I thought for sure Flaca was caught masturbating.

"Flaca was using the toilet water to clean my bathroom!"

Flaca wasn't masturbating. What was wrong with me? The strange consequence of having started swapping is that I have sex on the brain…all the time.

Tanya was completely distraught. "I saw her reach into the toilet with the cloth, ring it out into the toilet, and then use the cloth to wipe down my sink and counters."

Helen and Melissa pushed their food away in disgust.

"I think my breakfast just rushed into my esophagus." Helen put her napkin over her mouth.

"She had been to my house several times, and I had no idea that this was the way she was cleaning our home. With toilet water! Water from the toilet! Toilet water! TOILET WATER!" Tanya was yelling. People at the other tables could hear Tanya's protest about her cleaning lady.

"So, what did you do?" Melissa asked, appalled.

"I said, Flaca, what are you doing?" Tanya took a sip of her coffee. "I saw bubbles in the toilet basin, and the wet mop was lying next to it on the floor. I was dying."

"What did she say?" Melissa was on the edge of her seat. Helen still held the napkin over her mouth.

"She said, *What's wrong, Mrs. Tanya?*"

Helen and Melissa were in shock. I, on the other hand, was troubled that my friends were upset over the work efficiency of a cleaning lady.

"She did not react the way I thought she would. Flaca looked at me completely baffled, not one iota of *Oh shit! My boss just caught me with my hands in her shitter!*"

"So you fired her, right?" Helen finally removed the napkin from her mouth.

"No." Tanya kept her eyes down.

"You didn't fire her?" Helen was perplexed.

"No! Do you have any idea how hard it is to find good help?"

And then I thought I was the one who was going to be sick. I had nothing in common with these women I called my best friends. All of a sudden, I felt very alone until my phone buzzed on the table with a text message from Celeste. It dawned on me right then and there that perhaps Swap Club was filling a bigger void than I understood. I wanted to wait until I was back in my car to read the text, safely away from prying eyes, but my curiosity was overriding my good sense.

"Valerie, you are to be at 14380 Rosemont at 8 p.m. sharp. Ryan is to stay home this evening."

I sipped my coffee in silence, pretending to listen to my girlfriends' banter about nail polish and gossip about what's-her-face, but all I could think about was sharing the news with Ryan.

I was pretty excited about this change-up until I got home and saw Ryan doing math homework with Michael and Hallie eating a snack and watching cartoons. Ryan was going to stay home and have sex with his lady of the evening in our home. In our bed. In my bed. I didn't want Ryan to see that it bothered me, so I went secretly into our basement and had a mini-meltdown alone. I paced around from the washer and dryer to the couch and then back to the washer and dryer. I must have done that a couple dozen times before I was able to sit on the edge of the couch and pull myself together.

Ryan came downstairs and sat next to me on the couch. "What's up? Why are you hiding down here?"

"I got a text from Celeste with an address, but that means some woman is going to be in *our* bed." I looked at him warily and waited for him to respond.

Ryan put his arm around me, took my face into his hands, and kissed me.

"It'll be okay, Val. Just put the old sheets on our bed and I promise our house will look exactly the way you like it by the time you get back. You won't even know she was here."

But, what I heard was:

"For fuck's sake, Val, five other men have fucked you in our bed."

And technically he would be wrong. The last guy was in a car, and Neil was at the hotel, so really it was only three. I fake-argued the numbers as I went back upstairs and changed the sheets on our bed to the ones we never use. The crummy sheets. At the bottom of the pile. The ones that felt scratchy against my skin.

Before kissing Ryan goodbye, I turned to him with a pouty face and said, "Don't let her touch my stuff."

"Okay. If it makes you feel better, I won't let her lie on your side of the bed."

I made a fake-vomit face and then kissed him goodbye. He gave me a pat on my ass as I left.

At 7:59 p.m. I pulled up to a beautiful home on a popular crescent across the street from a park I often take the kids to on our way home from school. I'd never come to this street for anything but a good push in a swing or to build a sand castle.

Outfit of choice for this swap: jean shorts, black tank, and lace-up boots. Hot pink bra and matching G-string. I walked up the stairs and took a deep breath. A surge ran through my fingers as I pressed the doorbell. I heard the door unlock, and I lost the feeling in my legs as the door opened. It was Tyler, the teacher's assistant from my Art of Diplomacy class when I was at McGill.

My first instinct was to turn and run back to my car. So I did.

Tyler called after me as I fumbled through my purse for my keys.

"Valerie! Valerie, please." Tyler left his door open and chased me to my car, barefoot across his lawn. "Val, please don't get freaked out. Please."

His ice blue eyes were outlined with dark eyelashes.

"This is crazy," I muttered.

For all the times I would stare at him biting his lip listening to me discuss my essays, or purposely sit too close to him while he helped me work on my papers, or add one more spritz of perfume to my neck when I knew I would see him—I couldn't believe that I'd find him in this club as well.

"I didn't peg you to be a swap type." He stared at me with eyes that made me weak.

"I'm not," I lied with smooth conviction. "My stupid husband's idea."

I'd spent so much time training myself to be cool and collected in front of him. I would sign up for his extra-credit projects and conferences he would organize on "Effective Communication During Negotiations" and "How to be Persuasive and Assertive." We would go for coffee after to discuss my thoughts. I knew he liked being around me; there was an undeniable chemical thing between us. I started dating Ryan close to the time I was in Tyler's class because I was sure it was a transient crush that would never turn into anything serious. I had to ignore it, store it away in the deepest compartment of my being. Dating a teacher—even a teacher's assistant—was so cliché anyway.

I was afraid that once I got a taste of him, it would take me that much longer to close my eyes to that chemistry.

Tyler used his art of diplomacy to negotiate me off the road and into his house. First the assertiveness. "Val, please come inside." Then the persuasiveness. "Come on, let's be adults about this."

I put my keys back in my purse. He placed his hands on my shoulders, and I let him guide me towards his open front door. Where was I going anyway? Ryan was at home wooing some horny bake-sale-cookie-making housewife on my turf.

His home was simple, beiges and browns. The only burst of color came from the random artwork I could only assume his children made. He led me into his living room, the TV displaying the History Channel. A rasp with a piece of soapstone sat on the coffee table. My legs were trembling.

"Come, sit." Tyler had a warm, loving demeanor; he was the type of guy you wanted to get naked and cuddle in a cozy bed with while he caressed you. "Excuse the mess. I took up soapstone sculpturing as a hobby, but as you can see, I'm not so great at it." Tyler motioned towards the misshapen stone lump with shavings surrounding it. "I've been working on it for over a month." He handed me the oblong piece of soapstone that looked like a piece of…nothing.

We both laughed. I could stare at his gorgeous smile for hours. In university, I used to take long hot baths and fantasize about him holding my face between his hands and kissing me.

The last time I saw Tyler was about a year ago when I bumped into him at a Starbucks on Monkland. I remember he put his hand on the back of my shoulder as we caught up. He was telling me where life had taken him: two kids, a home close by, and still at McGill, but now as a professor. I could still feel the magnetism years later. I wondered if he could too.

"I can't believe I'm in your house." My voice was shaky.

Tyler looked at me, then placed his hand on my lap.

"Please, relax. I can tell you're nervous. I promise we can take it slow, and we won't do anything you aren't comfortable with." His warm hand on my lap felt so good; it felt like an eraser, wiping away my trepidation.

We sat on his couch and made some small talk, and I could tell he was trying to help me settle.

"So, you watch the History Channel?"

"Sometimes there's something worth watching on this channel believe it or not." We both gazed at the commercial for *Mountain Men*. "I said *sometimes...*"

We were quiet, and all we could do was stare at each other. The sexual tension was palpable.

"Truth or dare?" Tyler calmly asked. I was intrigued.

"Truth," I blurted out.

"Tell me a secret that no one else knows."

I knew exactly what I wanted to tell him, but I didn't want to freak him out. So, I took my time figuring out my answer.

"I melt when you look at me." Tyler smiled.

"Your turn, truth or dare?" I asked.

"Dare," Tyler replied.

"Tyler, I dare you to do exactly what you want to me." Tyler bit his lip—I loved when he did that. He moved in closer, and then he pulled me onto him, his hands on either side of my face, and kissed me passionately.

"I'm sorry, I don't have the willpower to control myself."

His kisses felt incredible, with his hands on my face, in my hair, on the back of my neck holding me on his mouth. I was already getting off, and all we were doing was kissing. He was hard; I could feel it through his pants. I wanted him, and I was finally going to have him after all these years.

Tyler stood up while still kissing me and pulled my top off. He kissed my neck, my chest, my clavicle, then unhooked my bra and took my breast into his mouth. My newfound sensitive nipple caused my knees to shake. The room spun. My legs grew weak with every lick, nibble, and stroke. He was in complete control; he knew what he wanted, and I was more than willing to follow his lead.

Tyler lowered himself to his knees as he kissed and licked and sucked. He turned me around to lick and caress my back. I stood with my eyes closed and let him have me, any way he wanted me.

Tyler took a seat back on the couch as he pulled me close to him. I stood there, half naked, while his hands explored my stomach and breasts. *A good negotiator has the ability to think like the other side to find innovative solutions.* I was reciting in my mind the lessons this man taught me. I couldn't believe my college-girl fantasy was coming true.

"You smell so good. Taste so sweet." He turned me around and continued to kiss my back and waist while he undid my shorts. His kisses grew more intense as his hand slid down inside my G-string.

He turned me back around to face him, and he stared into my eyes as he lowered my shorts to my ankles, and there I stood, completely naked in front of Tyler, my freaking T.A.

"You're so gorgeous." Tyler pulled me closer as he licked his fingers and started to rub me. I could barely stand up. His moans and fervent hands revealed how badly he wanted me too. He was enjoying pleasuring me as much I was enjoying receiving it. My mind was still recalling the course material: *create additional options when things are at an impasse.*

"Ty, I can't take it." I was at a physical impasse. In a matter of seconds I was going to come, his lips, his tongue, his fingers manipulating me so well I could barely breathe.

He turned me back around and rubbed me as he devoured me from behind. My legs gave out, and I landed on his lap.

"I can't take it." He continued to rub me as I gyrated on top of him. I wanted to feel his skin. I got up and unbuttoned his pants. His eyes were smiling at me. All I wanted was to remove anything that was between us.

I took off his pants, and then he laid me on his couch. His warm penis rubbed against me while he kissed me so intensely that I felt feverish. I reached down and slid him inside me; my whole body was in tremors as his lips were licking and kissing the side of my neck, and then every ounce of me wilted in his arms. My lips felt sore, but the rest of me was still tingling.

"I am so attracted to you, Val." I couldn't believe the words coming out of his mouth, words I had once daydreamed about but had since buried. Words that I couldn't script better myself. And here was my chance to tell him.

"Tyler, you have no idea how badly I wanted you when we were at McGill. There was always a connection. I can't explain. From the day I met you, all I could ever think about was being with you. Your lips, your hands, your eyes, I wanted them all but never said anything because I was afraid of being rejected."

Tyler sat up and took my face into his hands.

"Are you kidding? Look at you, Val. Nothing has changed—you're still amazing, funny, intuitive, and unbelievably sexy. If anything, I never went there because I couldn't imagine someone like you even thinking of me that way…and I probably would have gotten fired."

We kissed again and again all evening, and every time I looked at my watch I was hoping we had more time, but 11 p.m. was growing closer and my heart heavier. He held my hand while we talked, and he kissed me every so often just because he felt like it.

At 10:50 p.m. I got dressed, frowning as we cleaned up. I knew that it would be a while before I saw Tyler again. A part of me hoped that the next time we bumped into each other it wouldn't be at a McGill alumni event or a coffee shop, but rather right here, in an empty house where we could just spend hours with each other. As he walked me out, he also looked a bit sad. He pulled out his cell phone.

"Will you break a rule with me?"

"Depends on the rule."

"Give me your number." Tyler held his phone and waited for me to tell it to him.

"I can't. We shouldn't." I wanted to give him my number so badly, but my guilt was weighing on me.

"How about you give it to me in case of an emergency." Tyler's negotiating skills were still impeccable. Persuasiveness first.

"Val, please give it to me. I have to have it." Next, assertiveness.

It worked. I got into my car and could barely see where to put the keys in the ignition. My eyes welled with tears. Too overwhelmed to drive, I had to pull over. What was I doing? This wasn't just casual flirting. Exchanging numbers this time seemed to imply the rekindling of a lost love.

I had spent so much time trying to prove to myself that Swap Club was just about the sex, but at that moment I knew it was way more than that if three hours with an old crush could have me crying behind the wheel of my car. How is it possible to love my husband and have feelings re-emerge for an old flame? Was this just nostalgia? Midlife malaise? Was it a sign of a more fundamental issue with my marriage? Or with me?

I was only halfway through my Swap Club membership. Instead of rediscovering myself, I was feeling completely lost.

"I think the saddest people always try their hardest to make people happy because they know what it's like to feel absolutely worthless and they don't want anyone else to feel like that." —Robin Williams

CHAPTER 13

A Hot Mess

As great as I was feeling in June, the next month was the polar opposite. I have been edgy, impatient, frustrated, and most of all confused. Tyler turned my entire world upside down. Was it the sex? Was it the memories of old fantasies and the feelings of unfulfilled promise? Or was there really something missing in my life? How could I find myself distracted by someone who was not my husband? There were so many questions swirling in my head. How could I love Ryan and have thoughts about another man? What the hell was going on with me? I was like a kid with a loose tooth. I couldn't leave it alone.

It didn't help that the night I came home from the swap, I could smell the perfume and sex lingering in our bedroom from Ryan's conquest. I had to sleep on the couch that night and sterilize our room the next day.

Since then, I have been up at all hours tossing and turning. The flashback of Tyler and me together was causing an electric surge from my stomach right to my nether regions. Tyler's eyes burned a hole in my brain. I had to see him again, even though I knew we were restricted by not just the club's rules but by my marriage vows.

I wrote and deleted a text asking if he had five minutes to meet over and over again. And then I pressed *send* and buried myself under my covers to mask my shame.

Ryan had taken Michael and Hallie to Helen and Steve's house for the day to swim and stare at their giant new fence. I opted out; I didn't want them to see me. I just didn't have the energy to try and pretend like there wasn't anything on my mind. I felt like they would sense it, and I didn't want to face them and dodge questions.

I feel guilty to this day that I could have spent a wonderful day by the pool with our kids. Instead, I convinced Ryan that I couldn't go because I woke up with a fever; it wasn't that hard considering how haggard I looked. Ryan reluctantly left me alone in my misery, rubbing Purell into his hands and closing the door with his sleeve wrapped over his fingertips.

Now that I had sent the message, all I wanted was a response. My brain was dreaming up every possible reply. "I miss you like mad." "I can't stop thinking about you." "I need you." The only thing that would put it to rest would be Tyler's actual response.

It took Tyler more than four hours to respond. My phone battery nearly died from my constant checking. I started to worry that the mobile gods had sent my text to the wrong number, or his phone was rejecting my message. Either way, I was convinced that calling Rogers to make sure there was nothing wrong with the system wasn't completely mental of me.

It was.

Tyler responded with a simple "Sure." Amazingly, my brain hadn't considered that answer.

By the time I read the singular word, I was so angry that I couldn't help but respond with, "Sure?" I immediately regretted pressing send when my phone rang, and it was him.

"Hey, sorry it took me so long to respond. I just flew back from Florida. I was in line at customs when I texted you back. Everything okay?"

I felt like such an asshole. Worse, actually. I felt like a real loser.

"Yeah, yeah, everything is great," I lied.

The complete silence on the line punctured another hole in me, but this time it was right through my heavy heart.

"Val, are you okay? Tell me what's going on."

I felt a lump in my throat, and I felt the tears welling up in my eyes. I knew if I spoke he would hear me straining to speak.

"Val? Talk to me, please." I couldn't help myself; I was a complete hot mess as I stared at myself in the mirror. My gray roots were over-grown, my eyebrows unkempt. My skin looked dry, and my hair was pulled back into a dirty, messy bun. I was an absolute disaster. The only thing stopping me from getting into my car and driving it straight to see him was my reflection staring back at me.

"I'm so fucked up, Ty. So, so fucked up. I don't know what's wrong with me." I blurted it all out. "Now that I know what it is like to be with you, all I can think about is when I can be with you again. I'm a complete mess." (What the fuck was I saying?)

I sat on the landing of my staircase; my legs didn't want to hold me up any longer. My body was too heavy, too full of despair and sadness. Sadness imagining Ryan's face if he heard what I had just said to another man. Sad thinking about my kids' faces if they knew I didn't spend the day with them because I didn't want to, not because I was sick. Sad wondering what my life would become if Ryan ever found out I was cheating on him. Even though the Swap Club was consensual, these emotions were not.

"Val, please don't be upset. Please, I can't handle hearing you like this. What can I do? Just tell me what you want me to do, and I'm there."

A part of me wanted to tell him to drive right over and get me. Take me to some faraway place where he and I could just live anonymously. Sell kayaks on the beach, sipping fruit drinks and catching fish at sunset.

"Valerie?"

I couldn't speak; I didn't trust that what I'd say next wouldn't scare him into getting a restraining order.

"Meet me somewhere, Val. I'll tell my wife I have to get something from my office." I got up, with a glimmer of hope that I didn't look so crazy and could clean myself up enough to face him. But when I took a look in the mirror, I was horrified. With puffy eyes caked with mascara, I looked like the final scene of a horror flick—the part where the girl finally gets her head ripped off after being chased up the staircase.

"I can't meet you. I'm a fucking wreck. I just needed to hear you say something, tell me something to make me better." I was desperate.

I needed Tyler to take this burden off me. I couldn't handle this obsession I'd cultivated. If there was any way to get over him, it had to happen now.

"You're such an amazing person, Val. I am not worthy of your feelings. I want to take you into my arms right now and make you feel better. You just have to let me."

I wanted him to rescue me. I wanted him to grab me and comfort me and relieve me from having to consider the meaning of all these feelings. Then I imagined Ryan's face, my kids' faces, my mom's, my sister's, my late grandmother's—and her sounding like Woody Allen when I imagined her yelling at me. What a fucking liar I was, a fucking liar to all of them.

"I'll meet you. I need an hour."

"Where?" I had no idea how this would be possible.

"At my office." I guess he had already thought up a plan. Did this mean he was thinking about me?

"Same place? Leacock Building?" I had a good memory when it came to Tyler.

"Yes. See you soon."

I hung up, got undressed, and got into the shower.

I just stood there as the warm water washed over my body, clearing away all the sadness and all the anguish. I examined my body, and it looked awful. A diet of salt and vinegar chips and Diet Dr Pepper will do that to you.

I opened my mouth wide and let the shower spray inside my mouth. This wasn't just a shower, it was a cleansing. I got dressed, put my hair in a ponytail, and then made my way to Tyler's office on the twelfth floor of the Leacock building at the heart of the McGill campus, a place I have been many, many times. But this time it was going to be for a different reason.

When the elevator doors opened, I saw him standing in the hallway waiting for me. What was I doing? Such drama, such deceit. I was sure his wife was anxiously waiting for him, and here he was, standing in his office when he could be home with his family.

I walked up the dimly-lit concrete hall. He opened the door to his office and pulled me into his arms.

"It's going to be okay, Val. I promise." How could he promise me something he had no control over?

"Come in, let's talk." But I didn't want to go in. I didn't want to walk through the threshold with him in an awkward silence. I didn't want to have to sit in a fluorescent-lit concrete cube with a sliver of a window and explain my unhealthy fixation on him. This was not how I pictured it at all.

"Actually, Tyler, I'm going to be fine." I hugged him goodbye and left him standing alone and confused.

As I got back to my car, I realized that I watch too many movies. Scenes are set up for hours. Crews pre-light the Kinos to cast the perfect light onto the gorgeous lovers. A set designer creates the most romantic setting because a screenwriter spent years describing the perfect spot for their words to be spoken by the stunningly handsome male lead.

Ever catch the look of the female audience leaving a theater after the latest romantic comedy? They are pissed that they have to go home with *him* tonight and not Channing Tatum.

My reality check happened when I realized that Rhett didn't profess his love for Scarlett in his bleak office on a Sunday afternoon. I drove straight over to Helen and Steve's house and got choked up when I saw the look on kids' face when I walked into the backyard. Pure joy.

"Mommy! You're not feeling yucky anymore?" Hallie yelled from the floating donut in the pool.

"Nope, I'm feeling much better, my love."

"Then why are you crying?" Michael asked as he walked over to me.

I didn't answer. I just pulled him in and gave him a hug. I couldn't put into words how awful I had been feeling and how one look at my kids and Ryan made me recognize that I had made the right choice. This was where I was supposed to be.

Right?

Fuck.

"I told my wife the truth. I told her I was seeing a psychiatrist. Then she told me the truth:

that she was seeing a psychiatrist, two plumbers, and a bartender." —*Rodney Dangerfield*

CHAPTER 14

Swap #7: July 13, 2014

Leather, Fur, and Lace

Ryan and I were having dinner, just the two of us. Michael was at a friend's, and Hallie was out with my mother. We sat there in complete silence, eating bite after bite with nothing to say to each other. I'm sure it was magnified by the drama last month, but it was almost like I was dissecting our relationship to find reasons why I had wavered emotionally. Normally, I wouldn't think twice about a pleasant, quiet dinner, but here I was, anxious and looking for deeper meaning as to why we weren't talking.

We weren't in a fight. There was no argument to speak of. Perhaps we just had nothing to talk about. Simple as that. The truth was, Ryan and I were never big conversationalists. If it had to do with the kids, family, or finances, then yes, we had things to talk about. But put us at a dinner table—unless we had invited other people to come—and we just didn't talk much.

Could it be that I never felt smart around him? Even worse, did he only like the way I looked? I wiped my mouth and brought my plate to the sink. As I placed it down, I wondered why he never laughed at my jokes. Maybe he didn't find me particularly funny or charming. I thought about all the times I would hear him gasping for air when he was on the phone with his friends or his brother. I was starting to feel jealous as I imagined him laughing and talking for hours until I begged him for attention. How could he have so much to talk to them about and nothing to say to me? I walked back to the table and took his plate from him, even though he still had a few bites left.

"Val? I wasn't done." Ryan looked puzzled.

"Ryan, do you think we are mentally compatible? I mean, I know physically we have our issues, although I must say, the sex we have had since we signed up for Swap Club has definitely improved. But mentally, do I stimulate you?"

Ryan looked taken aback. "I was wondering what was going on in your head." Ryan brought his glass to the sink and then turned to look at me. "Yes, I think we are compatible, why?"

"Because you don't talk to me." I pulled myself onto the counter and sat with my legs dangling.

"I do talk to you. Since when are you afraid of silence?" Ryan stood between my legs and looked at me in the eyes. "Everything is okay. We are okay. This is our normal, Val."

"What if our normal isn't healthy?" I needed reassurance that Swap Club wasn't exposing the flaws in our marriage. That it was still just about sex.

"Being able to sit in comfortable silence with my wife is healthy for me. Not having to entertain you, placate you, or appease you, but just enjoy your company, is normal. Please stop overthinking everything, Val. Our normal is healthy."

Ryan leaned in to kiss me but this time he kissed me longer than *our normal*. We actually French kissed for the first time in years while not having sex. It was strange, and it caught us both off guard. It even, dare I say, turned me on.

The house was empty and we had some limited time before Ryan had to get the kids, so we went with it and had a Grade eleven style make-out session that had my pants and underwear at my knees, and my bra up around my neck.

After about ten minutes of saliva-filled making out, Ryan went to collect the kids while I cleaned up from supper, including wiping my ass marks off the kitchen counter. Maybe Ryan was right. I had to stop overthinking everything and ease up.

The Saturdays started to melt into one another. I was losing count of how many guys I had slept with. Was it six or seven? I went back to my calendar and stared at the little puppies in a basket of flowers next to the word "July." Seven. That was my number. By the end of tonight, I will have slept with more men in 2014, than I had in my forty previous years.

I went for a manicure at Mai's, my Vietnamese "other mother" I've been going to for years. Mai has no filter, and I love her for that. She makes a running commentary on my hair color being too dark or too light, points out my protruding pimple, compliments or frowns at what I'm wearing and wrinkles her nose if I don't pick a nail polish color she likes. I asked her to draw an ornate number seven on my pinky. She didn't ask why. Could she tell by smelling me that I was part of the Swap Club she hears the girls gossip about?

That afternoon while the kids were playing in the yard, Ryan sat on the porch reading his Grisham novel. I was tidying up inside when I noticed Michael's now-neglected science fair project. The spaces next to the dentist and roller coaster were still waiting for a pulse rate measurement. I had an idea.

"Let's go," I announced to Ryan and the kids. The three of them just stared at me.

"Did you guys hear me? Put your things away. We are getting out of here."

"Where are we going?" Michael asked, grabbing his soccer ball and tossing it into the vestibule.

"We are going to work on your science fair project."

A half-hour later, we were circling in the La Ronde parking lot for a spot.

"Mommy, what are we doing here?" Hallie had no idea we were at an amusement park. From the parking lot there was not much to see.

"We are at La Ronde, Hallie. It's an amusement park, like Disney."

Hallie took a look at the park entrance. "This doesn't look like Disney World, Mommy."

We bought our tickets, grabbed a map and found what I was looking for. 'The Monster.'

"Follow me!" I took Hallie by the hand and led my pack to the tallest two-track wooden roller coaster in the whole world. It said so on the map.

We could see The Monster and hear the sound of the screaming crowd from the other end of the park. The eerie sound of the wooden beams creaked and wailed as the ride sped through the track. When we got closer, the four of us stood at the base just gazing up at it.

"Mommy, I do not want to go on that!" Hallie started to cry.

"Don't worry, Hallie, you're not allowed on that one. You're way too small." Ryan picked her up and consoled her.

"Well, then I hope I never get big enough to get on."

Michael looked frightened, even more frightened than he was of Freddy Krueger.

"Mike, I'll go with you." Both Ryan and Michael looked surprised to hear me volunteer.

"Seriously, Val? I can go with him. It's ok. You stay with Hallie."

"No. I'm going."

"You sure?" I could tell that Ryan was relieved.

I grabbed Michael's hand, and we made our way to the line.

"Let's do this!" I was excited. I also got that cramp in my lower abdomen that sometimes meant explosive diarrhea.

Michael and I stood in line quietly, holding hands, both of us lost in our own thoughts. I was trying my best to appear calm, and every couple of minutes I gave Michael a reassuring smile. He just gazed expressionless at the monstrous roller coaster, all the while firmly holding my hand.

About twenty minutes later, we were fastened into our seats with a metal bar secured against our lap. All of a sudden Michael said, "Mom, I don't think I can do this!"

"It's okay, Mike, you don't have to if you are scared. I'll stay on and record my heart rate."

"I can get off?" Michael looked surprised that there was an "out."

I signaled to the ride operator. She unlocked Michael from our cart and escorted him off to the side so that he could watch from the sidelines.

I grabbed onto the metal bar as we climbed slowly up the track. *Tic—tic—tic—tic—tic* went the sound of the cables pulling us up. The wood creaking underneath teased us as we made our way to the top.

I tightened my hands on the bar as we reached the highest point; it was only a matter of time before we were cut loose. I hated roller coasters.

Dear God,

What have I done? Please don't let me puke.

Amen.

No sooner had I said the prayer in my head, our roller coaster zipped to the bottom of the track, then back up into the sky, racing over and under. Before I could catch my breath we were already plunging through the next drop. And I was laughing hysterically.

"Take that, fear!"

"Your pulse!" Michael yelled and signaled to his wrist from the gate. I placed my fingers on the side of my neck and tried hard to concentrate on counting before I reached the top of the next peak.

"154!" I yelled as we dropped again.

We got home from La Ronde later that day with a car jam-packed with more useless stuffies, a giant lollipop the size of Ryan's head, and airbrushed tattoos of Chinese letters I hoped really did mean "courage." My tattoo might have actually said "ugly-dumb-ass-fart-head," but I'd never know.

As I was packing the kids up for my mom, Ryan's phone beeped with an address. He stared at it and then looked at me.

"I've been here before." Could we have gone through all the possible couples already? There had to be more than seven couples in the club.

"Are you sure?" I asked, although I was more interested in knowing if I was going to have a repeat guest tonight. Ryan looked at his phone again and then back in my direction.

"Yup, I've been here before." He got up and left me alone in our sometimes-used-for-other-things living room.

I stared at the sofa, at the corrupted coffee table, and then I took a walk around my home. I toured the various locations I used for the different swaps and imagined any one of them re-entering my home again. Who would I wish for again? Nate? Neil? Would divine intervention bring Tyler to my doorstep? I didn't think I could handle that. The next two hours were going to be torturous.

Ryan skipped out the door at 7:50 p.m. I felt a pang of jealousy because whomever he was going to see tonight had obviously shown him a great time. Who was this woman my husband was so excited to see? This would probably manifest in a fight tomorrow about him not putting his dishes in the dishwasher.

At 8:03 p.m. the doorbell rang, and I took an extra second to compose myself. I made a wish with my eyes closed that if it were a repeat, it would be Nate or Tyler. I'd deal with the emotional hangover tomorrow. If I were going to have a repeat swap, at least the sex could be awesome.

I opened the door and found an absolute stranger waiting nervously on the dark porch to be let in. Hoping my disappointment wasn't showing, I smiled and invited him in. I spotted a black Ferrari shining on the street behind him.

Frankie wasn't Jewish; I could tell before he even opened his mouth. He was huge. Tan skin, dark eyes, small forehead, and hairy hands. This guy wasn't a guy. He was a carved mountain of man.

"Hey, I'm Frank or Frankie, call me *whatever*." He put his hand out for me to shake it and as I allowed my hand to be swallowed in his grasp, he squeezed the life out of it. My fingers cracked in his stony grip. This guy had money, but sadly no brains.

"You've got quite a handshake." I rubbed my poor hand and the indent my ring made on the side of its neighboring digit.

I could tell he was nervous. His forehead was shiny, and his shirt was sticking to his overly muscled back. *Wonderful. This should be a fun evening.*

I flashed back to Ryan's face as he hopped, skipped, and jumped out our front door to his repeat swap. It seemed unfair. First a broken heart, and now Swap Man number 7 was breaking my fingers. What was next?

"So, whass your name? Actually, don't tell me. I feel like namin' you myself tonight. So, *yer* name tonight is… uh… A… Am-ber. Yeah, Amber."

I looked at him with total disgust. I could tell because my bottom lip wasn't even touching my top one, and my eyes squinted slightly.

"Amber?" I asked.

"Yeah, I like duh name Amber, it reminds me of an old *girlfrien* of mine from St. *Leonar*."

I decided Amber was a sexy vixen who always got what she wanted. She walked with a sexy strut, drank vodka straight, and never let any guy tell her what to do. She was in charge. Always.

"Frankie, I want you to go into the living room, sit on my couch, and wait for me until I say otherwise."

Frankie looked at me and obeyed. There was something very satisfying about directing this muscle-bound man around. He clumped over to the only-used-every-second-Saturday-of-the-month living room, and I watched as his furry fingers slid up the armrest, wondering if he moonlighted as a pro wrestler.

I had to think of a plan, and I had to think fast. I collected two belts from the loops of my coats hanging in the front closet, my dog Camilla's leash (Camilla died, but I kept her leash because I couldn't imagine throwing it away; I knew someday it would come in handy), a Batman mask my son wore last year for Halloween, and some candles. I thought of getting my spatula, but I like my spatula. I wouldn't be able to cook with it again after I used it on Francesco "The Rock" McHairyballs.

Frankie was looking curiously at my set-up as I lined up all the accessories on my nefarious coffee table, closed my drapes, lowered the lights, and then lit the candles around the room.

"What's dis? Fifty shades of sumthin'? I don't want nuthin' in my ass, got it?"

"Frankie, stand up." My voice didn't sound like my own; it sounded like every teacher I had in elementary school when I was caught talking during the lesson. Then I moved the leather armchair to the middle of the floor and gestured for him to sit down.

"You want me to sit there now, eh? So, you's duh boss now, eh?" I put my finger over my lips.

"No talking? Now I can't even speak? What's dis, some kind of—"

I put my hand on his face and with my other one I ripped his shirt open. I had eyeballed his snaps when he walked in and couldn't wait to see how in one swift move, I could have this guy topless. Last but not least, I put the mask on him.

"Holy shit woman, you're freakin' me out."

He needed some reassurance that I wasn't about to do anything too crazy here. So I whispered in his ear, "Amber wants to have some fun. You like fun, don't you?" He nodded as his eyes and his chiseled, hairy pects stared right at me.

I stripped down to my black lace panties, matching bra, and cobalt blue Yves St. Laurent heels I bought for Tanya's wedding.

"Take off your pants." Frankie swallowed hard, and before I could bat an eyelash, he took a seat on the leather armchair in nothing but his plaid boxers. His legs were tree trunks and the chair looked like an elementary-school chair under his large frame.

I placed his hands on the armrests and then took Camilla's leash and tied them both down.

"Eh, be careful, *dose* hands are my moneymakers." I ignored him; those massive bristly knuckles couldn't be useful for anything but scrubbing pots.

Then I took the belts and fastened his thick legs to each leg of the chair. His calves looked like he was wearing two woolly socks; I couldn't believe how much hair this guy had on him. It stopped abruptly at his knee and his rippling quads were completely smooth. Same thing with his Lou Ferrigno torso; the front was a fur carpet, and his back was completely hairless. Upper arms, baby smooth. Forearms, werewolf. It was like he ran out of money at the laser clinic. I wondered if Celeste actually had included a strip down body-inspection as part of the initial meeting, would this guy have been granted membership?

I strutted over to my iPod and cued up "Madness" by Muse. Frankie was about to get the lap dance of his life. I'm sure he could have torn my bonds in two, but it was still very empowering to see a furry Vin Diesel restrained at my mercy in the middle of the living room.

First, the intro… a little tease as I turned and faced him and swiveled my hips to the minimalist synth-base. Frankie's eyes were fastened to my hips, following them from side to side in a trance. I loved it. Then I took a step closer to his legs, but not too close. I swiveled my hips even more, and then lowered my center of gravity all the way down until my ass was almost touching the wood floor. I rocked my hips from side to side, simulating how I gyrated on Tyler or Neil or Nate (but not on him, never on him). I would make this guy come without even taking his boxers off.

"You like this, don't you?" I said as I stared him in the eye and rubbed one hand on my breast and the other on my inner thigh.

Frankie nodded slowly and licked his lips.

"You want Amber to dance for you some more?" Frankie nodded again. I arched my back as I lay on the ground and stretched my legs into the air in front of him. His eyes looked glassy, afraid to blink and miss something.

I kept my eyes on him as I spread my legs wide in front of him. His eyes fell on my most sacred part covered only by my flimsy G-string. My hands caressed my breasts, then my sides, and then back onto my stomach.

"Where do you want me to put my hands, Frankie?" Frankie swallowed hard and then cocked his head to the side as he stared right between my legs. Something about the anonymity of the situation freed me from any second thoughts or inhibitions. I was fully lost in character. Amber had taken over.

"You want me to rub myself, Frankie?" His eyeballs nearly fell out of their sockets. The music was still pleading for me to move with it, so masturbating at this moment didn't feel quite right. I shook my head at Frankie and closed my legs as I shifted my weight onto my knees and got back on my feet where I moved around to the music with my eyes closed and imagined that it was someone else sitting and watching me. Actually, the attention-seeker in me imagined an audience was watching.

Ma ma ma ma ma ma mad madness.

Frankie's erection was lifting his boxers like a teepee. I could tell from the outline that like the rest of him, it was huge and hard. His eyes followed me around the room like a bouncing ball. It was time to take it up a notch.

I crawled on my hands and knees towards him, his eyes fastened on mine through his mask. His hands were in fists, and his chiseled jaw flexed as his teeth clenched his bottom lip.

I made it to his feet and then lay right below him on my back. I opened my legs and then took my fingers and traced a line down from my nipple to my belly button and then straight down my stomach to my G-string.

"You want to see?" I asked him, although I knew the answer.

"Fuck yeah." Frankie was hypnotized, his hardness straining in the confines of his boxers.

I started to rub myself with my fingertips over my G-string, arching my back as I stimulated my clitoris. I looked at him straight in the eyes and bit down on my index finger of my free hand.

"Dat's it, keep going, you makin' me so fuckin' hard." Frankie's hands were still in fists as he stared at me through the almond slits of Batman's mask. My goal was to get those tense fingers laying flat on the armrest by the time I was done.

Time to give him a peek. I could tell he was ready to see. I slid my finger along the bottom of the material; it was damp. (I'd become quite good at pleasuring myself.) His eyes followed my fingers as I pulled the material away, revealing my swollen clit to him.

"Oh fuck, ya look delicious, you gotta gimme a taste."

I nodded slowly at him.

"You want a taste?"

With one hand, I held my G-string away from my body, and with the other hand I rubbed myself slowly, in rhythmic circles, then up and down the slit of my lips. I was wet, I was pulsing, and as I snuck a peek through my squinted eyes at Frankie, I could see he was falling apart pretty quickly, too.

His knee was shaking, his breathing heavy, and his eyes were begging for a closer look.

"Please, Amber, lemme taste you." I liked the way he begged, with his hips gyrating in anticipation. I was happy to let him taste.

I slid closer to him, still lying with my back on the floor; I placed my feet up in the air and then on his knees. He had a bird's eye view as I slid my fingers inside me and moaned in pleasure.

"Jesus, you're smokin' hot." He was getting off too. Both his legs were vibrating, his head seeming to want to fall back. But his eyes stayed glued to me as I climaxed.

"Amber, a taste. Please gimme a frickin' taste of you."

He wanted to taste me, and I planned on letting him.

I was dripping as I slipped my fingers out, crawled up to him, and slid my entire body up between his legs until we were eye to eye. I placed my fingers on his lips and then into his mouth.

Frankie came a second later; his fuzzy paws still flat on the armrest. I got off, he got off, and then I sent him off with strap marks on his fleecy wrists and ankles.

I'm still not sure what drove me that night to act like that, if it was the anonymity of being "Amber" or if I had a latent exhibitionist side that decided to come out and play. Whatever it was, I liked it. I stripped in my living room for a complete stranger, and apparently I did it well. I was still buzzing from the power of the experience when Ryan and I turned out the lights to go to sleep.

Later that night, I was having one of my recurring dreams where I'm in high school and I can't find my locker. Because I can't find my locker, I can't find my schedule to tell me what class I have to go to. In a panic, I run along the rows of lockers lining the long hallway, but I have no idea which one is mine.

Desperately I try to find some kind of familiar insignia to indicate which locker is mine. All of a sudden the bell rings and everyone disappears into the classrooms, leaving me alone and cut off.

Then the bell rings again, and again, and again....

"Hello?" Ryan answered the house phone. I rolled over, and the clock read 12:42 am.

"We will be right there!" Ryan hung up and jumped out of bed. "It's Hallie. Your mother rushed her to the hospital. She had an allergic reaction. Her neighbor is staying with Michael." I immediately threw the covers off and grabbed the first thing I could find to throw on. We took off to the hospital.

Visions of my mother waving her hand in the air to shush me as I choked on the celery haunted me all the way to the hospital emergency room. I found her standing in her fur coat, which covered her Victoria's Secret cotton nightgown with a sleepy owl embroidered on it. Might I remind you, it was July. But Carol didn't want anyone to see her sleepy owl nightgown. I could see she was over-heating; her entire hairline was sticking to her forehead. It was the first time I had seen my mother in over thirty years without her signature red lipstick. I sent her back home to relieve her neighbor staying with Michael. I had to put the poor woman out of her misery. After all, she did save my life, and now my daughter's.

Ryan and I sat in the waiting room. I was slightly overdressed in my racy outfit from the night before and looked ridiculous in comparison to Ryan with his Abercrombie sweatpants and his McGill sweatshirt circa 1996. Maybe not as ridiculous as Carol had with her mink coat in mid-July, but my black-leather-leggings-and-bodice ensemble paired with Nikes was enough to make me look ludicrous all on my own. After enough looks from the orderlies and hospital staff, Ryan gave me his sweatshirt. I thought he was being chivalrous, but in retrospect I think he was worried about how it made him look, seemingly sitting there with a prostitute.

I lay my head on Ryan's shoulder, and we held hands for the first time in what felt like forever. He used to hold my hand all the time, and now it felt foreign to me. He'd said many times recently that he just isn't a public affection kind of guy, but I remember differently.

Ryan Martin and I met in 1995 working at a summer camp in the States. We were the only two Montrealers at the camp, so we instantly had a connection. I liked him. He was quiet, and I could tell that I made him nervous. I liked that, too.

One night, after the campers were asleep in the bunks, at a bonfire surrounded by chatty staff members all wearing trendy lumber jackets, ripped jeans, and sticky, gelled, carefully tousled hair, I decided that I would try and get Ryan's attention. I liked that he seemed more reserved than the other guys. I saw that as a challenge, a conquest.

Self-nicknamed Hobo, the head of the waterfront who had decided that Harold wasn't the coolest name, strummed his guitar. Everyone was having a good time singing along to "Hotel California," and all I could think about was getting Ryan to talk to me.

I walked up to him and asked if he could come with me to find a branch to roast marshmallows, but he just handed me his. So I sat next to him. We barely spoke, but every so often our eyes would meet. The oranges and reds of the fire glowed on our faces. I told him my cheeks felt warm and soft, so he felt them and then he did the unexpected: he leaned in for the first kiss. The flames in the fire pit weren't the only ones that got ignited that night.

I remember kissing Ryan for so long that night at the bonfire that at the end of the night when I got back to my cabin, my lips were raw and sore. The next day other staff teased and taunted us for being all over each other the night before. Ryan couldn't care less. We made out that summer every chance we could, no matter who was around. And tonight, twenty years later, I lay my head on his shoulder in the cold waiting room, holding his hand, knowing that a few hours ago we were messing around with other people to keep our spark from burning out.

A med student who looked like the kid who bags my groceries was standing in the doorway. "Are you Hallie Martin's parents?" We both nodded.

"Hallie is stable. We kept her overnight just to observe her, but you will have to keep a close eye on her for the next forty-eight hours, and make sure she stays away from mango from now on. The doctor on call will be here shortly to go over everything with you."

Hallie had an allergic reaction to mango that my mother gave her as a snack. It resulted in severe swelling of her lips, neck, and face. The doctor said later that the next time she is exposed to mango, it could result in an anaphylactic shock.

The last time I was in this hospital with Hallie was the day she was born. I didn't want to leave this place with her. She was so little, and the nurses were so helpful and kind. I was scared to go through the night feedings and colic that I had experienced with Michael all over again. But this time, tonight, I couldn't wait to wrap my daughter up and get her home.

Kept her overnight? I thought. Didn't he mean we *will keep* her overnight? It was the middle of the night, wasn't it? I looked at my phone. 6:33 am. It was morning, and I hadn't even noticed the sun come up. The med student nodded and then continued on his way, leaving Ryan and me breathing a sigh of relief as we hugged each other tight.

As a mother I laugh, I cry, I want to pull out my hair and then get it blown out. I bite my tongue when I want to scream, "Be careful!" and hold my tongue when I want to say, "I told you so." I pick my children up when they've fallen down or gotten their feelings hurt and wish I was the one injured, heart and soul. I praise them when they dance, sing, or spell it just right. I get on bended knee just to tie their laces. God knows the only people I would ever take a knee for are Michael and Hallie. I learned from my mom or whatever angel stepped in when my mom couldn't. I try, I sweat, I cringe, and then I do it all over again. Being a mom is the hardest, it is the sweetest, and it is the bravest thing I have ever done, and I pray my kids know I wouldn't have it any other way.

We walked into Hallie's hospital room, and I began to tear up at my little girl lying in a hospital gown fast asleep. She looked like a doll. A sweet-faced porcelain doll too fragile to play with. She was the type of doll you just sat and stared at and occasionally stroked its cheek. Her lips were still plump, but the swelling in her neck and face had gone down.

Dear God,

I promise I will be a better mother.

I promise I will be a better wife.

I promise I will be a better daughter.

I promise I will be a better friend.

I promise I will be a better sister.

Just please, let Hallie be okay.

Amen.

We stared at Hallie for hours as she slept in the hospital bed. When she finally stirred, we jumped to her side and waited for her to focus her eyes.

"I have to pee so badly." Hallie looked around the hospital room, confused. "Where am I?"

"You've been sleeping a while," I explained. "They had to give you special medicine that makes you sleepy because you had an allergic reaction at Grandma's last night."

"Okay, can I pee now?"

"Let's go to the bathroom, and then we'll get you something to eat. You must be starving." Ryan helped Hallie off the hospital bed.

"I told you Grandma's cooking was dangerous." Hallie always knew how to make us laugh.

Hallie was discharged from the hospital by lunchtime. When we picked up Michael, we had to deal with Carol's inquest, a defense mechanism for her guilt. Then we went home, got into comfortable clothes, and vegged out watching movies for the rest of that lazy Sunday afternoon. Exhausted from a night in the hospital, Benadryl still in her system, Hallie slept on my lap most of the afternoon. I stayed put for over six hours, without even a trip to the bathroom. Finally after my legs went numb, I moved Hallie off of me and stood up to get the blood circulating again. I called Melissa, but she didn't pick up, I texted her, but she never replied. I needed to vent to my friend about the last twenty-four hours.

Later that evening, when Michael and Hallie were fast asleep in their own beds, I found myself crying on the floor of our foyer, staring at my suede coat with Hallie's handprint on it. I couldn't stop thinking about the what-ifs. How shallow of me to be upset about her handprint when all I could think now was thank God she's still around to make handprints and messes and silly faces. How lucky we were. How lucky I was to have this suede coat to remind me.

Ryan sat down on the floor next to me and hugged me. I could feel his breath on the back of my neck. We just sat there. As he held me, I closed my eyes so tight that there we were once again, under the camp stars without a care in the world.

"You're a great mom, Val," Ryan whispered into my ear; he knew I needed to hear it.

Dear God,

Thank you. I promise I will try to keep my promise.

Amen.

"Nelson Mandela spent twenty-seven years in a South African prison getting tortured and beaten every day of his life for twenty-seven straight years. He got out of jail, spent six months with his wife, and said 'I can't take this shit!' Marriage is so hard Nelson Mandela got a divorce!" —Chris Rock

CHAPTER 15

Swap #8: August 9, 2014

Oral Fixation

After last month's hospital drama following my strip tease for Mr. Hypertrichosis, I was looking forward to tonight's swap. I wanted to have sex, and I was hoping my man tonight was hot.

I dropped off the kids at my mother's home in Cote Saint Luc this time. My mom was waiting with her front door open and was unimpressed to see Hallie zoom past her in a T-shirt that said "MANGO." I thought it was funny. My mother, not so much.

"Do we have to go?" Michael asked, knowing there really was no point. This was where he was *doomed* to spend the evening.

"Come on, Mike, it won't kill you to spend one night a month with your grandmother." And just as I said that, we remembered what had happened last month. "Sorry, poor choice of words. Next time we will figure something else out, okay?" Michael reluctantly passed my mother's threshold without looking back at me.

On my way home, I called Melissa, and it went straight to voice mail. This was strange for us. We never went a week without speaking, never mind a month. I called Jeff.

"Hello?" Jeff answered, his voice guarded.

"Jeff? It's Val. I've been trying to reach Melissa but haven't heard back from her. Is everything okay?

"Oh, hey, Valerie" He never called me Valerie. I could tell he was letting Melissa know I was on the phone.

"Jeff, give Melissa the phone. I know she is right next to you."

I heard some shuffling and muffled whispers, and then Melissa got on the phone.

"Hey Val, I can't talk right now."

"Melissa? What is going on? I haven't heard from you in forever. Is everything all right?"

There was silence on the phone. I could tell something was up.

"Listen, Val, I can't talk to you." And then she hung up.

This could only mean one thing: Melissa knew about Sam and me. *Fuck.*
Fuck, fuck, fuck, fuck, fuck, fuck, fuck, fuck, fuck, fuck, fuck, fuck, fuck, fuck, fuck, fuck.

I had to try and put this out of my mind and deal with it anytime after 11 p.m.—or start a pointless fight with Ryan to channel my aggravation.

I sat on my bed and watched as Ryan got ready to take his shower. I waited for him to take off his socks and like clockwork—4, 3, 2, 1—toss them on the floor right beside the hamper. My misplaced frustration all of a sudden had a target: my unsuspecting husband.

"SERIOUSLY?"

Ryan turned and looked at me, baffled.

"What? What did I do?"

"Well Ryan, one day if it wouldn't kill you, maybe you could figure out how to get your socks from the floor into the hamper. Better yet, maybe if you could figure out how to get your dirty clothes directly *into* the washing machine I would…"

And then he did what typically makes me completely nuts. He went into the bathroom and locked the door behind him.

So, I did what any normal wife would do. I put my mouth right up to the door and yelled through it.

"Don't you walk away from me. I am talking to you!" All I heard was the shower turning on.

"Open the door, Ryan! I was talking to you!" I proceeded to knock incessantly, completely normal behavior for any wife who has been ignored first by her best friend and now her husband.

Then I did what *any* completely immature wife would do. I emptied the laundry basket onto the floor, put back only my things and left all of his stuff on the floor with his socks. (Confession: I was completely aware that I would be the one on my hands and knees post-tantrum cleaning this mess up.)

In the madness, I took my phone out to check and see if I missed any calls or texts from Melissa. Nothing.

"I can't believe you are ignoring me! I am trying to have a conversation with you!" I screamed at the phone.

A few minutes later Ryan emerged from the bathroom.

"I was in the middle of talking to you."

"You aren't talking. You are yelling, and I am tired of being yelled at because one of my socks was on the floor." Then Ryan took a look at the ground covered in his laundry.

"It isn't about the sock, Ryan."

"It never is, Val."

I thought about Tyler. Was he the kind of guy who put his socks in the basket? I decided at that moment that he probably was. The socks are always neater on the other side.

While I was in the shower Ryan left without saying goodbye. I hated when he did that. But after collecting myself in the shower, I realized I didn't blame him. When I got out of the shower I cleaned up the laundry on the floor and then sent him a text:

I'm sorry I'm an idiot.

A few seconds later Ryan replied.

I accept. True. Sorry about the socks.

At 8:05 p.m. when my doorbell hadn't yet rung, I knew that the guy was not from Westmount or Hampstead. The Montreal timing parameters dictated that if this guy left on time and arrived between 8:05–8:10 p.m., then he was from the Mile-end, St. Laurent, or Dollard des Ormeaux, or possibly a slow driver from TMR. Any later than 8:10 p.m., then the guy was either lost or having a panic attack somewhere en route.

The doorbell rang at 8:07 p.m.; I guessed he was from Montreal West. Maybe. Outfit of choice: cotton maxi dress, white lace bra, and crotchless panties underneath.

Standing in my doorway was Jeremy. We knew each other well. The only thing we could do when we saw one another was laugh and hug hello.

Jeremy and I went way back. He went to L.C.C. high school, one of the all-boys institutions back in the nineties for the wealthiest families. I spent many Saturday nights in grade ten meeting up with a gang of guys from L.C.C. at Westmount Park. I would just hang around trying to get the attention of Keith Butler, Jeremy's best friend. Keith barely gave me the time of day. I remember he dated Monica, an average looking plain-Jane from The Study, the all-girls equivalent for the richest daughters of Montreal's finest.

I never understood what Keith saw in Monica, but he followed her around like a puppy dog. I was ultimately better off, because I wasn't sure what I would've done in grade ten if Keith showed any interest. I was a bigger prude than a Mormon on a prom date.

Jeremy and I also both went to Marianopolis College, and I think I might have smoked my first joint with him in his basement. Years later, we were both married with two kids bumping into each other at birthday parties and music in the park on occasion. Jeremy looked exactly the same as he did twenty years ago. Even better.

"You've got to be kidding me!" I laughed as I motioned Jeremy to come inside.

"What the hell are you doing in Swap Club?" he asked. "Better yet, how the hell did you convince Ryan Martin to join?"

Jeremy knew Ryan; they used to play on the same executive softball team. Montreal's executive softball league, as it pertained to the wives of the players, was understood to be Montreal's dad-league for thirty- and forty-somethings who played mediocre softball so they could miss bottle, bath, and bedtime a couple of nights a week.

As it pertained to the team members, softball was taken as seriously as with any MLB team in the big leagues. They even gave out trophies at the end of the season to the team that sucked the least.

"Man, Val, I have to admit, I always wondered what it would be like to be with you."

I was shocked by Jeremy's admission. At the door, no less. Jeremy actually thought about me? He wondered what it would be like to be with me? He did say it, so obviously it must be true, but for some reason I couldn't believe he thought of me as anything but an old friend.

"You wondered what it was like to be with me?" I had to ask.

"What guy hasn't dreamed of doing Val Matthews?" Jeremy said it like he was stating the obvious.

"I could say for certain that Keith Butler never dreamed of doing Val Matthews." I had him there. No question about it.

"Keith Butler? Are you fucking kidding me? He wanted you so bad but was afraid of rejection. Why do you think he dated Monica? Anyone could get Monica, nobody got Val Matthews." Jeremy was laughing at me.

Nobody got Val Matthews because she was afraid of rejection. Isn't it ironic? That and because Val Matthews had no boobs until she hit almost eighteen so she didn't waste any of the grade ten boys' time. Monica, on the other hand, had a beautiful set of knockers—enough to keep Keith's hands busy and his eyes from wandering.

"Well, after tonight you won't have to wonder anymore." I threw a devious smile his way, and then I saw a look I could only decipher as hunger.

"Um, Val, do you mind?" Jeremy motioned to the living room couch; he wanted to talk.

"Sure Jeremy, everything okay?" Jeremy waited for me to sit, and then he crouched down in front of me.

"I have something to ask you Val, and I've been waiting for the right swap partner to request this with. I think you would be perfect."

Jeremy looked down towards my privates and then licked his lips. I watched as he slowly rubbed his hands on his thighs, perhaps trying to wipe the sweat from his palms. He looked back up at me and smiled.

"Jeremy, I'm not sure what you're asking." I really didn't know.

I was so curious that it never occurred to me until after that it could have been something really freaky or kinky, and I was too naïve to realize.

"Val, I don't want to have sex with you tonight." Jeremy looked pleased with himself that he was getting this out of the way.

"You *don't* want to get laid?" I was halfway between shocked and insulted. Then again, there was an obvious history here, and it made sense that Jeremy was hesitant.

"No, I want to spend the night doing something else." Jeremy was being nebulous, and it was getting me even more upset.

"So, you want to play cards? Make cupcakes? Do heroin? What are you asking me?"

"Relax, Val! This is a good thing… a good thing for you." Jeremy sat on the couch next to me and took my hands.

"I want to spend the night with my face buried between your legs. All I want to do tonight is lick your pussy. Dine on your pussy and make you come and quiver and shake at the tip of my tongue until it is time for me to go."

And then I heard crickets.

"You want to eat me out for three hours?"

Jeremy licked his lips again and smiled.

"I don't get it. You only want to get me off tonight?"

Jeremy licked his lips again, and then shook his head.

"Oh no, I will get off too. You'll see. We've only got two and a half hours, so we better get started."

I didn't know what to think. Here I was being asked to receive oral pleasure over and over and over. Who was I to say no? I had also wondered over the years what it would be like to get with Jeremy. Guess that would have to wait. I had never really considered having my… *pussy* licked for three hours, but now that it was on the table it seemed worth trying. So I lay back onto the couch, hiked my dress up and gave in. Crotchless panties—not the worst idea.

First, he adjusted my body in front of him, moving my legs as far to the sides as they could go. Then he took one hand and tipped my pelvis towards his face. I watched as he examined me, felt the curves of my hipbones and pubic bone, and lined up his hands on my lower belly, just below my belly button.

"Crotchless? Holy Mother of God."

"Everything okay?"

"Amazing" he replied. (He liked my panties!) "You look good, you smell good, you feel good, and I can't wait to taste."

I lay my head back and stared at the pot lights; I was ready for takeoff. I felt his lips slowly run their way up my thigh, over my pelvic bone and then back down the other thigh. His hands were holding me from behind; it seemed as though he had fantasized about this moment forever, and now he was finally able to act out the scenario living in his mind.

His lips slowly kissed around my most sensitive parts, close enough to make me squirm but not on the money just yet. He did this over and over, kissing me, licking me millimeters away, but never on my lady bit.

He teased me and then teased me some more, every so often allowing a deep blow of air to tickle my clit, but then he'd recoil back to the lips or crease of my inner thigh. I heard myself beg him, but the more I begged, the further away he kissed. I wanted him to take the plunge already. I was wet, and I wanted him to hit the target. I knew he could tell I was ready for him.

"You want me to lick you here?" As he pressed his tongue against my clitoris, I jerked my knees together, almost crushing his skull. Thankfully Jeremy was a strong guy with crazy biceps that put me right back into the position he wanted me in.

"YES!" I screamed. I couldn't control my volume. It seemed like hours had passed while he had teased and taunted me.

"Val, I'm not sure I understand. Did you like when I licked you over here?"

Jeremy inserted his tongue inside of me and then slowly but firmly licked his way up my vagina, over my clitoris and then back down slowly.

I saw the light. Then I saw stars. And then I lost control of my legs and abdominal muscles because they all began to shake to the rhythm of Jeremy's tongue.

In circular motions he played with me in his mouth, and as my moans and groans escalated, so did the speed of his tongue, his mouth, and hands. The more I got off, the more Jeremy got excited, and the more Jeremy got excited, the more intensely he licked and devoured me, the more I reveled.

"I want to move you over there." Jeremy motioned to my staircase as he wiped his mouth.

He helped me off the couch that now had a perfectly round wet stain where my ass was. We both laughed when we saw it, and then I wondered how that would look tomorrow.

I quickly snapped back to attention as Jeremy placed me sitting with my legs spread on the sixth step, and he lay across the first five. He picked up right from where we left off but now he added his hands and fingers into the mix. He used his thumb and his tongue to play with me, and then what I could only assume to have been his index finger and middle finger to penetrate me with.

My head fell back and lay on stair number eight; I was 99.9 percent sure I came on the couch, and now I was pretty sure it was about to happen again. I ran my hands through Jeremy's thick hair, and the more aggressively I handled him, the more intensely he consumed me.

"Oh my God, Jeremy!" I couldn't help it. It was like a button he pressed; I didn't think I could take it anymore. My body was shaking, my knees were trembling, my head was spinning, and my stomach was in such a knot that the only thing I could do to release was to push Jeremy off.

"No, I can't."

Jeremy looked up at me, my body was restless, and my lungs were out of breath. He grabbed me firmly and plunged right back in.

I squealed and almost pushed him back off.

"I can't, I can't." I kept repeating the words, but Jeremy knew he could take me to a place I had never been.

He kept a firm grip on me, and I trusted him. I realized that I had to let go. There was no pretense here. No complex web of feelings. There was no excuse or worry or goal or consideration to rein me in. For the first time in my life, I could really allow myself to lose control, no matter what it felt like.

As a child, my dad would say to me, "Control your temper."

My mom would say, 'Control yourself."

My grandfather would say, "Control your emotions."

My teachers would say, "Control your mouth."

I had never really lost control. Every orgasm before this one had me unknowingly still holding on to something. When I let go and had that orgasm, it came from the innermost part of me. It came from the thunder in my mind, the lightning in my stomach, and the storm in my soul. When the elements were released, they fled from the most amazing part of my body in a tempest that left me at peace, and in complete bliss.

And here's the thing about control: it feels better when you lose it. And so I did, and then I did again and again. And so did Jeremy.

As I walked Jeremy to the door, both of us completely satisfied with our night, I had to ask him, "Jeremy, why? Why give up a night of sex just to please me?" Jeremy stood in the doorway and smiled. "Because my wife hasn't let me go down on her for over eleven years and man, do I love pussy."

Tonight I needed to lose control, and Jeremy needed it back.

"I believe that sex is one of the most beautiful, natural, wholesome things that money can buy." —Steve Martin

CHAPTER 16

Swap #9: September 14, 2014

Breaking and Penetrating

I love make-up sex. I never felt like there was any real resolution when I fought with Ryan unless we engaged in an emotional lovemaking session post-fight. I didn't always climax in the past, but when my overworked vagina finally healed a few days after Jeremy's oral frenzy, Ryan and I had mind-blowing make-up sex. I almost wanted to pick a fight with him an hour later.

We didn't necessarily establish who was right and who was wrong in the laundry fight. Ryan apologized for making me feel like he didn't respect my housework, and said he would make more of a conscious effort to make me feel appreciated. And then I apologized for taking my insecurities about Melissa out on him.

Ryan had no clue I slept with her brother, so out of context, Ryan just thought I was being too sensitive. If he knew I screwed her brother, then I'm pretty sure he'd agree with my anxiety. I had to tell him, so a few nights and many ignored texts to Melissa later, I caved. I sat next to Ryan on the bathroom counter as he brushed his teeth.

"I think I know why Melissa isn't talking to me."

Ryan spat out the toothpaste foam from his mouth, gave it a wipe, and then looked at me. "You are paranoid. I'm sure whatever it is you think is the reason, you're just making yourself crazy." Ryan opened the bathroom door, completely dismissing the conversation.

"My second swap was with her brother Sam." Ryan froze in the doorway. "I have a feeling Sam told her and that's why she's written me off." Ryan wheeled around back into the bathroom and shut the door behind him.

"First of all, Val, you don't know for sure that Sam told her. Second of all, I don't want to talk about this! I don't want to know who you've slept with. We made a pact!"

"I don't want to tell you who I'm sleeping with, but aren't you curious why Melissa isn't talking to me?"

"No, I think you're making yourself crazy over nothing. There could be a million reasons why Melissa isn't calling you and I'm certain her brother isn't one of them."

Maybe he was right. Maybe I was overthinking this whole thing. It could be nothing. I had to assume that if Melissa knew, she would have told me by now.

"We have four more swaps to go, and I have no interest in hearing about them." Ryan's hand was on the bathroom door.

"What if I do?"

We had been down this road before when I told him about Neil, and now suddenly my curiosity overwhelmed me again.

"Val, you want to know who I've been with?"

"Maybe." I wasn't exactly sure if making it even was a good idea, but the intrigue was clouding my judgment. "Do I know any of them?"

"Do you know any of them? Val, we joined a sex club in Montreal consisting of members all located within a ten-minute radius of our house. What do you think?"

My mind instantly ran a montage of every woman I had encountered in the last week. The Starbucks barista; the checkout woman at the grocery store; the crossing guard; every mom waiting in the schoolyard at pickup with long fingernails. Their faces flashed through my mind like a spinning Rolodex. Then my brain started to imagine each one having sex with Ryan, missionary, sixty-nine, doggy-style…

"Forget it. Don't tell me."

"Good idea. There's no good that comes from me telling you the names of the eight women I've been with."

He made a good point.

"Promise me, Val. For real this time, I don't want you to tell me anyone else you have slept with."

Then "Business-Ryan" held out his hand for me to shake, again.

"Okay, okay. I promise." We shook on it, and then we went to bed. Besides, the nail marks on Ryan's back had finally healed, and I didn't have the evidence of his extra-marital endeavors in my face anymore.

Saturday night rolled in and Michael didn't want to sleep at my mother's place. As I was arguing with him, I had a crisis of conscience. What was I doing? The kids just started school again. They were already inundated with homework every weeknight and Michael had been spending hours putting the last touches on his science fair project. Here I was forcing Michael to be miserable on his limited free time, just so Ryan and I could spend the night being intimate with other people. I spared my kids the "torture" of staying with my mother and called on my cool and eccentric sister Janet to save the day.

Janet was always the cooler sister. At fifteen, Janet always knew the lyrics to every song, even if it had just come out. I would have to study the lyrics written on the liner of the cassette jacket for weeks and by the time I could sing the song perfectly, it was already considered out of style. Janet knew how to whistle with two fingers, ride a bike with no hands, do double-unders with the skipping rope, hang out with boys and not be called a flirt, and chew gum in class without ever getting into trouble. I don't think she ever got a pimple or a mosquito bite in her life.

At thirty-five, Janet lived the life of a twenty-year-old. No kids, no husband, and no real career to speak of. Part of me was jealous of her, part of me felt bad. I couldn't imagine masturbating because I *had* to, not because I wanted to.

When Janet walked through the door in her Led Zeppelin T-shirt, ripped jeans, and floppy wool hat, Michael and Hallie busted with excitement.

"Let's go, brats. I have a ton of processed foods and gluten to feed you before I let you watch a movie completely inappropriate for your age."

Michael and Hallie threw on their shoes and grabbed their bags. They loved her, and luckily for me, she didn't mind having a sleepover party with her niece and nephew. Also, her most recent boyfriend Jake (or was it Jack?) had just broken up with her, and she welcomed the distraction.

"I have a ton of corruption in mind for tonight. Try not to call and check up on us every hour."

I rolled my eyes at her, and then blew them all a kiss as they ran down to her car. Check up on *them* every hour? Sorry, Janet, I'll be too busy screwing a stranger for the ninth time this year to be calling you.

About an hour before it was time for Ryan to hit the road, I was bored, so I sat on our bed while Ryan shaved his practically hairless face. I missed Melissa. So, even though I was sure she wouldn't reply, I texted her.

I miss u XO

I put my phone down and studied the lines on Ryan's forehead. The creases under his eyes were more prominent, the years having etched themselves into his skin.

"Hey," he acknowledged. "What's up?" I watched as Ryan readjusted his towel wrapped around his waist, and I nearly fell off the bed.

"What's up? Wow! What's up is that you have done some major landscaping! Are you kidding?"

I jumped up and ran into the bathroom to tug at his towel. He backed away protectively.

"Bug off!" He yanked his towel back up and then escorted me out of the bathroom and closed the door. "I'm pretty sure you've been doing the same, Val," Ryan yelled through the door.

He wasn't wrong; it just didn't seem fair that I've had to bushwhack my way through many blowjobs over the last decade. My muff was always trimmed and groomed, with the exception of 2005, 2006, 2010 and...okay. Whatever.

At 7:50 he was out the door, and I was left holding my glass of wine staring out the window.

Dear God,

If you could please go easy on me tonight and send me someone with a decent penis and personality I promise to fix the printer that I've been putting off for three months, fold and put away the beach towels that I laundered two weeks ago, clean out the Tupperware drawer, throw out the boxes of cereal from last year, and anything I can't recognize in the freezer.

Amen.

Man, I hope that works.

I paced around the house a little, and at 8:02 p.m. the doorbell rang. I opened the door and then thanked the good Lord. It was Nate, the perfect fucking boy next door—or, as you might remember, "March."

"Hi!" I sounded very happy. Maybe too happy—I should've played it cooler.

"Hi! I was super glad when Celeste sent me your address again; it's awesome to see you again." Nate came in, and we hugged and kissed hello like a couple that had been separated for summer vacation.

"Come in, I set up some drinks on my back porch. I'm trying to take advantage of the warm weather before it gets cold again. Fuck, I hate the fall. Do you like the winter?"

Shut up, shut up, shut up you imbecile. Don't do this again. For some reason, Nate still made me nervous.

"Sounds awesome. Let's sit outside and catch up." He followed me outside and we took a seat on my outdoor loveseat.

"You promised you'd keep in touch, Val. I thought you liked breaking the rules." His hand rubbed my thigh as I poured him a glass of wine.

"Why? Did you miss me?" I asked as I rubbed my hand along his crotch, getting my flirt on. I wanted Nate to tell me what I wanted to hear.

"Did I miss you?" Nate gestured to his semi-erect penis. I loved his penis. It was a great penis.

"I missed you a lot." Nate pulled me onto his lap and kissed me so hard our teeth collided.

Nate's hands found their way up my shirt and with one hand he unsnapped my bra and began playing with my nipple.

"You don't waste any time," I quipped. Nate thrust his hard penis against me and then retorted, "Nope."

We kissed some more and when we came up for a breath, he took a look around at my backyard and then became fixated on the high fence on one side.

"Why is there only a fence on that side?" he asked the same question most people asked when they looked at my backyard.

It did look pretty strange that we only had one-third of a fence up. The trees were so overgrown that it was hard to tell it was my elderly neighbor's fence and not that we ran out of money one-third of the way through this project.

"My neighbors have a pool, and that's their fence," I explained.

"Pool?" Nate shot me a devious smile.

"Yes, a pool." I wasn't sure what he was thinking, but I had to derail any thoughts of swimming. "We can't. They're out of town, and I don't have a key to their place."

Nate took a sip of his wine, stood up, and made his way over to the fence to get a closer look. He yelled over his shoulder as he peered in.

"Looks amazing, Val. Let's not waste any time debating this."

Nate climbed like a cat up the iron slats and then disappeared on the other side.

"Come on, Val, it's your turn," he yelled from the other side.

I placed my glass back on the table, hooked my bra back on, and hurried over. He was already navigating his way around the pool, moving chairs and umbrellas.

"What are you doing?" I was panicked. This was my neighbor's property.

They were an older couple away in France for three weeks. They had asked that I take any circulars or overflowing mail in for them. I don't know how they would have reacted to my using their pool as a sexual backdrop in exchange for my mail service. Their grandchildren frequented the pool, and it just seemed wrong to disgrace the sacred waters.

"Nate, stop! Come back here!" I had my mommy voice on, not the vixen voice.

"Let's go, Val!" Nate kicked his Sperrys off, peeled off his shirt and shorts, and then plunged into the pool in his boxers.

"Water's perfect!" He carelessly splashed around.

Fuck, fuck, fuck, fuck, fuck. I meditated on the word over and over until I finally got to the word *it*. I looked at Nate, then at the fence, then back at Nate, who was paddling around on his back. Next thing I knew I was climbing up the wrought-iron fence. I tried my hardest to slide myself over as effortlessly as possible, or at least look that way. Nate watched as I maneuvered my body over the top and then landed on my feet. I whispered "Thank God" to myself as I looked at my feet perfectly planted on the rocks, and then again as I looked back at the 7-foot-high fence.

Nate was standing at the edge of the shallow end leaning his hands on the pool's edge.

"Took you long enough," he teased as I made my way over to him.

"You know this is considered breaking and entering?" I was still nervous about being there. "I don't do this kind of stuff. I'm a good person! What if someone sees us?"

"Come, have a seat." Nate rubbed the edge of the pool in front of him. I crossed my arms and stood my ground.

"Come on, Val. We'll keep it down, and if anyone catches us, you can blame it on me. Tell them that you saw me swimming in here and you came to ask me to leave. Like a *responsible* neighbor." He was good. Actually, it seems a little thin when I think about it now, but it sounded reasonable at the time. Maybe he wasn't so good, but he was wet… and glistening… and sexy… and did I mention wet? He looked like an ad for some Hugo Boss Cologne.

I took off my sandals, hiked up my skirt, and sat in front of him with my feet in the water. He widened the space between my legs so that he could fit his body between and then wrapped my legs around his back.

"There's something about you that I trust." I might have spoken too soon because before I knew it, Nate shot me a devious look and then grabbed me fully clothed into the pool. I let out a squeal as the cold water rushed over me. I was just about to tell him what a jerk he was, but his lips and tongue interrupted. And, oh, that tongue.

His soft, perfect-sized tongue rolled around with mine. I forgot how much I loved his tongue. We circled around in the water kissing for what seemed to be an eternity, my hands on his shoulders and his firmly on my hips.

A list of things I forgot about while kissing Nate:

1. Trespassing.

2. My brand new Theory silk chiffon skirt clinging to my wet body.

3. The printer I still needed to fix.

4. The beach towels I still needed to fold.

5. The messy Tupperware drawer.

6. Last year's cereal and unrecognizable freezer items I still needed to throw out.

"You're wearing way too much clothes," Nate complained as I felt his hands release me in the water allowing my feet to touch the bottom of the pool.

My clothes floated around me like an opened parachute; I couldn't see where Nate went as he took a breath and submerged himself underwater. I turned to see where his head would re-emerge, but then it didn't.

All of a sudden I felt him beneath me, his hands navigating the waistband of my skirt. I stood there under the purple night sky waiting for him to disrobe me. He yanked my skirt down and let it float away, and then my lace underwear. I couldn't believe how long he was holding his breath. I removed my tank top and then felt his hands unhook my bra, *again*. All my clothing was floating around the pool.

The feeling of the water against my nudity turned me on completely. It was different than being in a bathtub, this sensation of the water tickling and tingling even the smallest of my body parts.

From behind I heard Nate come up for air and then plunge back underwater. His hands ran down my back and buttocks and then spread my legs. I felt him swim underneath me and then wrap his legs around my ankles to anchor him. I let my head fall back and float in the water like I used to do as a child in the bathtub.

My ears were submerged, muffling the sounds of the suburban streets. I was wary when he placed his mouth on me after last month's swap, but I closed my eyes and went with it.

The contrast between his warm mouth and the cold water totally messed with my senses. And then my concern for him drowning added an element of distraction but I figured as long as his tongue and mouth were moving, then he was still alive.

For a second, I actually convinced myself that my vagina was providing him with necessary oxygen. I was his lifeline so long as he kept eating me out.

After a few minutes, Nate finally resurfaced. He looked quite pleased with himself.

"You've got strong lungs," I called to him as I swam over to the stairs.

"Where you going?" I'd spotted the tented seating area, and as much as I wanted to have sex in the pool, I had already done the bathtub with Joe. I was more interested in having sex in a location I hadn't experienced already. The canopy looked like it could be exciting.

I made my way over to it, purposely swaying my hips because I could feel the burn of Nate's eyes on me. I was completely nude, and I couldn't have loved his attention any more.

"You coming?" I asked with my hands on my hips, tapping my foot on the ground.

Nate smiled and dove under the water, and with a few long strokes he made it to the stairs and out of the pool before I could count to five. He dropped his wet underwear at the side of the pool and walked naked, dripping wet and fully erect, under the canopy where I waited for him on the wicker sofa.

I could see the sky through the open seams, letting a breeze tickle my moist skin and give me goose bumps. Nate climbed on top of me. The friction of our cold, wet skin hurt but felt good at the same time. He kissed me deeply on my mouth, then moved to my neck and shoulders. He spun me around onto my stomach and kissed down my back and ass. He took his hand from behind and began rubbing my clit ever so lightly. Every time I put pressure down onto his hand, he moved it away.

"Ah ah ah," he teased. "I want to try something with you, will you let me?" Nate asked as he fingered the crease of my cheeks and spread them with his hand.

"What do you want to do?"

Nate kissed the lower part of my back and traced his tongue down the crease, then replied, "I want to taste." His tongue made its way down my crease and then back up towards my back. I was pretty sure he meant a taste of my rear end, but I almost hoped I was thinking dirtier than he at that moment.

I mean, I'd never really done anything like that before. Was I ready to let Nate lick my ass? The words resonated in my head.

Lick my ass.

Lick my… ass.

Lick… my ass!

Lick my ass?

I had to be sure we were on the same page.

"You want to lick my…?" Nate nodded as he grazed his fingers ever so lightly against my *other* hole. I perked up when a shiver ran through my body and shot out of my head like a teapot. I began to reason with my nerves: I had taken a shower before he came, we just got out of the pool, if there was ever a time to let someone do this, it was today.

I closed my eyes and gave my body to him. I relaxed my legs as he spread me open his strong palms holding my cheeks open. I felt so exposed. His tongue circled my rosebud and then every so often he would insert it inside me.

It felt good, it felt wrong, it felt weird, it felt intrusive and dirty, but it didn't feel bad. He used his fingers to play with me while he was doing it, and I have to say the combination made for conflicting yet highly pleasurable intimacy.

Slowly, Nate's finger moved from my clitoris to where his mouth was. I didn't know what to do. The thought of his finger penetrating me there made me wonder where my inhibitions had gone this year.

"I'm not ready for that just yet." I managed to decline his advance without ruining the moment.

"That's okay." Nate redirected his hands back to my clitoris as I arched myself in a sexy pose, legs still spread. I called on my inner Jenna Jameson to take over. His penis slowly penetrated me from behind, his slow thrusts in combination with the nibbling on my shoulder. The tender kisses on my back felt so amazing.

After what seemed to be several minutes, my arms and back began to get tired so I lowered myself and lay flat on the couch leaving my ass up in the air. Nate was sweating, his breathing heavy, and with every exhale the words *fuck* and *oh my God* would echo into the now-opaque sky.

Nate's grip on my sides firmed, his thrusts deepened, and his exhales turned into heavy groans. I could sense that this sex session was not going to be long. Our foreplay began the minute Nate received the text from Celeste.

"I'm going to come!" Nate roared. And then he did as he proclaimed. He pulled out and then came all over my back.

Nate collapsed next to me, and after a few quiet seconds we both exploded in laughter at the mess all over me. I could just imagine the look on Ryan's face if I told him I had sex tonight on our elderly neighbor's pool furniture after breaking and entering their backyard.

Nate used the pool equipment to fish out our soggy clothes, and then we hopped back over the fence. As we sat on my porch and finished off our wine, Nate thanked me for letting him do something he was afraid to ask his wife to do. I remembered what Swap Club was for every one of us: an escape from our lives for three hours a month.

A month later, I was watching out my window and saw my elderly neighbor cleaning his pool to close it for the winter. His wife was sipping her drink as she watched her husband trying to untangle something from the filter. I fell to my knees and hid against my wall when I saw him pull my lace G-string from the net and then examine it with his hands. I held my breath and took another peek when he handed the G-string to his wife as he scratched his head trying to figure out what it was.

"The truth is, everyone is going to hurt you. You just got to find the ones worth suffering for." —Bob Marley

CHAPTER 17

Adverse Possession

My truck was due for service. Instead of sitting in the waiting room staring at the filthy coffee vending machine, I ventured out on Jean-Talon to keep busy. I had an hour to kill so I walked over to Abe and Mary's, a stand-alone one-stop shop for over-priced jeans and salad.

As I crossed the busy street, I saw Ryan's car parked in the lot. I was confused and curious. Why was Ryan at Abe and Mary's? I had no idea he even knew about this place. He considered any piece of clothing over $100 exorbitant unless it was a gift. Maybe he was buying me a gift. I hung back in the parking lot and called him on his cell phone. I didn't want to potentially ruin the surprise, so I planned to let him know I was about to walk in, but he didn't answer. I walked around the side to take a glimpse inside, but there was no sign of Ryan in the store. A salesgirl spotted me peeping in, so I walked around the other side to double-check the license plate, and it was undoubtedly Ryan's car.

I walked up to the side entrance and looked through the glass door, and there was Ryan having lunch with Claudia DiSilva, one of Montreal's leading real estate agents. Claudia DiSilva was perfection. Her long, shiny, black hair looked silky to the touch. Her white skin was impeccable. She was an ageless, timeless beauty all put together in an outfit I couldn't dream up if I tried. The outfit I managed today included a coffee-stained sleeve and torn sweatpants that I might have slept in the night before. In my defense, I didn't think I would be bumping into anyone at the car dealership. I figured I could shower and get dressed properly before afternoon carpool.

I stood off to the side and dialed Ryan again. I saw him look down at his phone and then press "decline." I couldn't believe it. There was my husband, ignoring my call for a second time.

It was like a car accident. I couldn't stop myself from watching them through the window. Every time someone pulled into the lot, I pretended to be on a very important phone call.

I watched as his lips moved. What was he talking about? At one point he talked for over six minutes straight. I timed him. He seemed to have a ton to say to Claudia DiSilva.

I assumed that this was a business meeting until he said something and the two of them started laughing. When the laugh subsided, they were smiling and still looking at each other. I could feel the butterfly-filled tension out in the parking lot. His smile faded but his eyes were still sparkling, she seemed giddy, and I could tell by their body language that they had been together before. Intimately.

I had no idea how to react. My first thought was that I was wrong—I was reading too much into it. But all I had to do was watch for two more minutes, and I knew. I saw her touch his arm on numerous occasions. And every time she was speaking, Ryan would scratch his temple and smile while he listened. They ate their salads, but slowly, not in any rush to finish their lunch. Neither of them looked at their phones. Amid the hustle and bustle of mom-lunches swarming at tables around them, they were in their cozy little bubble at their table for two.

Then the weirdest thing happened. I began trying to convince myself that it was just sex from Swap Club. I mean, on one hand, you could imagine the strange "relief" I felt to have confirmation that Claudia and Ryan met in Swap Club. But on the other hand, what the hell was going on in my life that the consolation for my husband sitting and lunching with Claudia was that they did have sex... but it was only in Swap Club?

I wanted to gauge my eyes out. I ran back across the street to collect my truck and sped myself home to watch puppy videos. I tried to go about the afternoon with as much normality as possible when I picked up the kids from school. Homework duty with Michael, dinner prep, bath time, and then the routine peck on the lips when Ryan got home. I covertly sniffed when he kissed me to see if his upper lip smelled different. It didn't.

During dinner I tried to compose myself. I tried to ignore my feelings of sadness every time I looked around our table. After the kids were asleep, Ryan was watching TV and I heard him frequently on his phone texting. Was he breaking Swap Club Rule #1 and chatting with Claudia? I sat on the couch next to him and waited until I heard his phone vibrate in his pocket.

"Who are you chatting with?" I asked, but I already knew the answer.

"A real estate agent I'm working out a deal with." Ryan was telling the truth, technically.

I couldn't keep it in anymore.

"I saw you today." I kept it vague because I wanted to see if he knew what I was talking about.

"Really, where?" Ryan was calm, and still watching the hockey highlights on Sportsnet.

"At Abe and Mary's with Claudia DiSilva." I knew her name; I wanted him to know that.

"Yes," he continued, watching TV.

"And?"

"And what? You saw me having lunch with Claudia. Am I missing something? Is there a rule about having a work meeting at Abe and Mary's?" Ryan's calmness was making me more agitated.

"No. There's isn't a rule about working at Abe and Mary's, but there is a rule about fraternizing outside the Club."

Ryan turned off the TV and left me alone in the room.

"Where are you going, Ryan? I'm in the middle of talking to you."

"I'm going for a jog. I don't appreciate being questioned about my whereabouts. What were you doing there Val? Stalking me?"

"Did you have sex with her?"

"Today?"

I knew by his answer, catching me on a technicality that he had sex with this woman, maybe not specifically today, but they had been together in the past.

"What are we doing?" Ryan came back into the room, his hands in his pockets preventing me from reading any visual cues.

"Did you meet her in Swap Club?" I had to make sure that the only rule broken was meeting outside of the club, not having sex outside of the club.

"Yes. I met her through Swap Club. But we only had sex that one time in Swap, and never again. We've kept in touch. I know I shouldn't have, but I like her."

"What do you mean you like her, Ryan? What is that supposed to mean?" I was confused and blindsided. It never occurred to me that Ryan could also be getting more out of Swap Club than just the sex. How deluded I had become over the years, not even thinking for a minute that some other woman could turn his head.

"I don't know. I mean, I like her. She's just—interesting."

"I see." His words stung more than anything he's ever said to me. Ryan said, *She's interesting.* But what I heard was:

She's more interesting than you.

She's more fun than you.

She's smarter than you.

She's more woman than you… And that's why I met her for lunch.

Ryan's eyes were barely blinking, and he was rubbing his head. A combination of pissed off and done talking. He stood in silence and didn't move a muscle.

"I saw it in your eyes. I watched your conversation and her ability to get you to open up. Something I haven't been able to do. I want to be mad; I want to be mad so badly, but I'm not." I really wasn't. I could hardly blame him. "I made you sleep with other women. It would have been incredibly naïve to think that you wouldn't have a connection with someone. So how could I be mad?"

"Well, if you're not mad, then what's the problem, Val?" He was baffled.

"I'm sad, Ryan."

"Sad?"

"Yes. I'm sad because you have so much to say to her. I'm sad that you took the time to meet her for lunch. I mean, I love Abe and Mary's. How come you never meet me there?"

Ryan sat back down on the couch, absorbing my honesty. I continued. "This year I've been trying to figure out what I was missing, assuming that my malaise was the problem. That I needed to do something to find myself. I'd never really considered that you were missing something too. I'm sure I knew it implicitly. Relationships require two people. But if we're both missing something in our marriage, how much hope do we really have to fix things? Is sleeping with twelve different people in a year enough to solve it?"

Ryan stared at me in silence. What he didn't know was that along with my feelings of sadness, I was feeling an immense amount of guilt. How could I come down on him about his lunch with Claudia when I have been on an emotional roller coaster with Tyler since June? It seemed we were in an emotional relationship, just with other people. We were both culpable. Ryan looked at me. I couldn't read him at all. I felt like I was doing all the talking, but I couldn't bear the weight of the silence.

I broke first, "I think we should rethink Swap Club. Maybe it was a mistake."

Ryan stared silently at the floor, my admission just hanging there. Finally, after what felt like an eternity, he looked up.

"We signed up for Swap Club because it was something you wanted, Val. I did it to make you happy. What I want is to finish Swap Club."

"I don't get it. You were doing this for me, and now I'm saying I think it was a mistake."

"Yes, originally I was doing this for you, but now you are going to see it through for me."

"Then maybe you should consider following the rules." It came out more aggressive than I meant it. It was so strange that out of all of this—my husband telling me he finds another woman "interesting"—that the only thing I can gripe about is that he is breaking the rules of our sex club. Ryan looked like he was going to say something. I could see the storm brewing in his eyes. His eyebrows lowered, but then he ran his hands over his face and he was composed again.

"You're right." He said I was right, but his face was expressionless.

"I'm right?" I wanted more. More clarification. More explanation. More apology.

"Yes. I will follow the rules." He was still poker-faced.

"And that's how you want to leave things?"

"Yes." And then he got up and walked out the front door, past our cars in the driveway and up the street into the night.

"But I always say, one's company, two's a crowd, and three's a party." —Andy Warhol

CHAPTER 18

Swap #10: October 12, 2014

Happy Hallow "Threesome"

About two weeks prior to Swap #10 we received an invitation in the mail.

You are cordially invited to a Halloween Masquerade Party.

Date: October 13th

Time: 8 p.m.

Address: To be sent by text message an hour before.

Please come in costume & mask required to keep your identity a secret from all.

Celeste

Inside the envelope were two stamped return address envelopes marked with our names. This was mine:

Mrs._____ Will Attend

Mrs._____ Will Not Attend

And then on the back of the RSVP card to fill out:

I would like to fulfill the following fantasy:

❏ *S&M*

❏ *Threesome*

❏ *Anal*

❏ *Same Sex*

❏ *All of the above*

❏ *None of the above*

I stared at the blank line where my check mark should go next to "Will not Attend." This seemed like a step too far, and not the Swap Club we signed up for. Attend a crazy sex party? On the other hand, there were only three more chances for me to explore my sexuality, and if Ryan was determined to see his journey through, I may as well see mine through. Not to mention, if I decided to skip October, I would only be left with two. Given my track record, chances were one of those would be a dud.

I cast the RSVP aside. I wasn't ready to decide I wasn't going; I wanted to see Ryan's reaction. I was going to follow his lead now. That night, I showed him the invitation as he was tying the laces on his running shoes for an evening jog.

"Sweet, a Halloween party, sounds like fun."

And then I showed him his private envelope. Ryan's eyes widened, and then he paced a little with it in his hands.

"Did you fill out yours?" he asked hesitantly.

"No." Either my response gave him some courage or the shock of the invitation wore off quickly, because suddenly he seemed totally nonchalant about the whole thing.

"Well, if you're concerned, just check 'None of the above.' At the very least we can have fun dressing up and going to a party." Then he made his way out the door.

I didn't want to rock the boat too much with him; we had been navigating choppy waters for the last couple of weeks. It was extra hard for me to keep my composure because Claudia DiSilva's real estate placards, with her coy smile and crossed arms, decorated every lawn in suburban Montreal. Her eyes stared right at me, taunting *I'm Montreal's most interesting real estate agent.*

I looked at the rsvp and grabbed a pen, marked it up.

Mrs. Val Matthews *Will Attend*

Then I flipped over the RSVP card.

I would like to fulfill the following fantasy:

❑ *S&M*

☑ *Threesome*

❑ *Anal*

❑ *Same Sex*

❑ *All of the above*

❑ *None of the above*

I sealed it in the envelope and thought, "Why the hell not?"

It is absolutely no problem finding a cool Halloween costume in Montreal in October. Every second store on Ste. Catherine Street is a pop-up "Entrepôt de l'Halloween." Ryan and I had no idea what to expect when we walked through the doors.

Here's my observation: for kids there is every character you could dream up. Dora, Elsa, Cinderella, Rapunzel, Snow White, Tinkerbell, Cat, Bunny, Witch, Maid, Wonder Woman, Batman, Robin, Hulk, caveman and the list goes on. For men: Spiderman, Dracula, pirate, Batman, Superman, zombie, demon, astronaut, mad scientist, and that list goes on.

For women: cut the skirt about ten inches above the knee and then you get our selection consisting of a slutty princess, slutty Dora, slutty nurse, slutty maid, slutty witch, slutty Wonder Woman, slutty Tinkerbell, slutty cat, or slutty bunny. I'm pretty sure Salon Triple XXX got their inventory from the same wholesaler.

We split up, heading to the sections for our respective sex, and I saw Ryan head straight for the Masked Avenger. I didn't want to burst his bubble that the chances of us walking into a fleet of Zorros were high, given the mask requirement.

I began slowly sifting through the rolling racks loaded with the wardrobe selection for a Comic-Con strip club. I had barely made it through the second of a dozen racks when Ryan returned with his costume in hand.

"Will you just pick something?" We had been in the store four minutes, and he was already growing impatient with me.

"Do you have somewhere else to be?" Our kids were at play dates, so we had a few hours to kill. Why couldn't he just chill out? In the back of my mind, I was wondering if he had a secret rendezvous planned with Claudia.

"I just want to go to the Apple store and then maybe get a haircut before we pick up the kids."

Then my concern about his secret rendezvous changed to my concern that he wanted a haircut because Claudia would be at the party. Without even realizing, I shot Ryan my *You've got to be kidding me; do you know what I do for you on a regular basis; how many socks do I have to pick up off the floor and toilet seats do I have to flip down and then wipe before I sit* face.

Ryan took out his phone and entertained himself while I continued to peruse the slutty costume choices.

"Ryan, you could help me choose, you know?" I wanted his input, which in retrospect may have been a bit cruel given that I was going to wear it to fuck some other guy.

"They all look the same. Just pick. Slutty vampire? Slutty policewoman?" And then Ryan gestured towards a black latex bodice. "A slutty slut?"

All costumes require you to "purchase separately": fishnet stockings, six-inch heels, and a box of latex condoms. I took the Marie Antoinette costume, wig, and bejeweled mask. I left the domestic service costumes, perverted Disney cast members, and sexualized animals for the other ladies.

While we stood in line, surrounded by a plethora of Halloween doodads and gimmicky accessories, I remembered Halloween as a kid. My costumes, made from the same plastic they used as place mats at McDonalds, came out of a cardboard box and had to squeeze over my snowsuit. My paper mask was held on with an elastic band and staples that I could barely breathe in. The nose holes were poked with a pin. By the end of the night, my plastic costume was completely tattered, and my dad was wearing my mask on his head.

Ryan was staring at the costume in my arms.

"Marie Antoinette?" he asked.

"Yeah, I figure it's more age-appropriate."

"Age-appropriate?" Ryan was making fun of me. After all, look where we were standing—in a ridiculous pop-up Halloween shop filled with teenagers.

"*Suivant*, next," the cashier called out.

I placed my costume, wig, bejeweled mask, fishnet stockings, and some costume jewelry on the counter. Ryan placed his black cape and mask.

"*Cent quatre-vingt soixante dix-neuf.*" The cashier stared at Ryan waiting for his wallet to open, but the only thing that fell open was Ryan's mouth. He actually looked offended.

"WHAT?" Ryan didn't care how loud it came out. I, on the other hand, started inching away from him.

"One hundred and eighty dollars and seventy-nine cents. Make that eighty cents, we don't take pennies." The cashier waited for Ryan's wallet to appear.

"A hundred and eighty?" Ryan wanted clarification that he heard right.

"And eighty cents." I added, trying to be comical, but Ryan wasn't finding me, or the price of our costumes, funny at all.

That night we looked ridiculous wearing the costumes almost two weeks before Halloween. My masked swordsman sounded like Darth Vader breathing through a kazoo because the mask squeezed his nostrils too tight.

"How am I going to breathe tonight?" Ryan tried adjusting the nosepiece.

"Ryan, if you're having second thoughts about your same-sex fantasy, you should just say so." Ryan was not amused.

As we drove to a mansion on Upper Belmont in Westmount, I caught a look at myself in the side-view mirror. The costume was pretty amazing, I had to admit. The white and baby-blue short but thick and layered skirt attached to a tight-fitting corset gave the hourglass, legs-for-miles illusion. My lace-up stilettos provided the perfect hooker height, and my mask's almond-shaped eyeholes really changed my face. Unfortunately, the crinoline was itching my legs through my white fishnets, and my lace-up heels were so stacked that the angle hurt my calf muscles.

I needed to hold onto Ryan's hand as we walked up the circular driveway. We made our way through a maze of shiny black cars, and I recognized a few of them. There was the Porsche I tainted; I wondered if Douchebag McMoneybags ever got the wet spot off?

The stone mansion stood on the street like the godfather of the block, aged stone and wood trim framing the beveled leaded glass windows. I could imagine the century-old walls hiding secrets like a vault. No matter how hard Ryan worked, we would never live in a house like this. A house like this comes from family money, passed down through the generations. We did not have family money. We had our money, which was enough to keep up with the Joneses, but not *these* Joneses.

The giant door was locked, so I clanged the door knocker. Within seconds a masked and topless young butler led us into an empty den, or as I can call it now, The Holding Room. The butler offered us each a glass of champagne that we sipped anxiously while we waited for further instruction.

Ryan made small talk about the room. He wasn't really talking *to* me so much as talking *at* me. No response from me was necessary. He mumbled about the sconces, the Art Deco sculptures, the teak bookcases, and all the nervous chatter that usually comes out of him in the waiting room before his annual colonoscopy.

"Relax, Ryan," I said while I adjusted my mask. "I know you're nervous."

Actually, I was the one who was nervous; I was about to have my first threesome. The door opened, and a masked Celeste and the topless butler entered the room.

"Welcome to your fantasy night. Valerie, you will follow me, and Ryan, you will follow Antoine."

We didn't look at each other when we left the Holding Room. Ryan went to the left and down a staircase, and I was being led up a winding staircase where plaster cutouts along the walls held marble statues and ten-foot paintings. I held onto the polished mahogany railing for dear life. These shoes were not made for walking; they were *sitting* shoes.

"Valerie, the rules are simple. No names, no violence, and no discussion of tonight when it's done." Celeste pulled a piece of paper and a pen out of her bodice.

"Your safe word is *red*. Use it when you feel uncomfortable and want to stop."

A safe word?! What kind of debauchery am I getting myself into that requires the word *red* to end it? She handed me the pen. "Sign here." I looked at what seemed to be a legal contract.

"What is this?" I asked.

"Insurance you will keep tonight and the location a secret." I looked at the paper again; there were about fifty bullet points. Words jumped off the paper. *Confidential. Private. Secret. Discretion. Punishable. Liable.*

I signed it. I had no plans on telling anyone about this party. (Until now, of course.)

Celeste opened the door onto the most magnificent master bedroom I had ever seen. Standing in the middle of the room was a massive California King bed about three feet off the ground under a purple velvet canopy. Dimmed sconces lit the periphery of the room and flames from candelabras with wax candles twinkled against the wall. Standing on the far side of the room, a masked Dracula and a pirate waited patiently for my arrival. I turned as the doors shut behind me and then swung back around as The Count and the Pirate made their way towards me.

My knee was shaking. Not because the heels I was wearing were so stupidly high, but because I was so nervous. I knew it wouldn't be sexy to go into a full blown panic attack here, so in lieu of imagining cute puppies, I imagined Ryan was in the basement hanging in Shibari restraints and corked up with an anal plug.

The Pirate approached first, and as he came closer, I saw crystal blue eyes darting through the holes of his mask. His hands reached for my face and brought my lips to his. The minute our mouths touched I opened my eyes and looked straight into his as the electricity bolted through my stomach, then to my legs.

He kissed me deep, he kissed me hard, and when I thought my legs were going to give out he took one hand off my face and wrapped it around my waist. I almost forgot about the second guy until his hands grabbed hold of me from behind and he began kissing and biting my neck. Dracula… obviously.

It was hard for me to concentrate on kissing the Pirate while Dracula nibbled on my neck, then my shoulder, and then down my shoulder blade. My heels were wobbling beneath me, and my corset was squeezing my ribs and my chest so tight I couldn't wait for these guys to get this costume off of me.

Dracula turned me around to face him. I tried to look through the mask, but I couldn't tell if I knew him or not. I decided I preferred the mystery, so I stopped looking too hard. The Pirate got down on his knees and started kissing the back of my legs, then my ankles, and ran his hands up and down my inner thighs just as Dracula placed his lips against mine. They were moist and warm. He kissed me slowly, his pace differing from the intensity of the Pirate's kisses, the ones that screamed *I miss you. I need you. Come over here.* Dracula's were a more of a subtle whisper. *I want you. I want to suck your blood.*

The sensation of two mouths and four hands took some time to get used to. It was more than a little overwhelming, but it wasn't hard to allow myself to let go and enjoy. It just took some concentration to pace myself and not fly off the handle.

Dracula led me towards the red velvet French carved Recamier sofa floating in the middle of the room and sat me down in the middle of it. As both guys stood right in front of me, I wasn't sure how this was going to proceed. I took a deep breath and leaned back while pulling the Pirate towards me. I wanted to kiss him some more.

Our tongues rolled and licked each other's lips, and every so often he would kiss my chin and then my neck. It felt delicious. My eyes were closed, heightening my senses. I could feel the warm body of Dracula lower himself between my legs before he even so much as touched me. His hands traced a line up both sides of my outer thighs and then once he reached the top, near my hip joints, he ran them back down my inner thighs all the way down to my ankles.

He did that a few times as he placed random kisses on my knees. The kisses from the Pirate grew more intense as he began to untie my corset, exposing my breasts. He took my nipple into his mouth and licked and sucked until it was hard.

My breathing became heavier the minute Dracula got onto his knees and took my other breast into his mouth as. While each guy nibbled and sucked my breasts, I leaned my head back and raised my hands above my head and allowed myself to be taken.

The Pirate needed more; he craved something else, and he wasn't shy helping himself to it. He sat between my legs and spread my knees apart. He lifted my skirt up to reveal my thigh-high white fishnets, the tiniest white lace G-string and baby blue garter. Dracula took my head into his hands and kissed me softly and then made his way to my ear and whispered.

"When he's done, I'll finish you off."

I looked him in the eyes and then gasped when the Pirate placed his lips against my pulsing muff. He taunted my clit through the lace and then kissed his way towards my garter biting on it and then sliding it down my leg and then over my high heel. He placed my hands over my head and tied them together with the garter.

Dracula liked this idea and then began to undo his belt. He used it to tie my foot to the leg of the chair and then the Pirate used his handkerchief to tie my other one to the other leg. There I was, spread eagle, dressed like a whore-y version of Marie-Antoinette about to surrender to a vampire and a buccaneer.

Dracula lowered his pants and took out his erect penis and began to rub himself, watching as the Pirate got comfortable on his knees, adjusted my hips, and placed his mouth between my legs. I squirmed, I shook, and I whimpered with every lick and nibble, and he was just getting started; my G-string was still on.

His fingers separated the lace from my body, and he began rubbing the very tip of me with his soft finger. I could barely handle it. My legs were trembling and just as I felt a gush of wetness spill out of me, he placed his tongue in me. Dracula loved watching me quiver and moan; he continued to stroke himself and fell back onto the bed as if he was watching late night porn with his wife asleep upstairs… only tonight, the live show was knocking him off his feet.

The Pirate had a rhythm with his tongue, a clockwise circular motion that got interrupted every time I jumped and squirmed. My moans became increasingly louder, my fists clenched, and my heels dug into the carpet as I felt my body climaxing. We were in perfect sync, because just when I needed him to apply more pressure to the very tip and use his hands, he did just that. And when I needed him to thrust his tongue inside me while rubbing me with his finger, he did just that. I was going to come; I was losing all feeling in my hands and feet, and my lungs weren't filled with enough air because as I exhaled I nearly fainted.

My knees shook, my body convulsed and I don't think I ever yelled so loudly. The Pirate wiped his mouth and then continued kissing my inner thighs, my labia, and my clitoris while I continued to tremor.

Dracula got off the bed and came to untie me while the Pirate removed his pants. They both led me onto the bed and gently placed me on all fours. Dracula put a condom on and then took me from behind while the Pirate kneeled in front of me. Both gentlemen about it, they caressed me and showered me with affection as they both inserted their pulsating penises—one into my... *pussy* and one into my mouth.

The cadence took a few seconds, but after a few thrusts we were all in sync. I sucked and rubbed the Pirate's dick while I managed to swivel my hips and gyrate on Dracula's. The receiving of pleasure mixed with giving pleasure simultaneously was a feeling of complete satisfaction, gratification, and fulfillment.

My goal was for these guys to come at the same time, and I decided I knew the best way to do it. I sat Dracula back down on the Recamier sofa and then the Pirate on the loveseat. I lay on the bed, legs spread for them both to see. I licked my fingers and traced a line down my chest, down towards my swollen clitoris. They watched zealously while I played with myself, purred, and made sure to make eye contact while I masturbated for my intimate audience. I fingered myself vigorously and matched my intensity with theirs. I was so turned on by them watching me. And then, I wanted them back.

"Come here, boys," I demanded.

They obliged and made their way over to the side of the bed where I twisted myself onto my stomach and took both of them into my hands and mouth. Both of them rubbed my body down as they grunted and gasped with ragged breath as I made them both climax. With quivering sighs, Dracula and the Pirate collapsed on the bed next to me, all of us spent.

A few minutes later, the guys watched as I reluctantly tied my corset back on and put myself back together. The pirate was sweet enough to slide my garter back up my thigh.

At 11 p.m. on the nose Antoine knocked at the door to escort me out. Ryan was waiting at the base of the stairs, his mask bent, cape tattered, and lips looking chapped. I deduced just by looking at him that I had a better night.

I had to control myself the entire drive home, trying not to giggle while he rubbed his wrists and mentioned the need for a Tylenol and an ice pack for his balls.

The day after my threesome with the cast of Scooby Doo, I got a text from Tyler.

I enjoyed every second of you last night, I crave you today and I can still feel and smell you on my skin.

The blue eyes, how did I not realize? The electricity that jolted me when he kissed me? The signature move: hands on face?

I replied:

How did you know it was me?

Tyler:

I know how you taste, I know what you feel like. And there's no one I feel better inside of than you.

I didn't know what to reply back because I didn't trust myself not to type something I couldn't retract after touching the blue "send" graphic on my iPhone. I went with a simple smile emoji, and then I deleted the conversation. I left my phone upstairs in my bedroom and occupied my hands with preparing dinner. I didn't want to be a hypocrite, even though not-so-deep down, I knew it was too late for that.

Michael came into the kitchen and seemed preoccupied.

"What's up, Mike?" I asked casually.

"I have one last task for my project, and I really, really, really don't want to do it."

I knew he was talking about the dentist, although after watching a horror movie and going on a roller coaster, I didn't think a trip to the dentist was such a big fear he had to overcome.

"Don't stress about it, Michael. Look at the bright side, you get to miss school." I winked at him. The truth was, I promised God that I would take the kids to have their teeth cleaned in exchange for anal beads at Kate's shower. God delivered scented candles and Mrs. Gold instead. I put a reminder in my calendar to make an appointment for Michael at the dentist.

"Happiness is the highest form of health." —*Dalai Lama*

CHAPTER 19

Why I Love Pain

Claudia DiSilva gave me a swift metaphorical kick in the ass. I knew the only way to keep Ryan from craving another woman was to give him what he needed. A hot dinner on the table, and my hot *pussy* at least twice a week. One night, as Ryan and I were getting into some foreplay, he was fondling my breast when he stopped abruptly, sat up, and said, "Don't freak out, Val, but there's a lump in your breast."

And there you have it folks, the immediate erosion of Ryan's relationship with my left breast forever. First of all, there was no way to not freak out from that information. Second, finding things that make your partner freak out when he touches your breast might make him avoid touching your breast. It certainly did in Ryan's case.

I stared at the ceiling all night. What would happen if I had breast cancer? Was this it? Statistics said there was a good chance I wouldn't fucking die from it.

I snuck into Hallie's room and just stared at her. I studied her face, the shape of her nose, the way her lips parted slightly when she slept. I remembered how badly I wanted a girl and thanked God endlessly for giving her to me. I promised God I would be the best mother and make sure my daughter was the one to cure cancer.

But, alas, Hallie was still in elementary school and was nowhere near cracking the genetic code for the curse of the twenty-first century. She was barely able to remember to wash her hands after she used the bathroom.

I watched the sun come up. The sky turned from a deep purple-blue to pink and then yellow as the sun pressed through the clouds. The weather was getting cold again, and I resented my black leather boots sitting stiffly next to my closet.

I checked the clock. It was still too early to call Dr. Rosenberg, so I continued to stare at the ceiling until Ryan stirred.

"You okay?" Ryan asked as he turned to face me.

"I couldn't sleep. I'm scared," I admitted and then buried my head in the pillow. I knew that even in Ryan's best effort, he couldn't calm me down the way I needed him to. I needed Melissa, but she still hadn't replied to my umpteen texts. Maybe if I texted her that I was sick and had a lump in my breast, she would reply back. What kind of heartless person wouldn't, right?

Hi. I know u hate me right now, but I'm scared. I have a lump in my breast, and I need u. Please call me back :(

I hesitated. Backspaced the sad-face emoji. And then I pressed "send" as the tears rolled down my cheeks.

The sound of the radiators heating up clanked and echoed against the wood floors. Ryan held me quietly as we watched the six on the clock turn to a seven, and then he got the kids ready for school.

At 7:45, the house was completely still. Ryan did the morning carpool while I stayed frozen staring at the clock waiting for the seven to turn to an eight so that I could finally call Dr. Rosenberg's office. A few minutes later, the front door opened and shut with a thud. There must have been very little traffic on the way to school, or Ryan must have blown every light. The footsteps came swiftly up the stairs, the door to my bedroom swung open, and it was Melissa still in her pajamas and not Ryan who climbed into bed with me and held me tight while I continued to stare at the clock.

An hour later, my mother, Melissa, Ryan, and I sat in the waiting room. I knew that my mother would come even though I told her a dozen times to stay home. Typical Carol. Melissa sat on one side holding my hand, Ryan on the other. My mother just sat and stared at us while clenching her Chanel. I could tell just by looking at her she was calculating all the times she wished she reminded me to go for a mammogram.

When my name was finally called, I had the urge like I always do to yell, "Bingo!" as is always the case when I'm called into a doctor's office, license bureau, passport office, and any place you have to take a number and wait. I forced Ryan to come in with me. My mom jumped up to come but I immediately told her to stay in the waiting room.

As I got on the table I had flashbacks of the first time Dr. Rosenberg had to touch my boobs, and here I was at forty, cringing once again.

Ryan stood in the corner, Melissa sat on the chair, and both uncomfortably watched on as Dr. Rosenberg pressed on my breast. I winced as he prodded the lump.

"You have nothing to worry about, Val. Your lump is exactly what we hope for." Dr. Rosenberg slid my bra back over my breast and motioned for me to sit up.

"Exactly what we hope for?" I was confused.

"Round, hard, painful, all signs of a fibroadenoma, a benign cyst," Dr. Rosenberg explained.

"I will still send you to the breast clinic at the hospital for an ultrasound, and we will continue to monitor you, but you can relax. Cancer is called the silent killer because it sneaks up on you with no warning. When there's pain, it's a good sign."

Ryan dropped Melissa and me off at our house, where I stripped off my clothes and slipped into the bath and cried for over an hour. Melissa sat on the floor next to the tub in silence.

"You can be gorgeous at thirty, charming at forty, and irresistible for the rest of your life." —*Coco Chanel*

CHAPTER 20

Swap #11: November 8, 2014

Not Sorry, Wrong Number

The morning of Swap #11 was like any other typical Saturday in our house. Ryan complained that I forgot to run the dishwasher, my kids were glued to the TV, and all I wanted to do was enjoy my morning cup of coffee and pretend to read the *Gazette*. I scanned my way through the important news and headed straight for the Weekend section and the Arts and Entertainment. I am proud to say that I don't get my news only from the Facebook newsfeed.

November is a tough month, especially on the weekends when the kids need to be kept busy. It's not cold enough for winter activities and not warm enough for the summer ones. It really only left two options, bowling or a movie, and seeing as last weekend we took them to see *Big Hero 6*, we met Melissa, Jeff, and their kids at the bowling alley. Melissa and I still haven't spoken about Sam, and I was hoping it would just blow over.

While Ryan, Jeff, and Melissa were organizing the shoes, watching the kids and paying for the hour, I escaped to the bathroom to relieve myself from the residual tension between Melissa and myself. It didn't take more than her "Hi" to bring back the flashbacks of Sam's dwarf thumb pulsating in my hand.

Fluorescent lighting has never been flattering for my skin, I thought as I stared at myself in the mirror. With my summer tan faded, I wondered why my greenish complexion was kindly referred to as "olive" and not "puke." Maybe some iron would do me some good.

I lifted my sweater above my bellybutton and stared at my tummy. Once upon a time I had a six-pack without ever having stepped into the gym. At forty, the skin on my abdomen was starting to loosen, but if I stood really straight, I thought I could see a four-pack.

I spent the next few minutes shrugging and then straightening my back, completely engrossed in the many levels of "fit" I could fake my tummy. The good thing about living in Montreal was that I had only four months of straight-as-an-arrow good posture for bathing-suit weather each year to really worry about it.

Melissa walked into the bathroom and stopped abruptly at the doorway as I stood there gazing at my stomach in the mirror.

"Val? What are you doing?" she said, baffled.

"Nothing. I sprayed myself with water by accident."

Melissa came in and closed the door behind her.

"Liar. What is going on with you?"

"What is going on me with me?" I replied. "What is going on with you? What's with the silent treatment?"

"I saw you, Val. I saw you leaving that guy Tyler's house late at night a while ago. How could you cheat on Ryan?"

I lost the feeling in my legs. My heart was thumping in my chest, and I needed to sit down, but the nearest seat was a filthy toilet. I was prepared to discuss Sam; I had no idea she remembered my college crush, Tyler. I was still holding my sweater up, my stomach still hanging out.

"Melissa, you don't understand. I wasn't cheating on Ryan. You could ask him. He knew I was at Tyler's." Okay, so it was a half-truth.

"What do you mean, Ryan knows?" Melissa was genuinely confused.

"It's a long story, Melissa, but I assure you I wasn't cheating on Ryan and he knew I was with Tyler that night. If you don't believe me, I can go get him and you can ask him yourself." I was calling her bluff.

"I'm not asking Ryan, but what in God's name were you doing at Tyler's?" Melissa waited for an answer. "And why were you kissing him goodbye?" I should have just told her he was hosting a book club for my former department or something nonthreatening, but I couldn't lie to my best friend. I had to trust that Melissa could handle my secret, even if it meant breaking Rule #6.

"Ryan bought us a membership to a sex club for my birthday," I blurted out. It wasn't exactly how I imagined telling her.

"A sex club?" Melissa, making sure she heard correctly, regurgitated my words back to me.

"All the rumors you heard about couple swapping are true, and Ryan and I are a part of it. You can't tell anyone or I will get into trouble and Ryan and I could go to jail." (I didn't read the contract word for word so for all I knew, I wasn't *really* lying.)

Melissa just stood there trying to wrap her head around what I was telling her. We could hear the sound of the pins in the bowling alley being smashed.

"I knew it! I knew there was a swingers club!" Melissa looked proud of herself.

"Yup. You were right all along."

"So wait, you're not having an affair with your old T.A.?"

"Nope," I replied, hoping that my voice wouldn't betray the omission in my reply.

"I mean—that is crazy! Val! You have to tell me everything!" Melissa was energized.

"I can't tell you everything, but if you joined the club, then you would find out firsthand," I quipped, knowing Melissa was not the swap type.

I wanted to tell her everything. I wanted to tell her about Nate, Tyler, the Halloween threesome, Claudia DiSilva... but as all the details bubbled to my lips it felt like too much to share. Not to mention, I had no idea how to approach the subject of her brother. We both stood there for a moment, lost in our thoughts. Thankfully, she broke the silence.

"So, you aren't a cheater?" Then she thought for a second. "I'm a terrible friend."

"You're the best friend, I'm the one that has been a terrible friend." I turned back towards the mirror and continued to examine my stomach. "Do you ever feel old?" I wanted to know if I was speaking to a sympathetic audience.

"Of course I do. Can we just move this part of the conversation outside this gross bathroom? My shoes are sticking to the floor." Melissa was sympathetic. Kinda.

"What happened to us? We used to sit in your basement and chat for hours about everything and nothing. When did we become too busy to stand in a disgusting bathroom and talk about my non-existent stomach muscles? Besides, you owe me one."

Melissa moved closer. She faced the mirror next to me as she untucked her shirt from her jeans. She looked for my reaction as she lifted her top and revealed what she was hiding. Hers was worse. Way worse. I couldn't see her bellybutton as it was hidden in folds of loose, draped skin.

"Happy?" Melissa asked sarcastically, but still smiling, as we stood side by side staring at our stomachs in a dirty bathroom mirror scrawled with tags and indecipherable signatures.

"Here's the reason I could never join your secret fuck club. What man would want this?" Melissa stared at herself. "My own husband is working extra hours to pay for our house renovations along with mine." Melissa squeezed her belly fat.

I hugged Melissa, our bellies touching, and we giggled like the two high school girls we were deep down.

"Can we go now or are we going to do more comparisons?" She put her arm around me and gave me a squeeze as we walked out the door.

Here's the thing about bowling: I don't like bowling until I am actually doing it. That afternoon it took only three frames for me to finally get a strike. Ryan looked proud of me as I sat down next to him at the desk. He gave me a high-five and then kissed my head. I wondered if his emotional affair with Claudia had fizzled or he was just focused on winning the ten frames.

After we bowled, we were starving and I really wanted to hit that new BBQ joint that opened up on Décarie Boulevard. I pulled my sleeve up to show Ryan my *severe* jaundice and my need for iron at lunch. But what man doesn't want some barbecued brisket? It wasn't a hard sell. Melissa and Jeff opted out, though; the bowling was apparently enough activity for them for one day.

Montreal BBQ stood in the same location as Il Forno, an Italian place my late grandfather used to take Janet and me to all the time. As we walked through the door, the first thing that hit me was the smell of the mesquite wood from the smoker. Baskets of condiments stood like centerpieces on each table's gingham tablecloth. Even with the smoky smell in the air and all the hipsters running around the joint, I could still imagine my grandfather telling Janet and me about the time he boarded his first commercial airplane at age twenty-five to visit New York City. His ticket, he told us, was the same price as the chicken Parmesan he was eating.

Ryan ordered us a "Family Plank," which was exactly that: A plank of wood covered in piles of pulled pork, beef ribs, chicken wings, and the thing that would do me in for the rest of the day—the chopped brisket chili.

Unsurprisingly, Hallie nibbled on the corn bread and French fries and Michael tried a piece of this and that but also stuck with mostly fries. Next time, I decided, I would just order the *Martin* Family Plank: a trough of fries and loads of ketchup.

All afternoon my tummy rumbled and gurgled. I wasn't used to eating like that. By 4 p.m. I had been sitting my bathroom for a solid forty-five minutes, and I won't be too descriptive but I was sure that there was nothing left inside my body. I was also sure that all the iron I ate was now out of my system, and the green color of my skin was actually a shade deeper.

Over a decade into our marriage and I still ran the water and left the TV on outside in my bedroom for fear of any sound reaching Ryan's ears. I wanted to believe I was a goddess, and heaven knows a goddess never has a bowel movement.

By 7 p.m. I had consumed five Tums, four Peptos, two organic chewable Gravols, and two liters of ginger ale. My stomach was feeling much better; however, my bum-hole was a bit tender. There would be no ass-play tonight for sure. Although I doubt Celeste would send me Nate for a third time. I took a shower and got ready for Mr. November.

Like usual, Ryan skipped out of the house by 7:50 p.m. leaving me pacing around impatiently. Outfit of choice: loose-fitting boyfriend jeans, an old Rolling Stones T-shirt my sister Janet would love to steal, and underneath—nothing.

At 8:03 p.m. as I was putting on my Mereadesso sheer pink lip treats, my doorbell rang. I heard some commotion coming from my porch so I hurried and curiously opened the door. Arguing on my welcome mat were Tyler and some guy I didn't know.

My heart jumped. Another threesome? Was Celeste crazy? As much fun as it was, it was a fantasy and it was fulfilled and as far as I was concerned, no need to do it again.

"Dude, you must be mistaken. This is the address I was sent." The guy was so sure of himself, he even showed the text to Tyler.

"Listen, *dude*, unless you feel like sharing me tonight, take a hike." Tyler let himself into my house and began to shut the door.

"That's it? I don't get a say?" The poor guy looked defeated. The truth was, he didn't stand a chance.

"That's it," Tyler asserted and then shut the door.

I couldn't understand what happened; all along this club has been super organized.

"What happened?" I asked Tyler as he grabbed me close and started to kiss me.

"I think I just got myself kicked out of Swap Club, that's all." And then he continued to kiss me fervently.

"What are you talking about?" I pulled away from him, which was a hard thing to do. His arms were so damn strong.

"Val, I fucking miss you, and had to see you." Tyler stared intensely into my eyes and let out a sigh that instantly welled his crystal-blue eyes with tears. I felt bad Tyler was so emotional, but in a selfish way I was flattered. Here was a grown man overwhelmed about me, wanting so badly to be with me, and openly emotional about it.

I led Tyler to my used-more-than-ever living room and sat him on the couch. I cuddled into him, rested my face on his chest, and comforted him. Tyler placed his warm cheek on my forehead and caressed my hair while he tried to compose himself.

"A few months ago I thought we had a fun swap, and although I sensed there might have been something deeper there, I let it go when you left my office." Tyler took my face into his hands and looked me directly in the eyes once again.

I felt guilty about this whole interaction given the whole Claudia thing, but it also made me feel like I should explore this too. I liked how he looked into my eyes; I felt connected with him that way.

"What I do know is that when I'm with you I feel so good, so alive." Tyler leaned his head back and squeezed his eyes shut. His hand continued to caress my hair.

I had to say something. It had to be sweet, it had to be sensitive, and it had to make him happy. I sat up, straddled him, and took his face into my hands, whispering in his ear, "Ty, I will always be here."

Before I could even say another word, his mouth was on mine, and his impassioned kiss declared that he believed that somehow, someday, he would end up with me.

Tyler effortlessly carried me up the stairs and placed me softly on the bed. My drapes were open, allowing the streetlights to cast a hazy glow, and the window was cracked open slightly, filling my room with the crisp autumn air.

Tyler crawled on top of me and gently kissed my lips, my cheeks, my neck and then my lips again and again. Occasionally he would just run his nose against mine while his eyes held onto mine. Every so often he would pause while looking at my body and then place the palm of my hand against his chest. And somewhere between feeling his heart beating against my fingers and seeing the wet eyelashes from his tears, words fell from his lips and floated like clouds over our heads. "I can't believe the way I am feeling. I don't know how this is possible." Tyler shook his head, closed his eyes and smiled. "No words could ever do what I'm feeling right now justice. I know this is crazy."

These words still echo in my head. *This is crazy.* And it *was* crazy. It was unbelievably, undeniably crazy. The way I was feeling lying with Tyler was crazy. The way I felt kissing Tyler was crazy. The way I was completely, both physically and emotionally, captivated by Tyler was bat-shit crazy.

This was Swap Club, consensual play with another man for three hours once a month. I could feel I was crossing a line emotionally. I understood how easy it was for Ryan to do the same. We were opening ourselves up in a way we had never done with each other.

I could hear my late grandmother yelling, "This is vat you vant? Cheating vith a stranger?"

"It's not cheating, Bubby. It's Swap Club."

"Call it vat you vant. This is cheating."

My dead bubby was right, but at that moment I couldn't deny myself the intimacy I wanted so badly. A three-hour sex session with Tyler again—I had to have it.

This is just sex. This is just sex. This is just sex. My new mantra on autopilot drowned out the sound of my grandmother.

I got on top of Tyler and kissed him. I kissed his forehead all the way down to his belt buckle. I wanted to please him, and I knew how much Tyler liked the way I pleasured him. I stared into his eyes as I undid his pants. He tried to unbutton my jeans, but I playfully slapped his hand away.

"My turn first."

I slid Tyler's pants down and glided them over his feet and then his underwear followed suit. He was already semi-erect, exactly how I like to start off giving head. I don't particularly like the feeling of a flaccid penis in my mouth, and if it is completely erect, then I can never take credit for its growth. I like knowing I've made a difference.

I took him into my mouth; my hand held the base while I slid my mouth up and down, taking special time at the top where his body would jerk each time. I played with him as I lightly grazed my teeth against the shaft and taunted him with my tongue along the edges of the tip. His moans grew deeper, and his foot danced around on my bed. I used my hands together with my mouth; as I slid my mouth up, my hand would follow and rub the end, and as my mouth slid down, my hand would follow and then massage his scrotum.

Tyler took hold of my body and turned me onto my back. I sat up and removed my T-shirt and tossed it onto the floor.

"Val, I could just sit and stare at you." I loved hearing how much he liked my body, using words that were hardly ever spoken by Ryan.

I got up onto my knees and unbuttoned my jeans.

"Do you want to see more?" I flirted. All of my body hangups disappeared under his gaze. I felt beautiful. Tyler smiled and tossed me back onto the bed and pulled my pants off, revealing my completely nude body.

"Oh my God, what am I going to do with you?" Tyler kissed my breasts tenderly while his hand rubbed my already-moist crevice.

The truth was, I was wet from the moment I lay my head on his chest downstairs. As Tyler spread my legs apart, I took hold of his penis and rubbed it against me. We both jumped with delight, thrilled with the idea that he wasn't even inside me yet, and it already felt so pleasurable.

Slowly I applied pressure down against him, and his throbbing penis slipped inside me. We both held still for a moment enjoying the feeling of his body inside of mine. We were connected. From this moment on, we didn't talk. Our actions were the expression and validation of the way we felt. It was a physical declaration of our conflicted feelings towards each other. That night was about intimate revelry. We were on a journey together of desire and emotion.

Tyler held my hands above my head while he kissed me passionately and made love to me for over an hour and a half. We started slowly; he kissed me tenderly and with every thrust he moved deeper inside of me, both emotionally and physically. The emotion was overpowering, and both of us couldn't hold onto each other tight enough.

I looked up at my ceiling, Tyler's warm skin pressing against mine reminded me how amazing it felt being with him. Before I could prepare myself, tears were streaming down my cheeks, and all I could think of was not wanting this night to end. Not wanting to say goodbye to Tyler. Not being happy. Not knowing what I was going to do. Not knowing how it felt to make love until now. I couldn't help it. As I climaxed and felt a massive release, I wept.

Tyler kissed my wet cheeks and stroked my back as he lay on his side next to me. We stayed in contemplative silence for what seemed like forever. One hand propped his head, the other caressed my back, putting me into a trance until I finally looked at the clock through my blurry vision. It was very close to 11 p.m.

"You have to go," I said grudgingly.

Tyler looked at the clock, then jumped up and threw his clothes on. "Shit! I feel like a couple of kids with parents on the way home."

I lay still on the bed while Tyler raced around my bedroom looking for his belongings. A part of me just didn't have the energy to care if Ryan came home and found us. A part of me welcomed the possibility of evening the stakes by letting him see me with another man. I was emotionally drained.

"We'll talk tomorrow, okay?"

I nodded halfheartedly, and then he kissed me good night.

A few minutes after the front door slammed shut behind Tyler, Ryan was home.

"Val? Where are you?" I heard Ryan clump up the stairs, and then he came into the bedroom to find me pulling our sheets off the bed and cleaning up.

"Um," Ryan began. "Do you have something to take this off?" I spun around to find Ryan in full-on drag makeup. I examined Ryan's face, and then I took off out the door.

"I don't know where we'll go from here, There may be no way to fly.

And the cloud I'm in just makes it all to clear. That I can't leave you with a

bad goodbye." —Clint Black, A Bad Goodbye

CHAPTER 21

The Good and the Bad Good (Byes)

Some other things you should know about me: I suffer from a fear of smelling bad; at any given time I am wearing four different deodorants, body cream, and perfume. Also I don't like Broadway musicals; by the second act I have the urge to scream, "Shut the fuck up already! We get it. You can sing!"

And—

I hate goodbyes.

As I swerved off our street and pressed my foot on the gas, I realized that all I was wearing was a T-shirt and my Ugg slippers. I lifted my foot slightly and then thought, *Who gives a shit?*—and pressed it down even harder.

I sped through the streets, and as I grew closer to Westmount, I got a nervous feeling in the pit of my stomach. What the hell was I doing? What was I thinking chasing Tyler home? Had I completely lost all sense?

I wanted to blame Ryan because, after all, he was the one who facilitated my entry into the beds of other men, and then into the arms of another man.

Up ahead I saw his brake lights, so I flicked my headlights to catch his attention, but he turned onto the next street, bringing him closer to his front yard. I had to speed up.

237

I ran through the stop sign and then pressed my hand lightly on the horn when I saw his car again. He slowly accelerated, and my heart fell into my nervous stomach. What if he saw me and was running from me? Ryan must be wondering where I was. How would I explain this to him? I had to set things straight and clear my conscience. Just as I was about to give up and turn my desperate car around, Tyler finally stopped.

I parked behind him and waited until he got out of his car. He walked cautiously towards me, making sure to look over his shoulder to see if anyone was watching. I got out of my car. The night was filled with a brightness that seems to come only with the cold and the edge of winter. The wind rustled through the trees, causing just the last few leaves still clinging to the branches to succumb to the fall. I saw the brown grass fading on the lawns of the surrounding houses. I saw the sparse clouds moving past the stars in the sky. I saw Tyler.

A shiver ran up my spine, not from the cold air flowing up my body, but from watching Tyler making his way towards me. I felt like I was in one of my dreams. As the lights from my headlights lit him up like a ghost, he floated towards me.

"Ty! That was the worst goodbye!"

Tyler got closer, but I could tell he feared what this looked like.

"I know, Val! That was a terrible goodbye."

Tyler was an arm's length away from me, and I could smell him. I tugged the bottom of my T-shirt lower down to cover my ass. It was probably a good thing to have my hands occupied because the impulse to fall into his arms was overpowering.

"Ty, I don't know what's going on with me. What I know is that I need you to say goodbye tonight and let me go on with my life. You have made me feel things that I didn't know I could feel, but I'm married, and I love my husband, and I have to end whatever this is. I need to sleep at night."

Tyler looked at me, and then his eyes dropped to the pavement.

"This can't be goodbye, Val, I can't let you go. I know this is nuts, but I can't imagine not seeing you again."

Tyler refused to make eye contact. I didn't want to hurt him, but I needed to make things right.

"You're an amazing guy. A sensitive, loving, caring, and emotional man who hides nothing. I wish my husband were more like you in some ways. My life will forever be changed because you opened yourself up to me. Do us both a favor and go home to your wife."

Tyler raised his eyes from the ground and smiled slightly and said, "That is the nicest, most incredible, heart-wrenching, heart-warming, beautiful, sad, amazing, terrible, wonderful thing anyone has ever said to me."

I took a step closer and placed my head against his chest, still holding onto my T-shirt. Tyler wrapped his arms around me and kissed me on the head.

"Goodbye, Val."

"Goodbye, Tyler."

And with that we got into our cars and went to our homes. Where our spouses were waiting. Hopefully.

"How very little can be done under the spirit of fear." —*Florence Nightingale*

CHAPTER 22

The Science Fear

I told Ryan *the guy* left his cell phone, so I chased him down to give it to him. Ryan was too busy washing the makeup off to think anything of it. That night I felt released from the imprisonment of my secret and slept better than I had in months.

The following Monday I rolled up to Michael's school around eleven in the morning and waited so I could take him to the dentist. I never considered the dentist particularly frightening, and I could think of several other scary activities to get a heart rate above one hundred. Namely, sex with a stranger, sex with a family member, sex with your best friend's brother, sex with a pirate and Dracula.

Michael made his way down the school walkway and climbed into the car.

"I can't wait to get this over with."

"Having your teeth cleaned is nothing, Michael. The whole thing takes twenty minutes, if that."

A half-hour later I found myself in the dentist chair measuring my heart rate as Dr. Cairns was chiseling at my plaque. Michael made it to the waiting room, but no further. I couldn't convince him to get into the chair, and I didn't want Dr. Cairns to charge us for canceling so I took the spot, and one for the team.

When we got into the car, Michael just stared out his window. I couldn't understand why he was upset with *me*.

"Mike, why are you being like this? I took your appointment. Ninety-six beats-per-minute. You should be thanking me, not ignoring me!"

"It's your fault I'm such a pussy!"

"My fault?" I was shocked to hear Michael talking like that. I wanted to get mad at him for using that word, a word I have just recently been reunited with. A word that had changed how I viewed pleasure was now spewing out of my child's mouth in reference to his low opinion of himself. A pussy, in the negative. Even worse, he was blaming me for his fear.

"How is it my fault?" I was stunned by the accusation from my ten-year-old after I watched a horror movie, went on a roller coaster, and had my teeth cleaned for Miss Clarice's goddam punishment of a science fair project.

"The whole reason I decided to do my science fair project on fear is because I'm so anxious. I'm constantly nervous, and it's your fault. *Michael, be careful, Michael, watch out, Michael, look where you're going. Michael, I'm afraid you're going to get hurt, fall, throw up, Michael, Michael, Michael…*"

I pulled over because I couldn't concentrate on maneuvering my car through the snow banks and my brain through this conversation.

"My job, Michael, is to keep you safe and happy. I can't help if I'm trying to protect you." I had to stay calm; this was the first real conversation I'd had with Michael about what goes on in his head.

"Mom! Every time you think you're fixing it, you're making it worse. I had to face my fears and this project was supposed to help me."

Michael was ten years old, but his thinking was beyond his years. He was right. Trying to be helpful and shield him from his fears only validated those fears and made it okay for someone else—me—to face them on his behalf.

I lived in fear of the world every day. I feared what people were thinking about me. I feared what people were saying about me. I feared things I had no control over, and here I was, teaching my son that he should run away from his fears instead of just facing them.

Michael and I sat in my car in silence. It amazed me that my son could recognize that his fears were his to face, and that every time I thought I was saving him, I was actually reinforcing the issue.

"I didn't realize I was making it worse," I said to him, and I really didn't. I messed up, and he had every right to be frustrated.

"Mom, sometimes you think you're helping but you're not. What's that thing Dad always says? It's not helpful if it's not helping."

"You're right. I'm so sorry, Mike."

"Tough love works, Mom." Michael smiled.

"Let's get some McD's and face some fears. What do you say, Mike?"

Michael and I skipped the rest of his day at school and spent the afternoon at home eating McDonald's and watching horror movies. (With the lights on, upstairs in the living room.)

A few weeks later Ryan, Hallie, my mother, Janet, and I attended the grade five science fair. Michael had seemed remarkably calm the night before, and now he looked so small next to the other students. My heart was pounding. When it was time for Michael to present, we were the loudest group applauding as he took the microphone. He shot us a look to shut up. I had to belt out, "Go, Mike!" Then I shut up and took my seat.

"My name is Michael, and I decided to do my project on fear and its influence on our heart rate. I always thought that my mom was a worrywart"—giggles could be heard in the audience—"and that her job on this planet was to live in fear that something bad was about to happen. But after spending time with her during the research for my project, I learned that my mom is the bravest person I know, and I've never felt luckier to have a mom like her." That's when his eyes lifted from his notes and smiled at me. I bet there wasn't a dry eye in the room, not even Miss Clarice. (Suck teeth.)

I have to admit I didn't fully listen to everything that followed his opening statement. I was too busy relishing in Michael's words and the way my mom squeezed my hand just before she pulled out a tissue and honked her nose into it.

A week later, Michael climbed into my car after school and handed me his paper from his science fair project with an 87 percent written across the top in red.

"That's amazing, Mike!" I was so proud of him. I had literally walked around beaming all week.

Michael smiled and said, "Yeah. I'm happy."

But I could tell he didn't really care what Miss Clarice thought of his work because, as far as he was concerned, his project was 100 percent about more than just science.

"I blame my mother for my poor sex life. All she told me was 'the man goes on top and the woman underneath.' For three years my husband and I slept in bunk beds." —Joan Rivers

CHAPTER 23

Swap #12: December 13, 2014

Stranger Than Usual

I wasn't sure how to feel when I woke up the morning of the final swap of the year. Ryan had already gotten up when I rolled over and stared at the picture of him and me in Rio. We looked relaxed; the only thought on my mind then was whether or not the tourist we asked to take our picture would give us a "framer."

Thirteen years later, the list of things on my mind has grown into: *What should I make for dinner? What high school should we send Michael to? Is Hallie too overscheduled? How will we find the $3500 for the condo in Hallandale we overextended ourselves for? Do we have to go to all three weddings coming up, even though one or two of the couples will probably be separated by the fall? My gray hairs are spreading, and I think I saw a number eleven on my forehead... and is there anything left in my marriage beyond parenting and a requirement for membership in Swap Club?*

One year earlier I lay in bed staring at the frumpy lady in flannel pajamas who abandoned her sex life for Wheat Thins and the Kardashians. One year later and fully on the other side of forty, I was still uncertain. It felt like so much in my life had changed in the last year, but really, what was different? I was still worried my marriage was in trouble, but now I didn't have the sex to blame it on.

The door slowly opened to my bedroom, and Hallie peeked through the crack to see if I was awake yet. I gestured for her to come cuddle. She crawled into bed with me.

"Mommy, are you forty-one yet?" she asked.

"Not yet, my heart, next week," I replied and kissed her on her head.

"Good, because I want you to be young for a little longer."

And with that, my kid rolled out of my bed with a huge smile, leaving me thankful that she was making sure I was going to be around.

Tyler got into quite a bit of trouble for messing up last month's swap for two people. The woman he was supposed to be with called Celeste when he was a no-show, and so did the guy he turned away from my door. Celeste called me to find out what happened, and I played dumb. I told her I had no clue which of the men was legitimately supposed to be at my place, and I was certainly not welcoming both men into my home. Celeste expelled Tyler from the club and from what she told me, his wife was pissed. I think she moved in with her parents for a week.

The lines were so blurred. If he had gone to his designated home to screw the woman waiting there, then it was a swap. It would have been business as usual. He went to a different house and fucked another woman, and his wife moved out.

My mother picked up the kids around 5:30 p.m., so I was able to take some extra time getting ready for the last swap. At 7:00 p.m. Ryan got a message to leave the house at 8 p.m., drive to the nearest intersection, and then wait for further instruction. That message put Ryan into such a funk that before he left at 7:59 p.m., he chewed a couple of Tums.

I paced around the house with my glass of wine. When I stopped to check myself in the mirror, I got inspired to say a prayer.

Dear God,

You've given me a lot this year. I found my orgasm, I lived out my fantasies, and I discovered that I give great head. The only thing I ask for now is to make this last swap night memorable.

Amen.

The final doorbell summoned me. I placed my wine down and took a breath. Outfit of choice for the conclusion of Swap Club: lilac cashmere sweater, gray skinny jeans, and high brown boots.

The butterflies still made their appearance, but no deafening heartbeat. No anxiety. I was calm and sad that this was going to be my last time answering the door for a swap. I put my hand on the knob and pulled the door open to find Ryan standing on our stoop.

"What are you doing here?" I asked in a panic. "My swap is going to be here any minute!"

"Hi, I'm Ryan. It's nice to meet you." Ryan extended his hand to me.

"What are you doing?" I asked, baffled.

Ryan got closer, hand still out, so I took it and shook it slowly.

"Do you have a name?" he asked charmingly.

"You know my name is Val." I was so confused.

"Val, is that short for Valerie?" Ryan continued. "What a beautiful home. Do you mind if I come in? Before someone sees me?"

I was starting to get it. I widened the threshold for Ryan, then shut the door behind him. My husband took a second to compose himself, looking as if it was really his first time in our house. He was good at this play-acting.

"Can I offer you some wine?" I asked playfully, deciding to just roll with it.

"Sure, what have you got?" We both knew he bought the wine and knew exactly what we had in stock.

"Penfolds?" I asked, knowing it was one of his favorites.

"Sounds great." Ryan followed me into the now-used-for-the-first-time-with-Ryan living room and took a seat on the couch. I poured him a glass and sat next to him. He took a sip and smiled at me.

"You know something, Val, you have the most beautiful eyes, and I'm not just saying that."

I don't think Ryan ever told me I had nice eyes. They were brown and small and for most of my life I always wished they were green or blue—brown eyes, in my mind, couldn't possibly be considered beautiful.

"Thanks, that's sweet."

It felt enigmatic pretending to be strangers. I just spent the entire day with him doing mundane errands. We went to Costco, shoveled our walkway, and counted down the hours until 8 p.m. And now, here we were, enjoying each other's company.

"So Valerie, I'm going to put our wine glasses down, and then I'm going to do something."

Wine glasses now on our desecrated coffee table, Ryan took me by the hand and led me up to our bedroom. I felt the delicate butterflies in my stomach.

The idea of Ryan as a complete stranger was turning me on, and I actually looked forward to what would come next. Ryan turned around at the foot of our bed and placed his hands around my waist.

"I don't want to be too forward, but I'd love to kiss you. By the look of your lips, I bet you're a great kisser."

I leaned in and closed my eyes, meeting Ryan's mouth. His lips felt tender and warm, and I know this sounds cliché, but it felt like the first time we ever kissed. He held me tight and kissed me like I was the most amazing woman on the planet. He alternated between kissing my lips and my neck and then held my hair back as he kissed behind my earlobes. Where had he learned the art of seduction?

Usually in situations like these, I would climb into bed, he would make a smartass comment about my pajamas, then he'd get on top of me and four minutes later we were watching Jimmy Fallon.

Ryan slowly placed me on the bed as he peeled off his shirt. His body looked good. It had been a while since I had really paid attention to him topless. He reached over and delicately removed my cashmere sweater.

"You are stunning," he said, and then continued to kiss me more passionately.

Who was this guy? He was sweet, attentive, and romantic. He was taking his time, making sure I felt wanted and desired.

I felt his hand brush down my thigh and around to my ass to pull me closer. I could feel his firmness through his jeans, and it turned me on knowing that just kissing me excited him. I reached down, unbuckled his pants, and slid them down past his knees. I could see his stiff penis through his underwear, so I climbed on top and rubbed myself against it.

"Val, you're so sexy. Look what you do to me." Ryan sounded like his words were scripted for him, all the perfect things I wanted to hear.

"You like that? Do you like the way I feel, Ryan?" As the words came out of my mouth, I realized that I, too, knew all the things men like to hear.

Ryan pulled me off of him, placed me on my stomach, and then stripped me of my boots and pants, tossing them onto the ground. I lay there naked, on my stomach, and I had never felt sexier in my life.

Ryan stood there and looked at me.

"I've never wanted anyone so badly in my life." He started kissing my feet, and then moved his mouth up the back of my calves, stopping to lick behind my knees. His hands followed the trail of his tongue all the way up the back of my thighs until he reached my backside. He licked and kissed his way to my lower back and gave me shivers when he reached my shoulders and neck. He pulled my hair to the side and intensely sucked and kissed the nape of my neck. Ryan was making my whole body tingle. I was so proud of him. I didn't dare tell him that, though; I didn't want him to think I was condescending. Nor did I want to break the spell of the moment.

I turned over to face him so we could kiss again, and I wrapped my arms around his waist to pull him down on me. I was hot for Ryan, a feeling I don't think I'd had since 2006.

I reached inside his underwear and pulled his penis out. I loved the way it felt rubbing against my most sensitive pieces. Ryan began to make a sound I had never heard. With every swivel of my hips, he made a low sounding growl. Ryan was in a zone, a virile and carnal place that made me even more attracted to him.

And then Ryan did something so out of character, so level-10—he literally ripped my G-string off with his bare hands and threw it to the side, plunged face-first into my wet lips and ate me out like he had never tasted my sweetness before.

"Oh my God, Ryan!" I could barely stand it.

He had the technique down; his rhythm was next to perfect and his intensity made my legs twitch. I wanted to scream from the top of St. Joseph's Oratory. Ryan knew how to eat *pussy*!

The best part was that he was enjoying it too. He moaned and groaned with every jerk and jolt of my legs. When I thought I couldn't handle it anymore, he held onto me tighter.

I had an idea. I was going to try something new with my husband.
I twisted my body around and sat on his face, then leaned down and took his hard throbbing penis into my mouth. I couldn't believe it—Ryan and I were sixty-nining! Another thing I wanted to yell from the Oratory!

His dick was smooth and actually a pleasure to give head to. I am ashamed to say that it had been years since I had ever really paid attention to his penis. I don't mean servicing him; I mean admiring it. Appreciating the wellspring of his pleasure. Every time I let out a whimper with his penis in my mouth it vibrated and felt even better for him. The gratification for him to keep giving me pleasure was definitely a win-win for both of us.

I was ready for more. I needed more and I knew he did, too. I lay on my back as the wetness poured from me, aiding his stiffness to glide right inside me. He cradled my body and plunged deeper inside of me with each thrust.

His pelvis lined up perfectly with mine, his rhythm was perfectly in tune with mine, his body fit perfectly with mine. Instead of squeezing my eyes closed tight, I opened them and stared right into Ryan's eyes. I was transported.

At that moment, we were in our shoddy four-star hotel in Rio. The air-conditioner didn't work, our bodies were sticking to each other from the heat, and it smelled of rotting wood. But we couldn't give a shit. We had sex as often as our bodies could take, maybe more. We were young, we were in love, and there was nowhere we would rather be than in each other's arms.

This was the first time in over a decade that Ryan and I weren't parents. Each of us had had our "boys' nights" and "girls' nights," but this was just us. Just the two of us. No distractions. No friends. No restaurants. No television. No strangers. Just each other. Ryan and I were lovers, sexual beings looking to pleasure one another and make each other feel desired, sexy, and beautiful.

We made love for about twenty minutes, and for us that was the equivalent of an all-nighter.

As we both caught our breath, I started thinking about Tyler. I thought about his profound impact on how I felt about myself today, about feeling good enough for not just Ryan, but for me. Through Tyler's eyes, I was able to see my own self-worth and appreciate it.

Ryan came into my life that night as a stranger and displayed a variety of new talents he learned from his various coaches. I am so grateful to them for all their hard work.

"Thank you," I whispered into Ryan's ear, and he smiled. I think he thought I was thanking him for Swap Club. I was actually thanking him for something much bigger than that.

EPILOGUE

Celeste sat across from us in her luxurious living room and stared at us while sipping green tea. I couldn't believe a year had passed already. It felt like just yesterday Ryan and I had last been here.

"Did you two find what you were looking for?" Celeste asked.

It was a tough question to answer. I had started off looking to spice up my sex life. I did things I never realized I wanted to do, living out sexual fantasies I didn't even know I had. But all that made me realize I was looking for something else. Either way, I knew that the Swap Club provided me with a year of the best sex I ever had.

"I found exactly what I have been looking for," I admitted.

"Is that so, Valerie?" Celeste sounded interested in hearing more.

"Yes. I found out that I am sensitive, emotional, and in tune with my sexuality. I learned that I know how to seduce a man and provide him the pleasure that he craves."

Celeste looked intrigued and impressed.

"Ryan? What are your thoughts?"

"Well, I'm happy Val liked her birthday present and that I benefit directly from what she got out of it."

"You know, there is a penalty for breaking rules in this club." Celeste looked at both of us.

I had no idea if she knew I exchanged numbers with Nate and Tyler. Did she know about Claudia? Maybe she knew I told Melissa. Was there a rule about family members screwing each other? I didn't know if she was talking to Ryan or me. Maybe he broke more rules than I even knew about.

"Rookie year means rookie mistakes, but lucky for you both, no harm, no foul." Celeste took another sip of her tea, and Ryan and I stared straight ahead.

"Swap Club is a secret organization that prides itself in giving couples a life that includes hedonism, self-indulgence, and in some cases some mild debauchery. Based on what I see sitting before me, I would say that this club provided you with exactly what you were looking for."

Celeste got up and walked over to her antique Georgian mahogany desk and opened the drawer. We watched as she pulled out some paperwork.

"Happy Birthday, Valerie," Celeste said. "I hope this year treats you just as well as last year."

And she placed a new contract on the coffee table in front of us.

"What do you say, how about one more year?" Celeste smiled, and then slid the papers over.

The End?

ACKNOWLEDGEMENTS:

To Kari Hollend & Todd Breau (1Degree Pictures), Antonello Cozzolino (Attraction), Christina Kubacki & Mark Slone (Entertainment One) who believed in Swap Club from the beginning.

To Vincent Salera at World's Best Story who took a chance on me when no one else would.

To Case Cooper at Platinum Graphics- Your unbelievable imagination and purposeful thought in the creation of the cover art is incomparable. You're a true artist and a friend.

To Sandra Hume- Thank you for going above and beyond in your editing of Swap Club.

To my incredible friend and lawyer Joe Sisto - always there to listen, always there to help and never charged me enough for your hours. You're a real *mensch*. This never would have happened without you.

To Samantha K., Nini S., Kat M., Amanda W., Jody E., Lindsey M., Lee H., Amy F. & Lisa K. - Your feedback, support and overall encouragement will be forever appreciated.

To Carrie Kessner Cristofaro- For giving me the courage to write this book.

To my late Grandpa Lou who watches over me from above, you're the reason I chase my dreams. You're the reason I believe in magic.

To my Dad and Lori- The example you have set for loving your careers has been instrumental in my desire to pursue my passion for writing. Thank you for your support and encouragement.

ACKNOWLEDGEMENTS CONTINUED:

To my Mom- A woman who should write the book about commitment, undying love and devotion. You are my best friend and I thank you for always putting me first, even when you shouldn't have. Short of massaging your husband's heart with your bare hands- you kept Max alive with your love and inability to take 'no' for an answer. Always remember- *you* brought them to their feet, because they know who *you* are.

To Max- The coolest man I know, thank you for taking care of me like one of your own. You were a gift to my Mom, Andrew and I. You'll always be King Haberkorn to me. 2/23.

To Paige, my Heart. The world got better the day you were born and I thank your dad Adam for giving me the greatest blessing in life. I love you to the moon and back Peanut. Go to sleep. I love you, goodnight. I love you. Goodnight. Go to sleep. I love you. Goodnight. GO TO SLEEP. xoxo

To Mackenzie & Lyla- Thank you for letting me be a part of your life. I love you both so much.

And, to Jasen - the love of my life. How do I thank you for loving me even in my darkest hours? Even with my dirty bun and massive zit on my chin you make me feel like the most beautiful creature alive. Your love saved me and I am forever grateful you came into my life. I love you about a 43.

'It's such an unusual sight I can't get used to something so right.'
~*Paul Simon*